THE ANGELIC WARS

War of the Angels

JESSE CENTENO

Trafford
PUBLISHING®

Order this book online at www.trafford.com/08-0497
or email orders@trafford.com

Most Trafford titles are also available at major online book retailers.

Printed in Victoria, BC, Canada.

ISBN: 978-1-4251-5063-3 (sc)
ISBN: 978-1-4251-7631-0 (e)

*Our mission is to efficiently provide the world's finest, most comprehensive
book publishing service, enabling every author to experience success.
To find out how to publish your book, your way, and have it available
worldwide, visit us online at www.trafford.com/10510*

Trafford rev. 11/3/09

 www.trafford.com

North America & international
toll-free: 1 888 232 4444 (USA & Canada)
phone: 250 383 6864 ✦ fax: 812 355 4082

Contents

I

In the time of creation, the Almighty had made the heavens and the angels. It is written that it took six days to create the earth.

During those six days, while the Almighty was absent, the archangels are in charge of the heavens. One of them stood guard over the throne of the Almighty. His name is Satan, and archangel with many curious thoughts, who could no longer endure it.

Satan stood in front of the throne, walked around it, and wondered what it would be like to sit on it, so he did. The greed of power that he felt was incredible. Another angel who happened to scc this ran in front of him and bowed down.

"You're Highness," he said.

"This feels good, I like it. I feel like a king." said Satan, feeling very comfortable.

"I will be your prince," said Beelzebub.

"Satan! You can't do that! Get off the throne! The Almighty will be angry!" shouted Lama, a lower class angel.

"Come here and bow to me Lama," demanded Satan.

"No! I will tell Michael of this!" leaving the palace.

"I will spread the word around about our new king," said Beelzebub, as he walks out of the palace.

At another level of heaven, Michael is met by Lama.

"What's going on?" Michael asked seeing him disturbed.

Satan is sitting on the thorn of the Almighty, declaring himself king," replied Lama.

"We shall see about that!" He can't do that Lama!" said Michael, storming out of this level of heaven making his way to the palace.

By this time, the heavenly palace is crowded with angels. "What is happening here?" asked Gabriel.

"I heard that we are to honor Satan, he had made himself king," replied Raphael

"Greetings Michael," said Gabriel.

"Where is Satan?"

"In the palace, Michael," answered Raphael.

Michael walked toward the palace, followed by Gabriel and Raphael. Upon entering, they see many angels bowing down to him.

"This is wrong, Satan! You have no authority here!"

"I am king of heavens, Michael! Bow to me!"

"You are nothing, but and archangel, like the rest of us, and I will go against you and any other angel that joins you."

Satan looks at Michael with anger. "So, now I have an enemy."

Michael turned to the crowed palace of angels. Beelzebub stood standing in front of the crowd with his sword drawn out.

"Any angels who do not want to be ruled by Satan, may walk away now!" he stated, leaving the heavenly palace. Many angels did follow Michael out of the palace.

By the time the Almighty returned, there stood a great rebellion among the heavens. Satan and the angels were cast out. In his anger with the angels, God made man.

This made Satan very upset, for he knew man would take there places in heaven, and so it begins the angelic wars.

Lorenzo Alexander was a simple man of faith who refused to obey the laws of the church. He believed in the commandments of god. He's been a lonely man all his life, he's not a wealthy man, not a poor man, but he did lived in a home of his own.

In the sixteenth day of Gemini a visitor came to him in the night while he is asleep. A soft voice is heard within his bedroom.

"Lorenzo, I want to be your champion."

"Go away," he murmured in his sleep.

Ten minutes later the voice returns. "Lorenzo let me be your champion."

"Kings have champions, I ain't no king," he said.

A few minutes later he heard the voice once more.

"Am I to be your champion, Lorenzo?"

"Who are you who is to be my champion?" asked Lorenzo.

"I am Angel Topaz."

Lorenzo Alexander opened his eyes and sat up in his bed rubbing his eyes. He sees a vision before him, an angel looking at him.

"Angel Topaz, be my champion if you wish for I do not know why?" he said lying down in bed. He no longer hears the voice.

In the nights that followed in Gemini through Cancer, Lorenzo Alexander was taken by Topaz to a place known to him as Heaven. There he met a man in a robe standing outside his house. It looked like a castle.

"Who are you?" asked Lorenzo.

"I am Enoch," the man said.

"Are you flesh?" Lorenzo asked again.

"No, I am not, Lorenzo."

"Am I flesh?"

"You are a spirit, brought to me by the angle Topaz. You will return to your body later on," replied Enoch.

"Why am I here?" questioned Lorenzo.

"You are here to learn from me, Lorenzo. Remember everything that I tell you," answered Enoch walking into the castle.

"What and I supposed to learn from you, Enoch?" he said following him into his castle.

"I'm going to teach you the wisdom of the angels, the knowledge of the plants and astrology."

"Will I remember all this when I return?" asked Lorenzo.

"I say again Lorenzo, remember everything that I teach you and tell you," replied Enoch.

Lorenzo sat on an ivory chair and a large thick book was given to him by Enoch. "Read and learn it well, Lorenzo Alexander," said he.

Lorenzo opens the book and reads it. "Metatron, the second tallest angel in heaven, Angel Sandalphon is the twin brother of Metatron."

Enoch walked out of the room leaving Lorenzo Alexander alone in the room reading the book. When all the works of Enoch had been taught to Lorenzo, the angel Topaz took him to another man.

"I know who you are," he said walking up to him. "You're Moses"

"And I know you Lorenzo Alexander."

"What am I going to learn from you, Moses?"

"You're going to learn from me the power of prayer, Lorenzo the magical use of herbs and the secrets of a soul.

"Teach me, Moses all that I need to know," said he walking with him.

"Garlic as a whole or crush keeps away demons, Lorenzo. If you mix it with Bay Leaves you will have a powerful herb. Smoke your house with it and evil will stay away."

"Tell me more, Moses," listening to him.

The nights continued into Cancer. Lorenzo was brought forth by Angel Topaz to a man name Solomon. The man waited for Lorenzo outside his castle holding a book in his hand.

"Let me teach you the art of pentagrams and the secrets that lie within the elements," said Solomon, taking Lorenzo into his castle.

"What are the elements?" asked Lorenzo.

"Earth, wind, fire, and water, Lorenzo. You will learn the secrets of each element in this book," giving the book the Lorenzo.

By the end of Cancer, Lorenzo had learned all that had to be known to him. He had become a man of power on the side of God, but the questioned that bothered him was why?

In the early days of Leo, Ahab came to visit Lorenzo. He found I'm sitting on a picnic table outside having a glass of ice water.

"Greeting my friend, Alexander," he said sitting across from Lorenzo.

"Hello, Ahab."

"What's the matter? You look like you're in a deep thought."

"It's nothing, just a thousand things going through my mind," replied Lorenzo.

Ahab put his hand on his shoulder "I know what you need, Lorenzo?"

"What?" he asked, looking at Ahab.

"You need to come to my apartment; I have two friends I want you to meet."

"More women, Ahab?"

"You know me."

Lorenzo smiled, "Sure I'll be there," he said.

"That's tonight Alexander," said Ahab, as he got up.

"Don't worry, I won't let you down," said he as he watched him leave.

Throughout the afternoon, Lorenzo wrote his thoughts into his notebook. When he entered his house, he could smell a wonderful fragrance.

Lorenzo walked from room to room. "I know you're here, tell me your name?" he questioned standing still hearing a whisper in his ear

"Jade."

"Angel Jade, you shall be at my left side and, Angel Topaz, shall be at my right. Angel Jade shall be my guardian and Angel Topaz, shall be my champion," said Lorenzo, looking at his watch. "Come with me, I have a friend to meet," he said walking out the door.

At the apartment, Ahab and two female guests sat on the sofa talking to each other. Soon, a knock came to the door. Ahab answered the door seeing Lorenzo, and he looks at his watch. "Your late," he said.

"At least I didn't let you down," Lorenzo said walking into the room.

"Ladies, I want you to meet my friend Lorenzo Alexander."

"Hello."

"Lorenzo, I want you to meet Nelly," pointing to one of the ladies." And this is Carol," said Ahab, pointing to the other lady.

The four of them sat comfortably and got to know each other. Two hours later one of the ladies felt sick and Ahab could see this.

"Are you alright, Carol," asked Ahab.

"Yeah, just a headache coming," she said feeling very cold so suddenly. "Got some aspirin?"

"It's in the cabinet, in the kitchen, to the left," replied Ahab.

Carol walked to the kitchen for an aspirin. Her skin color is paled white, her eyes are becoming bloodshot, and her headache is even more painful than before.

"Is she going to be alright?" asked Lorenzo.

"She'll be okay," replied Nelly.

Soon, Carol walked in with a glass of water and an aspirin. She remains standing by the sofa not feeling like herself.

"Nelly! Look at me!" shouted Carol, as her whole body trembled.

"You don't look good, Carol," she said.

"What's happening to me?" as Carol fell to the floor in a rage.

Nelly and Ahab held her on the floor there was no time to be frightened seeing that Carol was acting like an animal. Suddenly, Ahab was thrown to the wall, and Nelly was pushed across the floor.

Carol raised upward facing Lorenzo. At first sight, he showed fear, but then words came out of his mouth. Ahab, stood up in astonishment

"You are not welcome in that body!"

"Who's going to stop me, you?" questioned a deep toned voice coming out of the mouth of Carol.

"Not I, but my champion will," replied Lorenzo.

Whatever was in Carol's body, felt the power of the sword. Carol screamed and fell to the floor unconscious. Lorenzo clapped his hands and touched Carol on the head.

She opened her eyes, and looked at him.

"Who are you?" asked Lorenzo.

"I am Carol."

"Who is she?" he asked again pointing to her friend.

"That's Nelly," replied Carol, sitting up from the floor.

"Who created the heavens and the earth and you?

"God," answered Carol looking around. "What happened?"

"You don't know?" asked Nelly as she got up from the floor.

"You freaked out on us Carol," said Ahab, walking up to her.

"I did?"

"Yes, you did," replied Ahab, picking her up from the floor.

"How do you feel Carol?" asked Lorenzo.

"Tired."

"I need to take you home girl," said Nelly.

"Yeah, take her home," Lorenzo said as the ladies walked out the door.

"See you tomorrow, Ahab," Nelly said.

"Take care ladies," he said watching them leave.

Lorenzo put on his coat." Where did you learn all that?" asked Ahab.

"Learn what?' questioned Lorenzo.

"All that stuff that you did to carol?"

"You don't wanna know Ahab," he replied walking out the door.

What happened on that night left many questions unanswered in the minds of Ahab and Nelly. Ten days later, Nelly learned the whereabouts of Lorenzo so she went to his house.

Pressing on the door bell, she waited. The door opened slowly and Nelly sees Lorenzo in his shorts and t-shirt. Lorenzo was surprised to see her.

"Well hello, ah" he said trying to think.

"You forgot my name already, Lorenzo?"

"I know who you are, I just can't remember right now."

"It's Nelly."

"That's it," said Lorenzo with a smile.

Standing by the door, Nelly smelled and odor coming out of the house. "I smell something good."

"I'm making my own incense."

"Really! Can I see?"

"Sure,' replied Lorenzo letting her inside the house. Once inside the house, Lorenzo continued to crush rocks into powder. Nelly is amazed and curious in what she sees around the rooms of his house. Hanging on the walls were portrait of Saints, Biblical prayers, statues of angels, lighted candles, and books of all kinds of religions. She comes to an herb plant that had red berries on it.

"Don't touch Nelly, just look at it."

"You sure are deep into this stuff, Lorenzo," said she watching him mix two ingredients of incense together.

"Did somebody teach you all this, Lorenzo?"

"Yes and no and I won't tell you who," replied Alexander washing his hands. "Now tell me why you are here?"

"I came here to ask you if you would smoke my house?" questioned Nelly watching him drying his hands.

"I can do that," he replied.

"Now?" asked Nelly.

"Tomorrow morning, same time, you come here and pick me up, Nelly."

"That would be fine, Lorenzo," she said walking out. "Bye."

"Bye Nelly."

What became a cold morning, turned into a bright warm afternoon. Carol entered an apartment building, making her way to a psychic room. The door was opened.

"I was expecting you," a young woman said dressed in a robe with signs of stars, moon, and a sun on it.

Carol walked inside facing her. "Then you know what I want to hear?"

"Shut the door, Carol, and sit," said the psychic lady dealing a deck of tarot cards.

Carol sat in the chair facing the women. To the left of her stood six lighted candles, to the right of her stood a lighted incense stick.

"Let's find out if what you are asking can be answered," said Edna, the psychic lady.

Laying one card a time on the table, she began to read to herself. Carol became restless and unable to sit still in her chair.

"What does it say?" asked Carol.

"Please be silent," answered Edna looking at the cards.

Carol stands up from her chair; she then takes out a pack of cigarettes. She opens the pack and pulls out a cigarette and began to smoke.

"Evil has touched you, Carol, and it will touch you again," said Edna.

Carol sat on her chair. "I want to know why evil is touching me."

"You have a friend, or know a person, who has great power. He's the reason why evil is touching you. He is an alchemist and a very good one, Carol."

"Is he better than you?"

"No, but he is more powerful than me."

"That's all I need to know," said Carol, tossing twenty dollars on the table walking toward the door.

"There's more!" shouted Edna.

"I don't want to hear it," said Carol, standing by the door.

"Carol, I want to see this man of power."

"So do I," Carol said, leaving.

With the arrival of evening, Nelly sat on her sofa watching television. A knock came to her door hearing a terrifying cry.

"Nelly! It's me Carol!"

"I'm coming!" shouted Nelly, opening the door.

"Help me Nelly," she said crying and falls down on her knees.

"What is wrong Carol?" asked Nelly, trying to bring her into her room.

"I'm so cold and I'm so scared, Nelly, entering her room on her knees. "It's happening again, Nelly."

"What is happening again Carol?" watching her go on her hands and knees.

"I don't feel like myself, Nelly," she said as her voice changed to a course sound. Carol began to bark like a dog and shook her head vigorously.

Nelly, jumps on her sofa as Carol tries to bite her. "Fight it, Carol!" shouted Nelly, knowing that her friend is possessed by a demon.

"I can't, it's too powerful," she said rolling on the floor.

Nelly runs to her bedroom and came out with a jar of water. By this time objects were flying across the room and the room itself was turning cold.

"Do something Nelly!" shouted Carol, unable to control her body.

Nelly splashes water on Carol's head as well as on her face. She lies on the floor in a deep sleep. Nelly puts her right hand on her head and reads the Lord's Prayer from the Bible.

Soon Carol opened her eyes and looked at Nelly. "Are you alright?" asked Nelly.

Carol sat up, took the jar of water away from Nelly and washed herself. "Where did you get this water?"

"Lorenzo made it for me," replied Nelly.

"I have to get some," said Carol, feeling herself once more.

"Lorenzo is going to smoke my house tomorrow morning, you can talk to him then," Nelly said, sitting on the sofa.

"I believe I will," Carol replied, getting up walking toward the door. "Can I keep this jar of water?"

"If it helps you, Carol, yes," she answered as the door is closed.

Early the next morning, on a rainy day, Nelly stood knocking on Lorenzo's door. The door opened and he finds her standing there.

"Are you ready?" she said with a smile.

Lorenzo put on his coat and picked up a box off the kitchen table. He steps outdoors closing the door and turns to Nelly.

"I'm ready now," he replied walking with her to her car.

Nelly drives her car two miles to her apartment. "This is where I live."

"You're not far from where I live, Nelly."

Parking her car the both of them get out of her car and walked up to her apartment. Nelly unlocks her door and they both entered her apartment room.

"Do you like it?"

"Nice place you have here, Nelly," answered Lorenzo taking off his coat.

"Can I help smoke my rooms?" questioned Nelly anxiously taking offer coat.

"In a moment, I will need your help," answered Lorenzo setting the box on the floor.

Nelly watched Lorenzo set a candle on the table and set fire to it. He then begins to burn incense. Lorenzo took out a container that had white powder in it. He then begins to put it upon himself.

"Take some powder, Nelly, and rub it on yourself."

"What is it," she said taking a small handful.

"It will protect you," Lorenzo said taking out his Bible.

"From what?"

"Negative influence."

Rubbing herself with powder she questioned Lorenzo. "Now what do you want me to do?"

"Take this incense and follow me."

With and incense burner on a chain, Nelly followed Lorenzo. He began to read from the Bible. Room by Room they went until her apartment was done. Nelly felt the peace in her rooms after the negative vibes were removed.

When all was done, Nelly blows out the candle and gives Lorenzo the burning incense. Lorenzo closes his Bible; soon a knock came to the door.

"That must be Carol, she wants to see you," Nelly said opening the door.

Lorenzo, kept quiet as he packed everything in the box and looked at the woman who came walking inside to see him.

"I remember you; you're that woman who has been touched by evil spirits."

"Yes, I am," said carol softly sitting on the sofa.

"Does the evil still bother you?" Lorenzo asked touching her hand.

"Yeah, can you help me?" she questioned.

"Come to my house, tonight, and I shall clean you."

"I don't know where you live?" she replied looking at him with sad eyes.

"I'll bring her to you, Lorenzo," said Nelly.

"I will also need you, Nelly, if you wish to help your friend," he said putting on his coat.

"I got a bingo game tonight," said Nelly.

"Cancel it and be at my house tonight," said Lorenzo, picking up his box. "If one of you ladies is kind enough to take me home, I am ready."

"I'll take him home," said Carol walking toward the door. "I'll see you tonight, Nelly."

It was mid-afternoon and the rain had stopped, the sky remained cloudy, but the sun poked through the clouds.

Ahab had walked home instead of taking the bus; it was such a good day for walk.

He arrived home and found the television on. There stood a young man sitting on the couch drinking a can of beer.

"What the hell are you doing here?" he asked.

"Mitsy invited me here, and I'm waiting for her," he replied looking like a freak.

"Mitsy!" shouted Ahab. Coming down the stars with a pillow case full of her clothing, she looked at her father.

"What's up?" she said chewing gum.

Ahab looked at his teenage daughter dressed like a hooker in the street. She had tattoos of a devil on both of her arms.

"What in the hell did you do to yourself?" asked Ahab.

"I joined an occult Dad, and this is my soul brother, and my protector," replied Mitsy, kissing the young man.

"What is all this?" questioned Ahab, pointing at the pillow case.

"I'm moving out and going with him."

"Like hell you are! Your only fifteen, you're staying here!" retorted Ahab.

"Sorry, Dad," Mitsy said walking toward the door.

Ahab stepped in-front of the doorway, not letting his daughter go. They both looked at each other with her father looking angry.

"I said you're not going!"

The young man grabbed Ahab by the shirt and throws him against the wall. Ahab sits on the floor to a corner feeling hopeless.

"I don't want to hurt you old man, but I will, and I can. Don't make me curse you."

"The power of evil is very strong with him dad, don't make him do it to you," said mitsy walking out the door.

"Mitsy! You don't know what you doing!" shouted Ahab as the door slammed in front of him.

Evening has turned into night; darkness covered the city, a moonless night. Nelly and Carol drove up into the driveway of Lorenzo.

"I'm a little scared about all this," said Carol.

"He's the only on that can help you."

"I know," she said getting out of the car and both walked up to the door.

There was a note posted on the door inviting them inside. Both ladies entered the house of Lorenzo. They saw a table with several candles burning. The room itself had a smell of church incense.

"Welcome," Lorenzo said wearing a green robe.

"I have to admit, Alexander, this is really strange to me."

"Don't be afraid, Nelly, especially you, Carol. I'm only going to clean you, fight that evil off of you," said Lorenzo.

"Okay," Carol replied nervously.

"I want the both of you to take off your jewelry, money or anything that you have, and put it on this table."

Both ladies did as they were told to do. Nelly watched Lorenzo put powder on himself and soon she put powder on herself.

"Protection?" asked Nelly.

"Of course," he replied looking at the other lady.

"Carol, I want you to take a candle lite bath," said Lorenzo showing her the bath tub. "Go ahead and fill it with water." Carol looked at the bath tub which had flowers all around it and candles were burning. She could smell a pleasant odor.

"What do I smell?" Carol asked.

"This oil," answered Lorenzo holding the oil. It will not hurt you, but it will hurt the evil in you," he said turning to Nelly. "You can stay with her Nelly, and I'll be in the next room," said Lorenzo giving the oil to Nelly as he left the bathroom.

"I feel so cold all of a sudden," Carol said.

"The water is warmed," said Nelly as she mixes the water and the oil together with her hand.

Lorenzo Alexander sat on a chair with a table before him. On this table stood five lit candles, burning incense, a Bible, and sacred oils. Lorenzo sat silent meditating.

Soon, Nelly and Carol came out of the bathroom into the room where Lorenzo was in. Carol had a bathrobe on as she stood.

"Now what?" Nelly asked.

"Sit, Carol," said Lorenzo as she sat facing him. "I want you to read a passage from the Bible."

"Okay," she said looking at the bible."

"Don't read it with your lips Carol, read it with your heart," he said.

"I'll try," she said becoming silent.

"Nelly, does not hear you, Carol, I don't even hear you," said Lorenzo

"You didn't sat I had to read it out loud."

"Try it again, and this time, let us hear you."

Carol read it out loud while Lorenzo splashed Holy powder on her. Carol finished the reading In the Bible and closes the book.

"What happens next?"

"Do you know how to pray?" he asked.

"Yes, I do, when I was a little girl, I prayed every night," Carol said.

"Stand up," Lorenzo said holding two oils in his hand. "Pray, Carol, and you too Nelly."

"What do I pray?"

"'pray anything that comes to mind, Carol."

There was a moment of silence and she looked at Nelly. Carol, scratched her head, closed her eyes, and a prayer came to mind.

"Alright," she said beginning to pry as Nelly followed.

While she prayed, Lorenzo rubbed oil over her and with the second oil he made the sign of the cross on her forehead.

"Amen," said both ladies.

"You are now cleansed," said Lorenzo sitting down.

"You mean evil won't touch me anymore?" Carol asked feeling good within herself.

"It might come back." He replied.

"What do I do then?"

Become a Christian now; don't wait until the last minute."

"How am I supposed to do that?"

"Ask Nelly."

"Me!" Nelly exclaimed in what Lorenzo said.

"Yes, you."

"Why me?"

"Because, Carol is your friend, you're a Christian, and you can show her how."

"Will you do it, Nelly?" asked Carol looking at her.

"Let's go home," replied Nelly, pushing Carol out the door.

"Answer my question Nelly."

"Bye Lorenzo and thanks," said Carol closing the door.

After what had happened that afternoon in his house, Ahab looked around the city for his daughter, Mitsy. It's late at night and Ahab hasn't slept. His anger overcomes his tired body.

By dawn, Ahab returned home dragging his feet, tried, and sad. He stumbled into a chair, and then made his way to his bedroom. The man is unable to find his daughter as he fell onto his bed.

In the days of Scorpio, a great day has come. Lorenzo prepared on this day, he knew the angels would come. In every room of his house stood a candle burning with incense. Lorenzo, in his white robe, recited a prayer inviting the angels to come and enjoy the comforts of his home.

He sanctified himself, and set quietly in his rocking chair. In the eyes of Lorenzo Alexander, he could see the angels and the saints gathering within his house. He smiled as the image vanished from his mind.

The feast of the Angels and Saints had begun. As long as the candles stay lit, the angels would stay. By nightfall, while Lorenzo slept with the candles lit a dream came to him, meeting the angels himself.

"Lorenzo Alexander, the man I wanted to meet face to face," one said.

"Who are you?" asked he receiving a drink.

"I am Topaz, your champion," he said looking like a man in a suite.

"Drink up," said another angel. "I am Jade, your guardian," he said shaking his hand.

"Allow me to introduce to you four generals," said Topaz, walking together toward the four angels sitting around the table.

"This is general Jasper of the North," said Topaz.

"A splendid feast you have here," he replied.

"Thank you Jasper," said Lorenzo.

"This is Garnet, general of the South," said Topaz once more.

"I've heard about you, Lorenzo," he said.

"Good things I hope, Garnet," he said with a smile.

Topaz, points to the next angel. "Over there is general Mosaic, who rules the west."

"General Mosaic, glad to meet you," said Lorenzo, shaking hands.

"Finally, we have Tigereye, general of the east."

"Tigereye? A funny name for an angel."

"Are you insulting me, Lorenzo?"

"No, I'm not insulting you Tigereye," he answered finishing his drink.

"Now that you have met them they are your generals," said Topaz.

"Wait a minute?" questioned Lorenzo surprisingly.

"What do you mean my generals? I thought they were under the command of God."

"God is our king and yours. I am in command of these generals, but I am also your champion, Lorenzo, and that makes you in command of my generals."

Lorenzo looked at the four generals. "I suppose you generals have armies?"

"No, we do not," replied Jasper standing up. "We have legions."

Lorenz stood in confusion turning to the angel next to him and looked at Jade, his guardian angel, receiving a smile from Jade.

"Why me? I don't even know what you angels want of me," he said.

"Tell him, Topaz," said Jade.

"You are chosen to lead us into battle."

"What battle are you talking about?"

"If the battle had been in the heavens, we wouldn't need you, Lorenzo. As it turns out the battle is on you world."

"I still don't understand topaz?"

"It's a spiritual war, Lorenzo. You have been trained to fight demons, save souls, and you have us at your side to battle the antichrist," replied Topaz.

"Are you sure you got the right person?" asked Lorenzo.

"Have faith, Lorenzo, we are with you always," said Jade as the entire group fades away.

"The sound of the phone ringing woke Lorenzo. He looked at the clock on the dresser. It's ten in the morning hearing the ring he answered the phone.

"Hello," he mumbled as he yawned.

"Lorenzo, this is Nelly. Have you seen Ahab lately?"

"I haven't seen him in over three months," he replied rubbing his eyes.

"Go see him, Lorenzo; he's not the same man."

"How do you know that, Nelly?"

"Yesterday, I saw him angry about something, I don't know what it is."

"Alright, I'll see him and find out what's bothering him," he said hanging up the phone.

Ahab has not seen his daughter throughout the entire days of Scorpio in to three days of Sagittarius. No letters, not even a phone call, which made him very angry.

He sat in a chair with a table full of guns and cans of beer. The clock on the wall was showing noon, and he hears a knock on the door.

"The door is opened!" he called out.

Lorenzo walked in, seeing a gun pointing at him. "Are you at war?" he asked.

"Damn right!" Ahab replied in anger.

Lorenzo looked around the kitchen where, Ahab, stood sitting in his chair. He sees beer cans, whisky bottles, dirty dishes, and garbage on the floor.

"What happened to this place, Ahab? Your house is a mess."

"Go home, Lorenzo, this is none of your concern," he replied drinking his beer.

"I am your friend and I can help you."

"If you can shoot a gun, you can stay, Lorenzo, otherwise leave my house."

"Tell me what happened, Ahab?" Lorenzo asked loading a gun. Ahab finished his can of beer looking at Lorenzo. He was wearing a dirty T-shirt and had not shaven for days.

"They got to my daughter."

"Who has you daughter?"

"That goddamn devil occult," he replied acting in a rage of anger.

"Calm down, Ahab, calm down," said Lorenzo as Ahab relaxed. "Do you know where the occult is?"

"No, but I know someone that can tell me."

"I got a better way," Lorenzo said walking toward the door. "Come with me, Ahab."

"Ahab put on his army coat and took four guns out of sis that stood on the table. He also put some shells into his coat pocket.

"No one is pushing me around anymore," he said to himself.

Ahab walked out of the house to the car with the guns. "We don't need that here," said Lorenzo.

"Just in case," said Ahab getting into the car.

Not saying another word, Lorenzo, gets into his car noticing that Ahab is restless. They drove out of the driveway and moved forward.

"Where are we going, Alexander?"

"To my house, I have to get something," he replied stopping by his house.

Leaving the motor running, Lorenzo, hurried into his house for a few minutes. Ahab continued to feel restless turning on the radio. Lorenzo came out running to the car.

"Okay Ahab, which way to your daughter?"

"Go west out of the city limits," replied Ahab as Lorenzo followed directions.

Thirty minutes later and three miles out of the city limits, Lorenzo came up to an intersection. This is the intersection, Ahab was looking for.

"Somewhere on this intersection is where I think she is," he said.

"You don't know exactly?" asked Lorenzo.

"No," replied Ahab as Lorenzo pulled to the side of the street.

"I want you to be silent and don't ask any questions," said Lorenzo pulling out a root from his pocket.

Holding the root in the palms of his hands, Lorenzo moved his arm left to right very slowly. Both men soon began to see the root jump.

"Your daughter is that way," said Lorenzo pointing to the left.

"If you say so," said Ahab taking over the driving and moved forward down the road.

Passing by houses and farms, Lorenzo held the root in his hand, but it didn't jump at all. The road came to a dead end, but ahead of them stood a broken down farm it was here the root jumped out of Lorenzo's hands

"We found her" exclaimed Lorenzo.

"At last!" Ahab shouted getting out of the car with a gun.

He hurriedly walked toward the old two story house with Lorenzo close behind him. Ahab stepped on the porch and knocks on the door.

"I think nobody is home," said Lorenzo, not seeing a single car anywhere around.

Ahab knocked on the door a second time. He was greeted by an old woman with a cane. "What can I do for you?"

"Where's my daughter? Ahab cried out with such anger in his voice.

"I don't know what you're talking about," said the old woman softly.

"I want her back!" demanded Ahab.

"Take it easy, partner," said Lorenzo.

"I know she's here! I'm going to look around!" shouted Ahab walking around her house.

Lorenzo looked into the eyes of the old woman. He smiles at her and just by her looks he knew that the old woman knew nothing of what is going on.

"Does your son lives here?"

"Yes" she replied.

"Does your son belong to an occult?" asked Lorenzo.

"No, but he has one of his own. I'm so proud of him."

"Were is your son now?" Lorenzo asked.

"I don't know he isn't here," replied the old woman, seeing Ahab coming. "Oh dear, here comes that awful man."

"You may not go inside," said Lorenzo to Ahab.

"She is here this is her coat and purse!" shouted Ahab as the old woman closed her door.

"She was here! Ahab, but she's gone and won't be back until tomorrow night."

"What do we do then, Lorenzo?"

"We wait," he replied walking back to the car.

Driving away from the farm they headed back to the house of Ahab, where he continued to clean his guns. Lorenzo looked at the clock showing six pm.

"You stay put Ahab. I'll be right back."

"Go ahead, I'm not going anywhere," he replied opening a can of beer.

Lorenzo Alexander drove back to his house to get his robe, book, and his wooden staff that he made. He walked to his car and drove away heading toward the farm.

At a private beach an occult ceremony was taking place. To the west stood the ocean, to the east was an acre of woods, to the south stood the sand dunes, and the north brought the cold winds.

Torches burned at the sand while a hundred candles burned around the ceremonial site. There are about fifty members all dressed in red and purple robes.

Of all the members, Mitsy was the youngest one there, dressed in a black robe. She walked with Taylor, who is the leader of the occult. Both entered a circle done by candles. Taylor picked up a torch shouting at the group.

"Tonight, we shall have a new member in our occult! Her name is Mitsy! Our master of darkness shall be proud, when she leaves!"

The occult members cheered, but mitsy becomes curious having a look of suspicion on her face. She turns to Taylor, and Taylor looked at here.

"What do you mean about me leaving?" asked Mitsy.

"Once I have christened you, making you a member of our occult, you shall be sacrificed," answered Taylor.

"Why me? Why not one of them?" she asked pointing at the other ladies.

"They are not virgins, but you are," replied Taylor.

"Am I going to die?" questioned Mitsy in a sorrowful voice.

"Death is not done here. You are moving from this world to the next world, the first to see it done," replied Taylor.

Mitsy showed fear within herself. "I changed my mind, I don't want to do this," she said.

"It's too late for that Mitsy, your already here," said Taylor waving his wand over her head.

Two members of the occult took the robe off mitsy and ripped her blouse. Mitsy struggles as she was placed down on the sandy beach.

The teenager was unable to move being held down by two men. She could feel the fingers of Taylor on her body as blood of an animal was poured on her body.

"I don't want to join! Let me go!" Mitsy cried out.

"I christen you Mitsy to the Prince of Darkness, let your soul be taken," said Taylor, holding a glass bowl containing a mixture of water and urine. He splashes the mixture on the body of the teenager.

"Hail to our new member, Mitsy!" shouted the crowd.

"Congratulations, Mitsy. You are now a member," said Taylor, kissing her on the forehead.

"I'm getting out of here!" shouted Mitsy, getting up from the beach sand, but the two men held her.

"The time has come! For sacrifice! Let us prepare for this!" Taylor called out.

The two men forced mitsy down on her knees. Mitsy, struggled for freedom, but in a hopeless situation she began to cry.

"I want to go home." She said.

"Show more fear, Mitsy, be very afraid, that is what my master of darkness enjoys most out of a mortal," said Taylor.

At the beach front, a large pot boiled over a roaring fire. A butcher block stood nearby, with a hooded man holding an axe. A silver tub stood at the bottom of the block for her head to fall in.

"Let's go, Mitsy, our master is waiting," said Taylor.

"What is gonna happen to me," she said, struggling and crying.

"Nothing is going to happen to you Mitsy, your leaving the world. On the other hand, your body will be very useful to us."

They approached the hooded man. "No! I don't want to do this! Let me go! Mitsy, pleaded.

Taylor, points to the two men that held Mitsy by her arms. Both men use force to put, Mitsy on her knees and out her head on the chopping block.

"God help me," pleaded Mitsy.

"People! My people! Our master has chosen Mitsy for a suitable sacrifice! May the blessings of our master be upon us!" shouted Taylor.

The hooded man looked at Taylor, waiting for him to nod his head. The man looked down at Mitsy raising the axe high in the air.

All at once a bolt of lightning came from the sky. It struck the axe, and killed the hooded man. The sound of thunder roars loudly.

Taylor was thrown to the ground and the people are in frenzy. Taylor got up from the sand and looked at his people in a state of panic.

"Calm yourselves!" he shouted looking among the crowd and saw a man in a yellow robe. "This is a private beach, you are trespassing!"

"Will you let Mitsy, come to me!" shouted Lorenzo.

Taylor stared at Lorenzo, not saying a word. A servant from the occult came up from behind him and asked a positive question.

"Do you want him dead?"

"Yeah, and take some men with you," replied Taylor.

"You all have sinned a great sin in the eyes of God! Mitsy, come with me!" Lorenzo called out.

Mitsy stood on her knees looking at Taylor, for he had anger in his eyes.

"You're not going anywhere," he demanded.

Immediately a servant touched Mitsy's shoulder and instantly received an electric shock. Mitsy, smiled at the servant pulling away from him.

"I'm going to him," said Mitsy.

"No!" shouted Taylor. "I want you to see what's going to happen to that man," he said pointing to Lorenzo.

"You can't hurt me," said Mitsy as she walked away from Taylor and met Lorenzo.

Lorenzo Alexander, saw three men walking toward him in a very unfriendly manner. He knew that those men were meant to harm him.

"Go back I say! Or you will suffer," Lorenzo shouted.

"Kill that man!" said the voice of Taylor

Lorenzo Alexander raised his arm and without warning three men fell to the ground motionless. Mitsy is dumbfounded in what she saw.

"They are not dead but they are suffering," said Lorenzo.

"I will kill you myself for doing that!" shouted Taylor.

"Come and get me!" Lorenzo called out, as he and Mitsy disappeared from where they were standing.

In a state of anger, Taylor looked at the sand dune seeing them run upward. He screamed like a madman chasing after them. The darken sky was lit up with bolts of lightning and a strong gust of wind blew about the occult. Everyone ran for cover, but Taylor reached the top of the dune only to see nothing.

"You can't hide from me! I'll find you! And I'll kill you!" he shouted.

Down below the sand dune stood Lorenzo and Mitsy. They watched Taylor walk away in disgust, disappearing from sight.

"Why could he see us?" asked Mitsy."We were hiding behind the wings of an angel," replied Lorenzo.

"Really?"

"Yes, really," he said as they walked together into the woods.

By morning of a new day, Lorenzo stopped by the house of Ahab. Both he and Mitsy got out of the car and entered the house only to find Ahab sitting on a chair with his head down on the table.

"Dad," said Mitsy softly putting her hands on his shoulders.

Ahab woke up to see his daughter standing in front of him. At first he did not know what to do, but then he cried hugging her tightly.

"You've come home."

"A man named Lorenzo brought me home," said Mitsy.

"Where is he?" questioned Ahab.

"I am here," replied Lorenzo as he saw Ahab stood up.

"You said we were going to get her tonight, but you went out and got her last night."

"I lied Ahab," said Lorenzo, walking out of the house.

"Thank you for bringing her home," Ahab said with a proud face.

At the private beach, Taylor walked among ruins of the occult. Bane, a member of the occult, walked with him. He knew that Taylor is still angry about last night.

"What do we do now?" he asked.

"Bane, we are going to get Mitsy back," answered Taylor.

"What about that man in a yellow robe?"

"If he's there with her Bane, I'm going to have his head carved and I will do it myself," replied Taylor as they leave the beach.

That same day late in the afternoon a car stopped by the curb. Four men walked out, with Taylor leading the way. They walked up to the house of Ahab, peeking through the windows.

"I don't see anybody in the room," said Bane.

"Gather up by the door," Taylor said as he puts his right hand on the door reciting a spell.

Before long his right hand passed though the wooden door and unlocked it from inside. Taylor looked at Bane and smiles.

"It's amazing what the power of our master can do for us," said Bane.

All four enter the room quietly. They see Ahab resting on a recliner with the television on. One of the men soaked a cloth with ether and attacked Ahab holding it onto his face. Ahab soon went unconscious.

The men walked upstairs hearing a voice from one of the bed rooms. From the inside of the bedroom, Mitsy was talking on the phone when all of a sudden the door slammed open.

Mitsy yelled over the phone as soon as she saw the men enter her room coming toward her. She stood in fear shouting over the phone.

"Lorenzo! Their back!"

The phone was hung up as she was put to sleep. Mitsy was taken down the stairs and Taylor looked at the both of them.

"Let's take the father with us," he said walking out of the house.

At his own house, Lorenzo hung up the phone saying to himself, "Taylor." He gets up, walks up to the cupboard and took out a large piece of chalk.

"I need your help, Topaz," he mumbled leaving his house.

With nightfall already approaching, Lorenzo reached the farm of Taylor. No one was in sight as he looked around the farm. He slowly got out of his car and walked toward the house.

A voice from behind him stopped Lorenzo from walking. "Going somewhere, Lorenzo?"

"Take me to Taylor," he said.

"Nah," Lester said striking him on the face. Lorenzo fell to the ground being kicked again and again.

"Get up," he said.

The house lights came on and Lester sees Taylor stepped out of the house. He stood standing on the porch and looked at Lester.

"Bring him here, Lester!"

Lester picked up Lorenzo from ground. He pushed him and kicked him toward the house where Taylor stood standing.

"You fight like a woman," said Lester.

Coughing out blood, Lorenzo looked at Taylor, trying to talk in his painful state. He could hardly stand up straight.

"I've come," coughing even more.

"I know what you've come for," Taylor said grabbing him by the shirt, leading him to the basement. "Do you want to join them, Lorenzo," he said tossing him down the stairs.

The noise caused a disturbance upon Ahab and Mitsy, who were tied to a pole. The both of them saw Lorenzo on the basement floor.

"Your hero came to your rescue," said Taylor, walking down the stairs. "I want you to know, that before the both of you die, you're going to see Lorenzo die first, by me. I shall behead him," he said looking down at Lorenzo. "Tie him up Lester."

Lester picked up the man from the basement floor. Lorenzo was slammed against a wooded beam and tied up. Taylor laughed softly with an evil look on his face.

"You're the devil," said mitsy.

"Yes, I am, and where I'm going your coming with me," he said laughing as he walked up the stairs with Lester.

"Taylor," Bane called out excited," the beach is ready to be reset."

"It's about time!" he said loudly turning to Lester.

"You stay here and watch our friends. I'll call you when were ready for them."

"Right," said Lester.

"Let's get going Bane," said Taylor heading toward the beach.

Down in the basement Lorenzo regain consciousness and his strength. He looked around the room finding Ahab and Mitsy tied up to a pole.

"Are you alright?" questioned Mitsy.

"Yeah, I think so," answered Alexander feeling a bit sore.

"I supposed we are all going to die together, so I'm sorry I got you in all this mess," Mitsy said sadly being looked at by Lorenzo.

"When I have friends among the heavens, nothing in this world can hold me captive," said he breaking out of his ropes.

"I knew I could count on you, Alexander," said Ahab being freed from the ropes.

"Go ahead and untie you daughter. I have something to do," Lorenzo said, taking out his calk.

The man went down on his knees reciting a prayer. He then proceeds to draw a circle on the cement floor, complete with symbols and words.

Mitsy became curious, "what are you doing?" she asked

"Making a shelter for protection," replied Lorenzo.

Ahab slowly and quietly walked up the stairs and peeked out through an opening. What he saw made him very unhappy.

"We don't stand a chance of escaping; there are too many men outside."

"We don't have to," said Lorenzo, finishing his circle. "Get inside, both of you and don't get out until I tell you."

"What about you?" questioned Mitsy.

"Don't worry about me, I'll be joining you soon," replied Lorenzo, hearing the door open.

"I can hear you talking down there!" shouted Lester, walking down the stairs. "How did you get loose?" he asked pulling out his gun.

"You cannot move!" Lorenzo called out.

"What have you done to me?" Lester shouted not able to move any part of his body.

"Stay in the circle, no matter what happens," said Lorenzo, as he walked up the basement stairs.

"Help me! Somebody help me!" shouted Lester.

The screams of this man was heard by the men outside. They came running toward the house and Lorenzo saw them coming. At once Lorenzo shouted out

"I curse this house, not by fire, not by water, not by earth, or even air, but by bolts of lightning!" he called out running back to the circle.

Within a few minutes the sky darkens and flashes of lightning brightened the dark sky. The man stood still while they looked at the sky. Suddenly a powerful bolt of lightning struck the house, causing it to explode with such force.

The entire house was destroyed; Lorenzo, Ahab, and Mitsy remained in the circle untouched. Ahab and his daughter were flabbergasted in what they saw.

"Ever in my life have I never seen this done. You have powers, Alexander," said Ahab.

"No, I don't. God has that power" Ahab."

"I knew it, you're a sorcerer, just like, Taylor," said Mitsy.

"I am not like Taylor. I am against Taylor," Lorenzo aid.

"How do you explain what happened here?" asked Ahab.

"I don't know, Ahab, only that the angels help me," replied Lorenzo reaching their car.

All three get into the car with Ahab sitting in the front seat with Lorenzo driving. They drive out of the property as Mitsy saw nothing standing.

"When Taylor gets back and sees all this, he's going to be very angry." Mitsy said.

"Let me worry about, Taylor," Lorenzo said driving away.

"Where are we going, Dad?" questioned Mitsy.

"To your uncle's house, he's having a birthday party right about now," answered Ahab.

Ninety minutes went by and they arrived at her uncle's house, which stood near a beach. A party was being held for the remainder of the night and everyone was having a good time.

"Mitsy, the fifteen year old, was concerned. She walked around finding her father. "Dad, did you see Lorenzo anywhere?"

"I saw him go up to the sand dunes."

Mitsy walked up the sand dunes finding Lorenzo sitting down. He did not hear Mitsy coming, but he only stared at the ocean.

"Do you like being here by yourself?" she asked.

"The ocean is talking to me," answered Lorenzo as Mitsy sat down next to him.

"What is it saying?"

"It's telling me the antichrist is here, but not yet in power," replied Lorenzo.

"You mean a false god?" questioned Mitsy.

"Yes," replied Lorenzo, "He will have great power to do anything."

"More powerful than you, Lorenzo?"

"Perhaps," he answered as he looked at Mitsy. He could see fear on her face.

"That sounds scary!" said Mitsy.

"It's more terrible than you could ever know, Mitsy. You should start strengthening your faith, because that will save your life."

Mitsy didn't say a word to him, but she left Lorenzo alone staring at the ocean.

II

THE MILLENNIUM HAS COME, life has changed. Laws were made to be broken. Killing becomes a pleasure and not for a purpose. Fear overcomes pain.

The rich and the powerful control the poor, and the poor becomes slaves to the rich. Cruelty has touched the hearts of men.

Hatred is good for the soul; love becomes a game that has no happiness. Religion stepped backwards, a cross is broken and the children of God are no more.

Open your eyes and look around you, because women are equal to men. No longer are things done by man alone. Women have rights as much as men. The privacy of man has been eliminated.

Whatever happened to the words of the Bible that says man shall have power over woman? Has man rewritten the Bible?

Lorenzo Alexander sat with Carol in his front yard, watching a church burn down to the ground. An angry mob stood near the church preventing the firemen from putting out the fire.

"What a shame," Lorenzo said.

"What, I don't understand, why did the government agents arrest the minister?" questioned Carol.

"He didn't want to change religion," replied Lorenzo as he was approached by Ahab.

"Can you believe this?"

"It's gonna get worse," said Lorenzo.

"How about your daughter, Mitsy? Is she doing okay, Ahab?" asked Carol."

Ever since Taylor got drafted into the army, she's been herself, and she has the steady boyfriend."

"Well folks, it looks like a show is over," Lorenzo said standing up.

"Bye, Lorenzo," said Carol walking with Ahab.

A new day in Aries brings curiosity to Alexander. At Hicky Incorporated, where he and Nelly worked, he saw two men dressed in suits walking with the manager.

Nelly walked away from her work station to Lorenzo. "Who are they?"

"Government agents, big shots," he answered.

"I wonder what they want?" questioned Nelly, walking back to her work station.

Three days later, a notice was posted on the bulletin board. A meeting is to be held today for all employees at the end of their work day.

At the meeting all employees were told to wear a mark if they wished to continue to work, and children are going to be marked. A day after the meeting employees were lining up to get their mark. Lorenzo walked out of the factory chased down by Nelly.

"Aren't you going to wear the mark?" she asked.

"No."

"You must Lorenzo! It's the way of life."

"Are you going to get one, Nelly?"

"Yes."

"Then you are not a Christian, Nelly"

"Lorenzo, this is not a devil's number, being a Christian has nothing to do with it. It's only a pyramid with an eye inside it."

"It's an evil eye, Nelly. That mark will control you, the government will own you," Lorenzo exclaimed, standing in the parking lot.

"What do you plan to do? Fight the government?" asked Nelly.

"Quit my job," answered Lorenzo getting into his car. Nelly stood alone in the parking lot watching Lorenzo drive away.

Throughout the city, hundreds of people were being marked. With evening already here, Mitsy and her boyfriend, Stark, came walking into her house.

Mitsy saw her father watching television as she walked towards him with a smile on her face. Stark, stood standing with his hands in his pockets.

"I'm home dad," she said kissing her father on the forehead.

"This is important, said Ahab listening to the news.

"When are you going to get the mark Mr. Ahab?" said Stark.

"Never," he replied.

"I got marked today," Mitsy said, showing her mark to her father.

Upon seeing the mark, Ahab turned and looked at her not paying attention to the television. Mitsy knew her father was not happy.

"You got marked without telling me?"

"I had to dad, there's no excuses," replied Mitsy.

"Everybody is doing it Mr. Ahab, you might as well get marked," said Stark.

"No," he said turning to his television.

"Why not dad?" asked Mitsy.

"I will not let the government mark my skin. That's why."

"You have to dad; it's the new way of life."

"I said, no," stated Ahab, turning up the volume on his television.

Mitsy and Stark stood there, looking at him, shocked that he refused to wear the mark. The both of them walked away out of the house, not saying a word.

So it is done, through out America, everyone was being marked. There's violence among the people who protested against the mark.

By the end of the month rewards were being offered, to anyone, if they knew someone who wasn't wearing the mark. Government agents' would use force on these people, just to put the mark on them.

Mitsy stood standing on the sidewalk, across the street, holding a thousand dollar reward check. She had told the agents about her father. Within a few minutes agents were knocking at his door.

"What do you want?" questioned Ahab in a snotty way.

"We would like to know why you refuse the mark?" asked the agents.

"I do have the mark," replied Ahab.

"May I see it?"

"No!" Ahab cried out.

"Then, we assume you do not have the mark," one agent said while the other pushed Ahab into the house and shut the door.

"You damn agents aren't going to touch my skin!" shouted Ahab, running to his bedroom. "No way in hell!" he shouted being chased by the agents.

Ahab, slammed the door on the agents, but it was kicked opened. Ahab, jumped on the bed trying to reach for his bat, but is captured by the agents.

"Let me go goddamn it!" he cried out.

In a struggle one of the agents hit Ahab on the head with a rubber baton knocking him out. Both agents looked down on him.

"Mark him," said one of the agents placing the mark on the palm of his left hand.

On the other side of town the phone rang at Carol's house. The woman walked up to the phone and answers it hearing a voice shouting over the phone.

"Run, Carol! The agents are coming to your apartment!"

Dropping her phone, Carol escaped from her apartment by going out the window and down the fire escape. Unfortunately, two agents were waiting for her down below.

"You must be Carol, or you wouldn't be running from us," said one agent while the other grabbed Carol by her arm.

"Don't touch me," she said pulling away.

"Why aren't you wearing the mark?"

Carol retorted "Christians don't wear that kind of mark"

"We found one," said one agent.

"We have to make an example of her," said another agent turning to Carol. "Take her to the chamber."

"Let me go!" shouted Carol, fighting for her freedom, but was taken away.

Lorenzo Alexander left his house in the morning and had not returned. By late afternoon, a van entered his driveway. Taylor stepped out, dressed in a uniform.

"Do you want me to get him out of the house, sir?" asked an agent.

"No, I'll do it myself," replied Taylor.

"Yes, sir,"

"Alexander and I know each other personally. I've been waiting for this moment for a long time," said Taylor, walking up to the door.

Taylor did not knock on the door, he only turned the knob and the door opened as it was left unlocked. He also found the house empty. Walking out of the house, he gave out a loud shout.

"I want this house watched!"

"Yes, sir!"

"If you see him, call me, before you arrest him," demanded Taylor.

"Yes sir," said the agent.

"I'll find you, Lorenzo," said Taylor to himself, walking to the van.

At the compound headquarters, Carol was taken to the chamber room where she was tied to a street post. By evening, Taylor walked into the room carrying an electric branding iron.

"How do you do, Carol?" he said.

"Stay away from me!" she shouted.

"Why did you refuse to take the mark, Carol?" questioned Taylor looking at her.

"Cause I didn't want to be controlled by people like you."

"She said she's a Christian," said the agent.

"Is that true, Carol, you're a Christian?" asked Taylor.

"What if I am, so what?"

They both looked at each other eye to eye and Taylor showed a smirk on his face. With branded iron in his hand he walked back and forth in front of her.

"I was going to stamp the mark on you, but now I going to brand you,"

"You don't scare me," she said.

"You're going to feel a lot of pain, Carol," he said with a smile.

"Mark me and I'll kill you," she said.

"Are you threatening me, Carol?"

"Am I scaring you?" she questioned. Taylor stood still and looked at her. He did not smile or even winked and eye. He then shut off the hot iron and got close to her face.

"I guess I can't mark you, Carol," he said. "Since you threaten a government officer, you must die. Such a waste on a beautiful woman like you, Carol," said Taylor, walking out of the chamber.

"You're gonna burn in hell Taylor!" shouted Carol angrily.

Far away from the city, Lorenzo was in the wilderness, away from life. With a knapsack on his back, he rested on a log, watching two fawns drink water from a pond.

"I will camp here tonight," he mumbled to himself.

A Fire burned in the forest, giving light in the night. Lorenzo ate his meal by the campfire. The night creatures were making their sounds heard to the ears of Lorenzo who sits against the tree by the campfire.

The moon is full, the night is calm, and Lorenzo Alexander, is getting comfortable. Within a few minutes a white dove landed on his knee.

"My goodness, you sure are friendly," he said.

The white dove flew off his knee as Lorenzo watched. The dove leads him to a vision, about fifty yards from him as he stood up walked slowly toward the vision.

"Lorenzo, get over here and look at his," said Topaz.

Lorenzo walked inside a tent, joined by Topaz, jade, and the four generals. He looked down at the marble table seeing large formation of legions.

"This is our legion of angel warriors, guided by you," said Jade.

"Our legions are not yet set in positions," said Tigereye.

"Are we at war?" asked Lorenzo.

"Yes," replied Topaz. "The antichrist is now, somewhere in your world, in the flesh. You will have to find him."

"The antichrist is not yet in power here," said Lorenzo, looking at Jade.

"That is true. That is why you need to find it before it finds you," said Jade.

"There will be war in your world. Call on us and we will be ready," said Jade.

The antichrist will have legions of its own, Lorenzo. We are prepared," said Jade.

Lorenzo looked at the angels at how they were dressed. "Will you look like that during battle?" he asked. The six angels' looked at each other in their robes.

"How would you like us to look during battle?" asked Topaz.

"The Bible says, you angels wear armor, can that be true?"

"Yes, that is true, Lorenzo," replied Topaz.

"Wear them, and legions shall also wear their shiny armor," said Lorenzo.

"So be it. The next time we meet Lorenzo, we shall be in our shiny armor, said Topaz.

"Well then," Jade called out. "Everything seems to be in good order. The next time we see you Lorenzo, will be at the battle field."

"You all seem so anxious."

"We are all willing to fight, Lorenzo," said Topaz as the vision faded away and Lorenzo found himself standing in the darkness of the forest.

A new day in Gemini brought Ahab and Nelly to a Café to have coffee. Both sat down with their cups of coffee and a donut.

"I can't believe my own daughter turned me in," Ahab said in disbelief.

"You would have been caught anyway, Ahab. Its better being caught by your daughter than by the agents. Besides you got the reward money."

"What do you mean, I got it? My own daughter kept all the cash. That's how greedy she has become, Nelly."

"Does she still live with you?" asked Nelly.

"Yeah, but she is over eighteen, she can do what she wants, Nelly."

Both get up and leave the café to go into the neighborhood for a walk. They walk by the house of Lorenzo and they see the house is watched by agents.

"They won't catch him, and they won't find him," said Ahab.

"Where do you suppose Alexander went?" questioned Nelly.

"If I were him, I would be out of the city. Somewhere in the forest far away where they can't catch me," answered Ahab.

They pass by a party store; Ahab went inside and bought a couple of drinks. Nelly picked up a newspaper to see a picture of Carol on the front page.

"Ahab, looked at this?"

Ahab looked at the newspaper, "It says Carol has been executed for betraying the government."

"How can they do that to her? She was my friend," replied Nelly.

"That's what happened when you don't wear the mark, Nelly. What I don't understand is why they didn't arrest me when I didn't have the mark. Something is wrong here."

"That's what's going to happen to Lorenzo if they catch him," said Nelly walking out of the store.

Deep in the forest and rocky terrain, Lorenzo rested on top of a large boulder looking down the cliff. Soon he heard a voice behind him.

"Don't move, or will shoot."

"Your guns will not work on me," Lorenzo said turning around.

The patrol open fired, but not a single shot was heard. They pointed their guns in another direction and the guns did fired. Again, they aimed at Lorenzo and the guns failed to shoot.

"I will come with you peacefully!" shouted Alexander. He got off the boulder and walked with the soldiers.

A six mile walk brought Lorenzo to a camp, where he was taken to General Hemkock. Lorenzo stood in his office watching the general eat.

"You do not wear the mark, your running away."

"You're not working with the government," said Lorenzo.

"We are rebels against the government," Hemkock said.

"Why? You're wearing the mark,"

"This mark only gives us what we want, it means nothing else to us," Hemkock replied.

"Then, what is your purpose of all this?" asked Lorenzo.

"To start a war," answered Hemkock.

"Against the government?" questioned Lorenzo.

"To fulfill a prophecy," replied Hemkock.

Lorenzo looked at him eye to eye. "What is your name?"

"You tell me first," replied Hemkock.

"I am Lorenzo Alexander, and I think you are absolutely mad. Your whole idea is madness."

"I am General Hemkock to you, and I will start a Holy war."

"You can't start a Holy war here in America General."

"No, but I can gather an army here and leave this county to go to another."

General Hemkock stepped away from his empty plate. He stood up and walked around Lorenzo. "How about you, Alexander, would you like to join my army?"

"No, thank you, general; you're too crazy for me." He replied.

"You already know too much, Lorenzo, I can't let you go, or I could turn you over to the agents, you have no mark," said the general.

"If you turn me over to the agents, I will tell them how crazy you are," Lorenzo said.

"They won't believe you," said the general, opening the door. "Ceepot!"

A high ranking solider entered the room. "You call me, Sir?"

"Put this man in chains," said Hemkock.

Ceepot stood next to Lorenzo. "General, I think that you have the needs of becoming and antichrist," said Lorenzo walking with Ceepot out the door.

Outside, the two men made their way to the jail house. A lady walked up to Ceepot in an emotional state. The woman grabs a hold of Ceepot.

"The minister of the church has given up on our son," she exclaimed.

"That only leaves one thing to do."

"You can't mean that, Ceepot, he's our son," she cried out.

"I'll talk to you later, honey," he said leaving her on the ground crying.

"What is wrong with your son, Ceepot?" asked Lorenzo.

"The ministers tell me that my son is possessed by a demon, and that they have given up on him. The only other way to free my son from a demon is to get rid of the body," he replied reaching the jail house.

"Tell your wife to bring the boy here," said Lorenzo.

"Why?"

"Do you want your son saved, Ceepot?" questioned Lorenzo, walking into the jail house.

"I will bring my son, Simon, to you tonight," he replied.

"Is that his name?"

"Yes," Ceepot answered.

"Ceepot, I will need my knapsack that you took from me," said Lorenzo.

"You'll get it back," said Ceepot, locking up the jail house door.

By late afternoon, a lady showed up at the jail house with food and a knapsack. They saw each other and Lorenzo walked up to the door.

"This is what you asked for," she said.

Lorenzo took his food and knapsack looking at the woman. "You must be the mother of Simon."

"Please help my son, don't let him die," she said to him looking very sad as she walked away.

With the coming of nightfall in the camp it remained quiet, but outside the camp a man was carrying his son followed by a woman, hurrying toward the jail house.

Ceepot unlock the door and took Simon, his seven year old son, inside. His son fought and struggled in his arms while being put on the floor.

"Goddamn it Father! I hate you for this! I will kill you!" shouted Simon.

"Be silent," Lorenzo said in a soft voice touching the boy and Simon, immediately blacked out.

"Can you help, Simon, Lorenzo?" questioned Ceepot.

"Your son will be a boy as he once was," replied Lorenzo.

Ceepot hugged his wife, and together they walked out of the jail house. "We will wait outside." He said.

Simon crawled to a corner and began to laugh. Lorenzo turned and saw the boy laughing very aggressively.

"What is your name?" Lorenzo asked.

"They call me, Simon."

"That is the boy's name. I want to hear your name," Lorenzo said watching the face of Simon turn pale white.

"To you, my name is not important, for I am very powerful. I defeated the ministers. Nothing can beat me, not even you," be said showing its dark red eyes as saliva ran down from the boy's mouth.

"Do you know who I am?"

"You are Lorenzo Alexander. Your name is well known throughout my world. I also know what you are looking for, you will never find him."

"You're talking about the antichrist," said Lorenzo.

"You will never know who it is because you'll be dead," said the demon within Simon, laughing vigorously.

A tap on Lorenzo's shoulder frightened him, but it turned out to be Angel Jade, standing behind him. Angel Jade is dressed in his suit of Armor.

"Do you wish for me to take that demon out of that little boy?" questioned Jade.

"Jade! You son of a gun! I'm not ready to fight you, but there will be another time," the demon said leaving the body of the little boy.

Alexander turned to Jade. "It was afraid of you," he said.

"You know what to do," said jade, disappearing from sight.

Lorenzo walked out of the jail house door to see the mother sitting on the ground and the father pacing by her. He walked toward them with happy news.

"Your son is himself, go and see him."

The mother gets up from the ground and gives Lorenzo a hug, she then ran into the jail house, Ceepot looked at Lorenzo and shakes his hand.

"When I go to see my son, you better leave, because I see nothing and I know nothing," he said as he walked toward the jail house.

At this time, Lorenzo Alexander made his getaway. He hurried down the road, away from the jail house, away from the compound, into the night.

Sunrise, a new day, three in a half hour into the morning, Ceepot entered the general's room and woke General Hemkock.

"The prisoner has escaped from his jail cell, Sir."

How did this happen?" questioned the general in anger.

"Don't know, sir," Ceepot said standing at attention.

"Get a squad of soldiers and find him. I want that man!" shouted Hemkock.

"Yes, Sir!" shouted Ceepot.

The sun raised high from the East and light was shown onto the land. Alexander stood on a steep hill, looking at two squads of soldiers coming toward him.

"General Hemkock doesn't know when to give up," Lorenzo said to himself.

From the north side, a group of agents were also observing the new squads of soldiers moving toward the hill.

"We have no army this far?" questioned Taylor, watching them through the binoculars. Bane walked next to him.

"There's a compound about ten miles from here."

"Who's in charge of that compound?" asked Taylor.

"General Hemkock," replied Bane.

"Why would the General bring a tank and two squads of solider in that area? He's after something," said Taylor, watching through his binoculars.

"Or, someone," Bane replied.

Lorenzo Alexander has put five incense sticks into the ground. He lighted them and stood up to face the eastern sky.

"I wouldn't do this, but those soldiers carry their mark of evil. So I call on thee Tigereye! Bring forth the legion and challenge the army before you."

A sudden silence stood about, and then a sound of thunder is heard throughout. The earth rose like a giant sand storm, rolling down the hill side. Rocks flew about; trees tumbled down in the path of the storm.

"What the hell is that?" questioned Bane, looking through his binoculars.

"I believe it's a storm cloud moving toward the army," said Taylor.

"Do you hear that noise?" Bane asked.

"Yes, I do, and it sounds like a bunch of horses," replied Taylor.

Ceepot is sitting in a jeep following a tank, he could also hear the thunderous sound of horses and it gets louder.

"Stop the jeep soldier!" he shouted looking through his binoculars. "I can hear them, but I can't see them," said Ceepot. "They must be in those clouds of smoke." The officer puts down his binoculars and turned to a soldier.

"I want you to call headquarters and tell the general we are being attacked by an army led by Lorenzo."

"Yes, Sir," said the soldier making the call.

Once again he watches through his binoculars and he becomes startled to see what is happening. His face turned white and mouth became dried.

"It's unbelievable!" he mumbled seeing body parts flying into the air, while the ground turned red with blood.

Taylor, witnessed the entire event as he puts down his binoculars and sits down in his jeep turning to Bane, who also saw what had happened.

"Take me to the compound; I want to see General Hemkock."

Right away, Sir," said Lester, as they all got into the jeep and drove away.

Ceepot is sitting in his jeep being driven back to the compound. He is talking to General Hemkock, over the Phone.

"I don't know where Lorenzo got his army, but they hide in the clouds. Our men didn't have a chance, they were slaughtered, sir." He exclaimed.

Remaining silent he hears what the General had to say. "Yes, sir, over an out," said Ceepot, hanging up the phone.

"The general is not very pleased."

"Sir, if the general had seen what we've seen, I say forget about the man, let him go," said Lester.

"I would do the same soldier, but that is not our decision."

At the compound, Taylor arrived with curiosity. He stood up and stepped down from the jeep. He looked at the general's office.

"Wait here," Taylor said walking into the general's office.

"Lieutenant Taylor," said the General.

"General Hemkock," he said as they saluted each other.

"What brings you here, Lieutenant?" asked the general.

"I have just witnessed the slaughtering of your men, General."

"Exactly what did you see, Lieutenant?" asked the General.

"I saw a cloud come down a hill and kill your men, General."

"Did you see an army, lieutenant?"

"No, sir but I heard an army, General," he replied.

General Hemkock leaned back on his chair, he is puzzled at what Taylor had said, and he remained in deep thought not saying a word.

"Lorenzo Alexander is my man, leave him to me, I know him more than you do, General."

"Where did Lorenzo get such an army so soon, Lieutenant?"

"He has his ways, General," replied Taylor.

"Well then, it just so happens that I want him too, Lieutenant."

"I want him because he has no mark, General."

"I want him for killing my men, Lieutenant."

At this time, Ceepot entered the general's office and finds the two officers. He stands at attention and salutes the both of them.

"Sir!"

"Not now, Sergeant," said Hemkock.

"Yes, sir!" he replied leaving the room.

"You want him dead, general and so do I," responded Taylor.

"What's your reason for wanting him dead, Lieutenant?"

"It's personal, General."

"Since you want him more than I do, go then see to it that it is done and bring me proof, Lieutenant."

"I will bring you this head, general," he stated leaving the office.

In the far regions of the desert, Lorenzo Alexander walked under the heat of the sun. The man was dusty, has been in the desert for many hours, yet he does not sweat, or is tired, and shows no signs of thirst or hunger.

Lorenzo came to a town somewhere in the desert sands. A town cut off from the outside world, a town in which no one carried the mark.

People stared at the stranger, but Lorenzo made his way to the church and stood by the steps. He dusted himself off as he saw the reverend walking toward him.

"Are you thirsty?" he questioned holding a bottle of water.

"I could use a drink," answered Lorenzo, taking the bottle of water.

"I am Reverend Daniel, and you must be Lorenzo Alexander."

"How do you know who I am, Daniel?" he questioned.

"The lady in the church told me about a stranger coming into town, and that person is you. Come inside the church and meet her."

Lorenzo took a drink from the bottle and looked at the reverend. He pours water over his head and takes a second drink giving the water bottle back to the reverend.

"I believe I will meet this lady," he said walking up the steps into the church.

Inside stood and old lady in front of the pews, she was kneeling and praying when Daniel came to her. Lorenzo stood at the altar.

Daniel whispered into her ear and then he sits down. The old woman finished praying, got up, and slowly walked toward Lorenzo.

"Let me feel your hand," she said in a kind voice.

Lorenzo put his hand onto hers noticing that she was blind. The old woman felt his hand, rubbed his hand, and placed his hand on to her cheeks.

"I am sister Isidore and you are the stranger I have been waiting for."

"The reverend tells me you know who I am."

"Come and sit with me Lorenzo Alexander," said sister Isidore, sitting on a pew together.

"What do you know about me, Sister?" questioned Lorenzo.

"I know what you are looking for? I know that the angels are on your side, but do you know why the angels chose you?" questioned sister Isidore.

"No, I don't," replied Lorenzo.

"Do you know why you are here?"

"I am here to fight the antichrist," Lorenzo replied.

"That is the purpose of you being here. It does not answer of why you are here," said Sister Isidore.

"Do you know the answer to that question, Sister?"

"You and I, and everyone in this world are being tested by the lord. We are to take the place of the fallen Angels. Remember that, Lorenzo Alexander."

"If what you say is true, then that explains why this world is in such turmoil."

"Yes. The fallen angels want us to fail the test, and if they succeed, we all are doomed as they are."

"Thank you for telling me what I needed to know, Sister Isidore," said Lorenzo as he stood standing by the church doors. Lorenzo stared at the sky, while Daniel made the sound of coughing.

"That woman is very good in what she says, take care of her."

"The sun is setting, Alexander, you cannot walk in the desert at night. Rest here and leave at sunrise," said Daniel.

"I shall do that," said Lorenzo, walking away from the church into town looking for a place to stay.

The night sky covered the town and a mass was being held. Outside the church doors, they hear the rumbling of trucks and sounds of a jeep.

The church doors were kicked open and soldiers enter, led by Lieutenant Taylor. The mass was interrupted.

Everyone watched the lieutenant walk down the aisle toward Daniel, the reverend.

"Where is he?" asked Lieutenant.

"Who wants to know?" questioned Daniel.

"I am Lieutenant Taylor, I am looking for a man that you have hiding, his tracks brought us here." He said grabbing Daniel by his collar, "So I know he's here, now tell me, where is Lorenzo Alexander?"

Without hesitation a voice spoke out somewhere in the audience. Taylor stood listening to what it had to say.

"He went west into the desert, about two hours ago."

Upon hearing this, Lieutenant Taylor throws reverend Daniel to the floor. Taylor turns around to face the audience.

"This church is closed by the order of the government. This reverend disobeyed the laws of the government and is under arrest."

"Lieutenant" shouted Hemkock, standing by the church doors. "Nobody in this town is wearing the mark"

Taylor looked at the audience and turns to Ceepot. "Sergeant!" he shouted.

"Sir!" he replied.

"Take the men and surround this town. No one is to leave until they all received their mark."

"Yes sir," said Ceepot.

"And take this man in irons," Taylor said having two soldiers pick up the reverend form the floor and take him away.

Taylor walked down the aisle up to General Hemkock and turned to the audience. The audience themselves were talking among each other.

"Everybody out of this church, now!" he said walking out with the General.

"We'll spend the night here, Lorenzo can't go far by foot, we'll find him tomorrow," said Hemkock.

"This town is surrounded, sir no one can leave," said the sergeant.

"You can now start giving out the marks sergeant," said lieutenant.

"Yes, sir."

"Ceepot!" the general cried out.

"What is it, General, sir?

"Burn the church down, Ceepot,"

"Right away, General."

"I am leaving here lieutenant; I will leave you in charge."

"Where are you going general?"

"I'm going back to the compound. I have an idea of how to capture Lorenzo, lieutenant."

"May I ask about your idea, General?"

"A hostage, lieutenant."

"Find Ahab and Mitsy. Then Lorenzo will surrender to us, general."

"That's my idea, lieutenant," he said getting into the jeep "I'll be back," being driven into the night.

Somewhere in the dark regions of the desert, under the stars, Lorenzo Alexander was asleep upon the sand, yet a restless night.

"Wake up Lorenzo," he heard a voice, feeling the touch of an angel.

Lorenzo sat up, looking at the angel. "What is it, Jade?"

"In the morning, look to the south, Lorenzo you will see soldiers looking at you."

"Let them watch. I have nothing to hide, jade, but I am sure that you and my generals will not let them get close to me."

"As you say, Lorenzo," said Jade fading away.

The sunrises and a hot day, the temperature has rising in the hours of the morning. Lieutenant Taylor and his soldiers stood in the desert, looking through their binoculars.

"I believe he knows we are watching him, Sir,"

Lieutenant Taylor grind his teeth watching Lorenzo through his binoculars. The man sits on the desert sand waving his hands, knowing very well he is being watched.

"Sergeant Ceepot, I want you to send four men down there to arrest Lorenzo. Bring him to me alive."

"Yes sir," said Ceepot, going to his men.

At the hot dessert, Lorenzo sat on the hot sand watching them at what they were about to do. Lorenzo smiles to see a jeep come his way.

"Here comes company, jade, you know what to do." He exclaimed.

Driving down the desert, heading toward Lorenzo, the tires of the jeep pop. There sat a jeep with two flat tires. Two men are about to get out of the jeep when the jeep itself explodes in flames, setting fire to the men.

"Damn," said Taylor.

"Shall I send more men, sir?" Ceepot said.

"No, we will wait here, but do keep a close watch on Lorenzo. Let me know if he makes any sudden moves."

"Yes, sir," Ceepot said.

Early afternoon in the city, general Hemkock and two agents knock on the door, answered by Mitsy.

"Is your father home?" asked Hemkock.

"No," replied Mitsy.

"You are his daughter?" questioned Hemkock

"Yes."

"Where is your father?" asking once more.

Mitsy stays silent, looking at the agents and the General. She felt very uncomfortable as if she had done something wrong.

"Your government people, my father already has the mark."

"That's not why we're here," Hemkock said.

"Is my father arrested?"

"No."

"Wait one minute," Mitsy said, going into the house and takes her coat to join the men.

"We only want your father," said Hemkock.

"Where my father goes, I go," said Mitsy.

She stood standing as the men looked at each other as if they had no choice. General Hemkock turned to her with a smile.

"Very well," he said walking to the car with Mitsy sitting in the back seat.

Ahab is with Nelly at her house. At this time Nelly prepared herself for work. She made her way toward Ahab and kissed him good-bye.

"If you are leaving, lock my house," she said.

"I will," said Ahab as Nelly left for work.

Two hours later, Ahab walked out of the house with trash bag. A government car stopped by the road side. The car window rolls down and he sees Mitsy.

"Hello, Dad."

"What have you done now?" he asked.

A car door opens and General Hemkock steps out. They stare at each other for a moment as the General spoke with a strong voice.

"Ahab you are to come with us, now. It's very urgent."

Not saying a word, Ahab set the trash bag down on the ground and got into the car next to Mitsy. They drive away as Ahab looked at the general.

"What has my daughter done, General?" questioned Ahab.

"In what way, General?" "Nothing, but I am in need of your help, Ahab."

"I will tell you when we get there, Ahab."

"Exactly where are we going, General?"

"Bownet, Ahab."

"Bownet is in the desert. What am I going to do there General?"

"In the desert, there's a man that we want. We cannot get close to him, but with your help, we can catch him."

"It sounds like Lorenzo Alexander," said Mitsy excitedly. "Am I right?"

"Is it Lorenzo Alexander?" questioned Ahab.

"Yes, it is."

"I will never betray my friend, General."

"Not even for a great sum of money, Ahab? The government is willing to pay; I know you're in debt."

Ahab showed greediness in his face. A thought comes to mind in what it would feel like to be free from debt, and have extra cash in his pocket

"No," he responded.

"Maybe not you, perhaps your daughter," said Hemkock.

"What do I have to do?" asked Mitsy.

"No!" shouted Ahab.

"Dad, the government is going to give us money. If you don't want it, I'll take it."

"No, Mitsy. It is wrong doing this."

The both of them looked at the General as the General is staring at each of them. Father and daughter kept silent turning away from the general.

"Don't mind me, talk amongst yourselves, we have time," said Hemkock, resting on the seat, smoking a pipe.

In the land of the hot desert sand, Lorenzo sat under the heat of the sun. Drinking water, Jade sat next to him watching the soldiers.

"Why don't you let us attack that force?" asked angel jade.

"I do not wish to start a fight. Let them start first," replied Lorenzo.

"This is going to end in a standstill, Alexander."

"I do not think so. They are up to something, Jade."

The sun is now beginning to set. Arriving in the town of Bownet, the government car stopped by the sheriff's office. Everyone got out of the car and Ahab saw a burn down church.

"Is that one of your doings, General?"

"A candle started that fire, Ahab."

The sheriff came out to greet them and they all entered the sheriff's office accompanied by the sheriff himself. The general sits down looking at Ahab.

"You had time to think Ahab. What's its going to be? Are you going to help me or not?"

"Lorenzo is my friend, General, I can't do it."

"Sheriff, lock this man up," said Hemkock, as Ahab is taken to the jail room.

"What about me?" questioned Mitsy.

"Are you willing to help?" asked Hemkock.

"Depends how much you give?" questioned Mitsy.

"Five thousand," replied Hemkock.

"That kind of money, I would cheat you."

"Ten thousand."

"A hundred thousand, general," said Mitsy.

"You are greedier than your father. You could cheat the devil in his own game."

"Do you want Lorenzo or not?" questioned Mitsy.

"You'll have it," replied the General, "But you better earn it."

Don't worry, General, You'll have Lorenzo in an hour," as they walk out of the Sheriff's office.

"What is your plan?" asked Hemkock.

"Take me to the desert," Mitsy said getting into the jeep.

"What is your plan?" asked Hemkock a second time.

"I'm going to drive this jeep to meet Lorenzo. You wait with your army and I'll bring Alexander to you."

"You make it sound so easy," said Hemkock.

"Lorenzo will not hurt me, General," Mitsy, being driven to the desert.

Not far away, Lorenzo sat on the desert sand under the heat without a shade. The sun was setting and the evening sky was approaching. Lorenzo stood staring at the army when all of a sudden he saw a jeep coming toward him.

"Shall I stop her?" asked jade.

"Did you say her?"

"Yes," answered jade.

Lorenzo stood silent for a moment, and then he said, "No, let her through."

At the army camp site, General Hemkock, stood standing on a jeep watching through his binoculars. He nods his head with a smile.

"She's going to do it."

"I knew Lorenzo wouldn't let Mitsy down. They are good friends," said Taylor.

Mitsy stopped the jeep next to Lorenzo. She remains sitting in her jeep looking at Lorenzo, who doesn't look tired or thirsty at all.

"What are you doing here Mitsy?"

"They are holding my father hostage. They sent me to get you, and if I go back without you, they will shoot my father in the morning and torture me when I return."

"So they have my friend, Ahab," said Lorenzo standing up. "It looks like I have no choice," he said walking around the jeep.

"Does that mean you'll come with me?" Mitsy asked.

"I'm afraid so," replied Lorenzo getting into the jeep.

Mitsy turned on the jeep as Lorenzo wipes the sweat off his face. They were about to drive away when they hear a faint voice from behind them.

"Mitsy."

They turn around to see a female angel descending onto the desert sand. Mitsy is astounded for she has never seen anything like this before.

"Mitsy, a lost child, a child not wanting to be found, what lies ahead in life is not very promising," said the angel fading away.

Lorenzo and mitsy looked at each other and she smiles at him with a surprising look on her face. The man showed no emotion.

"What ever happens tonight, Mitsy believe in what you see."

Keeping herself silent she drives toward the army camp. Her amazement turns into confusion and she becomes disturbed.

"That is the first time I saw an angel, and I don't know what she meant in what she said." Mitsy said.

"She's telling you, that you need to be saved," said Lorenzo as they reached the army camp.

"So now we have you," said Taylor, standing next to General Hemkock.

"Release my friend, Ahab!" shouted Lorenzo.

"Not so fast," Taylor said with a smile of hate.

"Take Lorenzo Alexander in town and tie him up in chains against the poles."

"Yes, sir," Ceepot said, taking Lorenzo away.

"What about my payment, General?" questioned Mitsy.

"Oh yes, your payment," Hemkock said walking up to mitsy and hands her a check.

"This check is only ten thousand, general?"

"That's all you're getting."

"You bastard!" she shouted in anger.

General Hemkock walked away from Mitsy and up to the government agents, which they were standing by the car. Hemkock pointed at Mitsy.

"Take this lady back to the city and make sure the father is with her." He said as the agents came walking toward Mitsy.

"You're nothing, but an asshole!" shouted Mitsy, as she was taken away.

By this time, night has taken over the sky. Lorenzo was tied in chains between two poles facing a full moon. A guard stood on watch. Jade appeared in front of him.

"Do you wish to be free?"

"It won't do any good," he replied.

"Who are you talking to, Lorenzo?" questioned Taylor walking in front of him.

"Shall I punish him for you?"

"No, but make him see my warriors before I die," mumbled Lorenzo.

"I'm going to let you stay there until you dry up like a prune," Taylor said slapping him on the face.

"On the day that you kill me, you will see my legion of angels and on that day, you shall never sleep until you take your own life," said Lorenzo.

"Go ahead; bring your invisible army here. A lot of innocent people will die," said Taylor walking away.

The morning sun rose and Lorenzo felt a cold wind blowing. He opened his eyes to see lightening in the sky. Even more than that, he saw a legion of angels on horseback among the clouds.

"We are going to wait for you," Topaz said standing next to him.

"If I'm going to die, what happens to my mission?" questioned Lorenzo in his weak voice "Do not worry, Alexander, there is another."

"I'm so tired and thirsty, Topaz."

"Have no fear, Lorenzo, soon you will join us. Taylor will see you more powerful than he ever imaged."

Three hours later, Taylor and Hemkock walked up to the dying man. Taylor poured water over his head awakening Lorenzo.

"What do you want?" asked Lorenzo in a low, weary voice.

"I want to see your invisible army," Taylor said.

"You will see it, Taylor. After I'm dead, but General Hemkock won't be, because he will be dead before me."

Hearing this, Hemkock becomes angry. He walked toward Lorenzo, and pulled on his hair looking at a face of a tired man.

"Who said so?" he asked.

"Look at the sky, General. It's cloudy. A storm is brewing just for you."

"I'm going to enjoy this day, watching you die," said Hemkock, letting go of his hair.

"How am I to die, Taylor?" asked Lorenz, hearing the sound of thunder.

"A slow death," he replied looking at him." The general wants your head and I want your heart."

"Remember what I said Taylor?"

"Am I supposed to be scared, Lorenzo?"

A lightning flashed and a cold breeze blew about, the sound of thunder in the air. Hemkock and Taylor looked at the darken sky.

"Your death is at hand, general," said Lorenzo.

"You will die first! Kill him now, Taylor!" shouted the general in anger.

At this time a bolt of lightning hit the ground, setting General Hemkock on fire. Taylor was also thrown to the ground. He saw the general burning.

Taylor got up from the ground and wipes himself clean. He then walked toward Lorenzo with hate in his eyes.

"It is done, just as I said."

"Die Alexander as you should have died," said Taylor stabbing him in the chest with a dagger.

From behind him, Taylor heard a voice. He turned around and saw an army of angels, it frightened him unable to speak a single word.

"We have been waiting for you," said Jade.

"I'm happy that you are wearing your armor, Jade, and to all that is here I am proud," said Alexander.

Taylor rubbed his eyes and saw four angels on horseback. A thousand or more angels stood behind at a distance. His mouth is dried, and he showed a shocking expression on his face.

Lorenzo Alexander mounted on a horse. The animal reacted, but it behaved itself. Lorenzo joins the angels and looked down on the officer.

"I'll be waiting for you, Taylor," he said with a smile. "Angel warriors! We march!"

Taylor is overwhelmed with fear, yet he only watched Lorenzo Alexander lead an army of angels up into the clouds.

III

THREE YEARS PASSED SINCE the death of Lorenzo Alexander. Nelly had joined a new religion that has formed among other religions. It's become popular in the minds of young adults and it has put other religions out of order.

It's in the month of Taurus, and the children were camping. Nelly, a leader among the campgrounds helped in keeping the children happy.

Evening has brought forth a campfire. There was singing and the children were roasting marshmallows. A woman, dressed in red with a dark cloak, sat in front of the campfire.

Nelly never saw her before. She only knew that she's from the pasture and came to the campgrounds. It didn't bother Nelly, nor did she show no harm to the children.

She talked like a librarian telling a story who knows a lot about the knowledge of Sorcery. She made herself known by telling a believable story that made Nelly curious.

"I, Jessica Sentena, will tell you to open your hearts, clear your minds, and listen to me with your ears. I will tell you, yes I will, about Jetson Mo-Billy, a man of mystery.

Jetson Mo-Billy is a humble kind of guy. He never married, or could not understand the love between a man and a woman. The kind of love that he had, touched the hearts of many. Even the animals were kind to him.

Many people say he could have been a saint, but that's not to be. He could have been a man of God, but he chose not to be. He lived alone, learning the ways unknown to man.

From his heart came forth knowledge. From his mind came forth wisdom and the works that he did came forth power.

Some say Jetson conquered darkness and learned the secrets within it. Friends who know him say, he conquered loneliness and learned what lay beyond it. Others say Jetson holds the key to other worlds, think of it, all that power he had within his grasp."

The lady drinks some water and put some wood into the campfire. She looks at those who are listening to her story and then she stares at the fire.

"There came a day to Jetson Mo-Billy when a question came to his mind. 'Is there life after death? Is there a heaven? Is there a hell?' this bothered Jetson, so he set himself to do a task.

This man came forth to me, Jessica Sentena, asking me to be his servant. I became thrilled about this, for I knew I would be at his side, eager to learn his secrets. I am to be contacted at later date."

At this time Nelly walked slowly toward the campfire. She holds a paper cup of water and she remains standing while all others are sitting on the ground. Nelly called out to the lady.

"Are you really Jessica Sentena?" she asked.

"What do you think?" replied the lady continuing her story.

"Passing days led me to forget what I have said to Jetson Mo-Billy, until my phone rang one morning. It was him telling me that I should come on a Saturday afternoon.

At long last, it has come I was determine to know all about Jetson Mo-Billy. I told myself. "Here is a man that is a mystery to me, a man not like any other man I know. He doesn't drink or smoke, stays very quiet, and works hard at his job I don't even know what he does."

Once more the lady drank water from a water bottle she brought. She was about to continued her story when Nelly asked her a questioned to her.

"Is Jetson Mo-Billy a living person?" she asked.

"What do you think?" replied Jessica.

"Is this a true story?" Nelly asked.

"I'm not likely to say," answered Jessica knowing that Nelly is interested in her story as she continued.

"Let me explain about his house. It has religious paintings on the walls, sculptures, and magical artifacts. So many things I wanted to know, but Jetson Mo-Billy would not tell me. That's the kind of man he is.

I did not say a word to him, but only listened to his instructions that he gave me. With incense burning and a lit candle, I watched Jetson Mo-Billy go into a trance, a deep sleep."

At this time, Jessica Sentena got up from the campfire and walked away from the group toward the pasture where she came from.

Nelly ran after her until she caught up with the lady. Jessica Sentena, knew then she was interested in her story looking at her

"I want to know one thing," said Nelly.

"What?"

"What happened to Jetson Mo-Billy?" questioned Nelly.

"Let him tell you," replied Jessica.

"Then this man is still alive," Nelly said.

"You said that. I didn't," said Jessica.

"I want to meet jetson Mo-Billy," Nelly said.

Jessica Sentena paused for a moment looking at her eye to eye. Nelly stood standing scratching her head and stared at her

"Let me see your left hand," said Jessica.

"Why?" asked Nelly putting out her left hand.

Jessica looked at her palm of her left hand. She remain silent staring at her palm. Nelly knew she was reading her palm.

"If you want to meet Jetson Mo-Billy, it must be now.

"Let's go," Nelly said walking together, away from the campgrounds.

Jetson Mo-Billy, a man on a mission, lives in a seven bedroom house. He sits on a sofa with a lit candle on each side, meditating. Deep in his heart within his mind he's saying.

"I know a great many things, good and evil, angels and demons, magic of all forms that's the kind of man I have become. Call me anything you want, but I know what I am."

Nelly and Jessica enter the house, making their way to where Jetson stood. They find him on the sofa staring at a candlelight, meditating.

"Be very quiet. He will soon talk to you," Jessica said leaving the room.

Nelly walked around the room looking at the religious paintings, rosaries hanging on the walls, a bible on a glass table, and beautiful flowers.

Why are you here?" Jetson asked.

Nelly sat on the couch talking to him. "I want to know what you saw in the supernatural world."

"That is not true. You want to know if I met Lorenzo Alexander," said Jetson.

"Do you know Lorenzo Alexander? Did you meet him?" Nelly asked.

"Listen to me, Nelly," he said as Jessica Sentena returns. "I will tell you about the world of the supernatural," he said calmly, opening his tiresome eyes.

"I, Jetson Mo-Billy, am a man on a journey into the unknown to see if there's life after death. In order to do this, I must perform an out-of-body experience. I did just that I can see myself lying in the bed and I see Jessica at my bedside. I float away into space without time. I see light, I see darkness, I feel cold, I feel warm, I float into mist, and finally into a fog. I find myself in a place, I know not where. I see many people wandering around like zombies. Some are in pain, and others are crying. I tried talking to them, but they only ignored me. I then hear a voice behind me, which I turn around. I saw a woman dressed in a gown of blue, white, and pink.

'Are you an angel?' I asked softly.

'I am Gabriella Angelina, here to guide you.' she answered.

'Were you sent to me?' I asked her.

'Yes,' she replied, giving off a wonderful fragrance.

'Who sent you?' I asked. To me she smelled so grand.

"'The angels,' she replied.

'I want to see an angel,' I said.

'You will, all in good time,' Gabriella said walking by me.' Come.'

I followed this woman and her fragrance made me feel peaceful. She brought me to a pond where I saw many people drinking from it.

'What is this place?' I asked.

'You are on an island, Jetson, between heaven and hell the water from this pond comes from the River Lethe. Dead souls drink this water to forget everything that they did in the mortal world.'

'My dear Angelina, this river is not meant for me.'

'That is true, Jetson Mo-Billy, for you have a body to return to,' she said walking on a path made of pebbles of stones.

It's a long walk on this path I now see the river Lethe and I have seen many things. I could not believe my eyes. We stayed close to the river seeing people swimming in it. At long last, Gabriella stopped and turned around.

'Do you know why you are her?' she asked.

I smiled at her. 'I am here to explore the world of the absolute.'

'That is not what I asked,' said Gabriella standing at the edge of another river. This is the river Acheron. Some call it the river of sorrow. Notice its color is different that the river of Lethe, Jetson Mo-Billy,' she said walking on the edge of the river.

'What's on the other side?' I asked looking at the water that seemed to be infested with body parts.

'The beginning of Hell,' Gabriella replied reaching a boat.

'Is that where we are going?' I asked.

'Yes. Jetson Mo-Billy,' she answered talking softly.

'Do not say a word just look. This is the Ferryman Charon, he will take us across the river,' as she got into the boat

We did not have to wait long. I watched the oars strike the water, rolled by four skeletal men, two on each side of the boat.

Charon stood at the back of the boat steering. I watched this man whose eyes were heavy blue, without a blink, or even a wink. An old man with large finger nails, a beard down to his chest, and long bleached hair, that shines in the dark without light.

We reached the other side of the River Acheron without any trouble. I got off the boat with Gabriella Angelina. I saw the beginnings of the Darker Regions.

'We can always turn back if you fear Jetson Mo-Billy,' said Gabriella.

'I choose to keep going, I must see,' I said to her without being afraid, even though I was, but I hid it well.

I'm standing on beach sand that is solid black, which matches the surroundings that stood quiet and frightening I felt fear like I never felt before.

'Stay close to me, this way darkness cannot separate us,' said Gabriella Angelina.

I was confused when she said that. 'You mean to tell me that darkness around here is alive?' I asked.

'No, I'm talking about the Prince of Darkness,' said Gabriella.

From out of the darkness, a scream of a woman frightened me watching her run pass me. I was amazed to see children, women, and men wandering. They all act dumb, not knowing what they were doing.

'This is limbo, the first level of hell. What you see here are those unbaptized, unbelievers, and the forgotten. Their minds have been taken, they do things without thought,' Gabriella said.

Our journey continued to the second level of hell. A strong wind blew about within the dark from all directions. Sand got into my eyes, and when I cleared them, I stood face to face with heads on a tree. They were snarling and growling at me. I screamed running toward Gabriella.

'Did you see where I was?'

'Yes I did, what you saw is Zaccrnu, a tree with the heads of devils.' She answered standing on top of the hill 'look down there Jetson Mo-Billy. Minos judges of hell, tossed over and over in a howling wind,' Gabriella said walking on top of the hill.

It would seem to me the further we went into the darker regions, the darker it got. I was now stepping into mud, or at least I thought it was mud. It felt like mud, I hoped it was mud and nothing else.

'We are now in Cerberus, the third level of hell, where sinners are wallowing in mire,' said Gabriella moving forward. We came out of the mud and onto hard rock. It was becoming difficult to see in the dark, but I find myself on top of a mountain I saw sinners rolling boulders at each other. It must have been some kind of game.

One of them stood up and walked up to me. 'You do not belong here, you are not dead. I should have taken over your body, but I cannot,' it said going back to what it was doing. The sinner gets behind a boulder and pushed it down the mountain.

I stared at the sinner and it stared right back at me. Something that it said I didn't understand looking at its bloody body. I then turned to Gabriella.

'What did he mean by that?' I asked.

'I asked you again Jetson Mo-Billy, why are you here?' I didn't even understand her either so I said nothing to her. Our journey took us to a strange river. It looked strange to me because there were no waves and no ripples. It didn't even react like a river, it stood lifeless.

'You are here at the river's edge Jetson Mo-Billy. The River Styx, the river of gloom. Look at its color, polluted with the blood of souls trapped within it,' she said reaching large rocks going across the river, and the both of them crossed the river by the way of the rocks.

'Do they call this the River of Lost Souls?'

'You can call it the Jetson,' she said standing on top of one of that rocks.

I stood behind her as we jumped from one rock to another entering a fog-like cloud. It had a foul stench that made me stop. I was coughing and gagging, it smelled like that of a dead corpse, and I began to hear voices screaming in my ears.

'Do not stop Jetson Mo-Billy! You must move on!' Shouted Gabriella Angelina. I continued to do what she asked, one rock to the next. I also noticed that the river cast no image of me. It looked so dark, empty, and very spooky looking. I was totally amused when I reached the other side. I danced around Gabriella, knowing that I made it

'We are now on level five Jetson Mo-Billy. Here you see the poor souls fighting and arguing in the mud of Styx.'

Moving on a path made of mud it took us into the Forest of Doom. Trees were tangled with other trees, branches and limbs were twisted, and long vines with thorns crossed our muddy path. I was surprised to see animal parts, as well as human parts, scattered about the forest. A mist overtook the forest that seemed to be alive in the darkness. As we walked through the Forest of Doom I do not hear any sound of insects or see any kinds of life. I also see that the path of mud has been mixed with blood.

Stepping out of the forest the heavy darkness turned into semi-darkness. I am able to see the surroundings, so I am looking at a city ahead of us and there were bonfires.

'I didn't know a city existed in the darker regions Gabriella.'

'They do, Jetson Mo-Billy. This is the City of Dis,' she said walking toward the city

Upon entering the City of Dis, I saw demons leaving the city in a hurry. I also see many souls entering the city. One of these poor souls came running near us shouting.

'It's party time! Demons are leaving! Time to party!' I stopped him.

'Why are the demons leaving?' I asked.

'Their leader wants to see them in Pandemonium,' he replied running and shouting like a mad man.

The city of Dis is nothing compared to the cities of the organic world. The entire city is built on blocks of stone, sand, and wood. They come in many shapes or forms, from squares to cones, rectangles to sea shell shapes, without windows or doors. Everything is so tightly enclosed, that only one person can walk between structures.

To my astonishment I heard my name being called. Someone knows me here. I looked above a circular structure after hearing my name a second time.

'Jetson! Goddamn it! I know all about you!'

'You know my name, but I do not know yours,' I said looking at a terrible demon.

'They call me Bitu, and you have a mortal body that I want. I am coming to your world, Jetson, and I will find you,' he said flying away.

'You have now seen the city of Dis,' said Gabriella Angelina. I, on the other hand, became worried.

'Is that demon, Bitu, really coming to my world to look for me?' I asked.

'He has the ability,' answered Gabriella.

'How can that be?'

'It all relates to my question Jetson Mo-Billy. Why are you here?' Gabriella asked as she walked out and away from the city of Dis.

Once again the darkness returned and it felt hot beneath my feet. The ground is hard and the air has a sulfur smell.

'We are approaching level six, the Burning Tombs, where demons put their captured souls into tombs The souls do not burn, but they feel the agony of the heat,' said Gabriella as we passed by the tombs.

Soon I was standing on a petrified log where there was a river without a shore. A river, alive with waves caused by fire burning upon it. A raging fire that swirled like a tornado, shooting fifty feet into the darkness.

Gabriella stood next to me and said 'What you see here is the River Phlegethon, the river of fire.'

'How are we going to cross this river?' I asked.

'We fly over, Jetson,' replied Gabriella.' After all, we are spirits.'

I'm now floating over the river of fire and I see flames without light. Darkness swallowed the light of fire. Flames burning with no light, it was so strange to me.

We finally reached the other side of the River Phlegethon. I landed on the ground which is of desert sand, and very warm.

'This is the beginning of level seven, Jetson Mo-Billy,' said Gabriella making her way into the desert.

Up the hill and down the hill we went, until we came upon pits that looked like well holes. Some were empty and others had poor souls in them.

'Violence against the demons is immersed in the waters of Phlegethon,' said Gabriella, passing by the pits.

I followed her, watching the fire come out the pits, and listening to the screaming of the souls in agony. Yet, not one could get out of the pits they were trapped inside.

We then come to a valley of giant trees. All of these trees are dead, up-rooted, and most of them were tree trunks.

I could not believe my eyes when I saw souls enclosed into these tree trunks; I was very disturbed to see them naked.

'This is a place for suicides, for those who took their own life without reason. Also, for those who took their own life because they wished to do so, are here to suffer,' said Gabriella.

I see an animal hidden in the darkness. Its blood shot eyes stared at me. The dog beast growled, showing its pale yellow fangs with green saliva falling from its mouth. The dog beast stood still and was about the size of a tiger with two inch claws.

'Away with you dog beast!' shouted Gabriella.

For once I felt fear, and Gabriella could see the fear in me as we watch the dog beast run into the darkness. I could hear its bark echoed in my ears.

'I do not like it here, let us leave this place,' I exclaimed.

'I will lead you to the desert of burning sands, Jetson Mo-Billy,' she said making her way out of the valley.

The further I went into the desert, the hotter the sand got. The heat that dwells within the darkness is so immense in a desert land. I don't see any sand dunes just a desolated desert region is all that I could see and feel.

The hot air stood still and dry, so dry that I could choke. The heat felt like the breath of a dragon, my spiritual body began to sweat.

I don't know how long we been walking in this desert heat, but for a spiritual body I was becoming exhausted. At long last we stopped to observe a city sparkling with black lights.

'Behold, the city of Pandemonium, the capital of the Infernal Regions,' said Gabriella.

From here the city looked magnificent, although deep inside I felt its true evil. I stared at the city and I knew the most powerful demons stood within the city.

'I do not wish to enter this city Gabriella,' I exclaimed.

'We will walk by it, Jetson,' she said not wanting to enter either.

I stay hidden in the darkness away from the black lights, when all of a sudden a demon stopped in front of me. I was speechless in the sight of him.

'Well! What have we here?' it said.

'Leave him alone Murmur!' shouted Gabriella.

'This is not your concern, you bitch,' he said staring at Jetson.

I looked at the demon as he was wearing a dull armor. An evil warrior I knew then, he was on a griffin and wore a dull crown upon his head. It seemed as if he just got back from a battle. Holding a lance he jabs it into the sand near me, looking at me with those flaming red eyes.

'Why are you here, at our place, you worthless good for nothing Jetson, so stupid.'

'Is Satan in that city?' I asked as Murmur laughed loudly.

'You came into this world to fight the devil himself,' he said laughing.

'I wanted to see what he looks like,' I said.

'You don't stand a chance against him, Jetson, so stupid. Right now he's in your world as I will soon be. And I'll be waiting for you,' he cackled and he headed for the city.

'Did you hear what he said Gabriella Angelina? The devil is in my world.'

'Yes, I heard, and I want you to remember what he said, Jetson Mo-Billy,' she said to me moving on, away from the city.

We remained on the burning sands of level seven. It was very quiet in the desert land. I could hear myself breathing in the darkness, and I was the only one leaving footprints on the burning sands, Gabriella did not.

Soon all this quietness came to an end. I heard a roar in the darkness the desert sand has turned into gravel, and the roar got louder and louder.

'We are reaching the Great Chasm falls, and beyond that is level eight,' said Gabriella.

I could hear the sound of the falls, but it remained so dark that I couldn't see the waterfall at all. I could smell rotted flesh coming from within the waterfall.

We now entered level eight of the Darker Regions. We saw demons pushing souls off a mountain. The land below where the souls fell was unknown to me.

'I will tell you this, Jetson Mo-Billy. As we go through this level,' Gabriella said picking up her gown. 'We are in the land of Malbolge, where trenches for the fraudulent exist. The seducers are scourged, the erroneous are afflicted with awful diseases, and others are immersed in reptiles.'

To me this was a terrible scene to be in, a disgusting sight that made me sick. I stayed at the outer edges of level eight.

'Level nine is also known as Malbolge, Jetson Mo-Billy. Here you see the soul sowers of discord, which are constantly being cut in half by demons as you can see?'

I felt even sicker watching this repulsive sight. I turned my head away so that I could not see this ugliness. The smell on this level is very unpleasant, I could not stand it.

'This is worse than level eighth, Gabriella Angelina,' I said.

'You must see, Jetson Mo-Billy. Counselors of fraud are wrapped in flames, hypocrites are weighed down in lead lined capers, barraters is plunged in the boiling pitch of blackness, and sorcerers have their heads twisted back to front,' said she leaving level nine behind them.

I became aware that the heat was no longer with us. It felt warm, but the further we went, the colder it got. The ground became frozen, and within the darkness stood a frozen vapor all around us.

'Look, and behold the river Cocytus, Jetson Mo-Billy. A frozen river of lamentations, which empties into Lake Cocytus of ice,' said Gabriella, walking toward the river.

The river itself stood frozen solid along with the land which we were standing on. I could see icecaps and giant stalactites. Trees were frozen down to their roots, but the strangest of all was the quietness that stood all around, as if evil had been frozen still in the cold darkness.

'Here is level ten jetson Mo-Billy, the frozen lake of Cocytus, where all feelings are lost forever. The gripping sounds of the souls of traitors buried to their necks in ice. Others have their eyes frozen shut, still there are a few wholly immersed in icy waters,' Gabriella said standing on a frozen chunk of ice.

'I do not enjoy the kingdom of the infernal regions Gabriella.' I said.

'Know one thing, Jetson Mo-Billy, that worse than all that I have shown you is the Lake of Fire,' she said as we followed a cold wind out of the Infernal Regions. I Jetson Mo-Billy has spoken."

It's now two forty five in the morning, when Jessica entered the room with three cups of tea. She sets the silver tray on a table. "Thirsty?" she questioned with a smile.

"Thank you, Jessica," taking a cup. "Drink up Nelly, you must be thirsty, I know I am," said Jetson.

At this time Nelly stood up stretching, and gives out a yawn. She then pours herself a cup of tea and sits back down.

"All those places you've been really exist?" she asked. "Maybe yes and maybe no. I'm only telling you what I saw during my out of body experience," Jetson replied.

Nelly finished her tea and gets up. She walked to a window looking out at the moon. She then pours herself a second cup of tea.

"Are you leaving Nelly?" asked Jessica.

"It is getting late," she replied.

"If you must go, Nelly, leave. But remember, I will repeat the story only once," said Jetson.

"Is there more?" questioned Nelly.

"Much more, Nelly, besides, you wanted to know if I met Lorenzo Alexander," replied Jetson Mo-Billy, pouring himself a second cup of tea

IV

NELLY SAT ON THE sofa with a cup of tea. Jetson also sat down after stretching out. The clock chimed at three o'clock in the morning.

"Now then, let me continue with my story, and please, no interruptions," Jetson said looking at the two ladies. He drank his tea to clear his throat.

"I, Jetson Mo-Billy, found myself back on the island of the dead. I don't remember how I got there, nor did I see any sign of Gabriella Angelina.

I sat on a log watching people swim in the River Lethe. 'Jetson Mo-Billy I presume,' said a voice behind me.

I turned around and saw a man in armor. He looked like a knight ready to do battle. I stood up to face him and said.

'I am that person.'

'Allow me to introduce myself. I am Lorenzo Alexander. I am here to guide you in the worlds above.'

'I will be with you, Alexander.'

'Halt, in the name God! You demon!' shouted a male voice behind me. I turned to see another man that looked like Lorenzo Alexander.

Both drew swords on each other and began to do battle. I got out
of the way and watched the fight. It was then that one of Lorenzo's
lost his sword and ran.

'Are you the true Lorenzo Alexander?' I asked.

'Jetson Mo-Billy, you must always test a spirit, cause demons
comes in many forms,' he said putting his sword away.

'Are you to be my guide?'

'Come with me Jetson Mo-Billy, and see what I have to show
you,' Lorenzo said walking to a carriage which had two of the most
beautiful horses I had ever seen.

The carriage itself was of many colors, and sweet smelling. Once
I got inside, the horses pulled the carriage without a driver knowing
exactly where to go.

'Enjoying the ride, Jetson Mo-Billy?' asked Lorenzo. I did not answer him. I was staring at a man that I have heard in my world. I never
knew him, but I do remember him in what he did in my world.

'Is something wrong, Jetson?'

'No, Lorenzo,' I said to him. 'Everything is okay.'

Outside, the sky turned dark. Clouds acted like smoke as if we
were going over a volcano. Lightning streaked across the sky from
all directions.

'Why are you looking at me like that, Jetson?' asked Lorenzo.

'When you were in my world, I know who you are. You're the
man who knows all about angels.'

'That is correct, Jetson, when I was like you. Right now that is not
important, Jetson. I know you have all the keys to open doors of the
supernatural, which makes you powerful and dangerous.'

'You know about me, Lorenzo?'

'I know all about you, Jetson, and you better guard those keys
with your life. Don't let it get into the wrong hands,' said Lorenzo,
taking out a chalk board.

'What are you doing?' I asked.

'Let me tell you about the world of the absolute, Jetson Mo-
Billy.'

I looked at him awkwardly' Have you ever been asked why are
you here?'

'An old blind sister asked me that question, Jetson, when I had a living body.'

'What's the answer, Lorenzo?'

'You will soon know as I have, Jetson,' Lorenzo said drawing the Star of David surrounded by seven planets. Mercury, Saturn, Mars, Jupiter, Moon, Sun, and Venus. Below all this are the heavens of his creation.'

"Should I know all about this, Lorenzo?'

'You wanted to know if there was life after death, Jetson,' he said when all of a sudden the carriage came to a stop. 'We are here.'

'Where is here?' I asked.

'We are here in the first heaven. The abode of the stars each with its own angel wonders. Do not get out, Jetson Mo-Billy, but see in what your eyes can see,' he said to me.

I looked into the night sky and saw thousands of stars everywhere as far as my eyes could see each star cast its own radiant light, making the night sky shine.

'I don't see and angel Lorenzo.'

'That's because we are far from each star. I assure you they are there,' he said clapping his hands. The carriage moved on.

'The entire first heaven is like this?' I asked.

'Just about, Jetson.

I became silent, looking at the stars in which they faded away. The night sky turned into evening, smothered by clouds. The carriage itself seemed to be riding on a cloud.

'It's here in the second heaven, where Jesus spends most of his time. John the Baptist also likes living here, Jetson.'

'Can I talk to them, Alexander?'

'I doubt if they are here, Jetson.'

'Then let me see the palace of john the Baptist?' I asked excitedly.

'No. we must move on,' replied Lorenzo, clapping his hand. The carriage continued above the clouds.

'How many heavens are there?' I asked. He did not answer me.

The clouds faded away and the carriage was on the road of gold. A heaven without sunlight, yet a radiant light shone brighter than the sun itself.

There's much more peacefulness here than I have never felt before. Prosperity in every way. The air was filled with such a fragrance, that it could calm a spirit of anger.

Soon the carriage stopped at a nearby village. We were greeted by peaceful villagers. I remained in the carriage looking at the villagers at how they were dressed in long white gowns.

'Welcome to the third heaven, Jetson Mo-Billy,' said a female, holding a silver platter with loaves of bread.

'May I ask who you are?'

'I am an angel,' she replied.

'Where are your wings?' I asked.

'Some angels do not have wings, Jetson Mo-Billy. Does that make you unhappy?'

'No,' I answered.

'I admire you for that, Jetson,' she said with a giggle. 'Are you hungry?'

'Have one, Jetson Mo-Billy,' said Alexander.

'Thank you,' I said to her taking a loaf of bread.

We stared at each other as I bit into the bread, it's as if I knew her from somewhere before, but that cannot be, cause she is an angel and I am not.

'You are eating Mana Bread, Jetson Mo-Billy. Food of the angels. It is made here and stored here,' Lorenzo said.

'I must go now, Jetson, but I'll be watching you,' said the female angel with a smile, and walked away.

'She sure is beautiful in that light blue gown, Alex.'

Lorenzo only smiled as the carriage rolled on the golden road. We remain in the third heaven arriving in paradise. I couldn't believe in what I was seeing.

'This is the Garden of Eden, Jetson Mo-Billy.'

'I never realized the garden would look like this Alexander.' I said smelling a strong aroma. 'The fragrance I've smelling came from here.'

'That's correct, Jetson.'

'I would love to take a walk through this garden Alexander,' I insisted.

'We don't have that much time Jetson,' said Lorenzo moving on.

I finished the angel food which was given to me. 'That's a good loaf of bread,' I said.

'One loaf will fill you up, Jetson.'

'So I notice, Alexander. But it has something in it that brings out the flavor.'

'I can't tell you what it is, Jetson, but it's a secret ingredient from the angels.'

I didn't know it, but we approached the forth heaven Clouds as white as snow, mixed with incense turned the clouds to blue or pink. The golden road disappeared within the clouds and the fragrance faded away, overcome by the sweet smelling incense.

'Look there,' said Lorenzo pointing to his right.

I was astonished in what I saw. A temple as long as three football fields and as high as a mountain. It stood like a cathedral, very well structured.

'Take a look at the left side of me, Jetson,' said Lorenzo.

I saw a large and colorful rainbow with angels flying over it and under it. Some angels were sitting on it. Below the rainbow stood a magnificent altar, dcorateed with untold riches like I had never seen before.

'You have just seen the fourth heaven, Jetson Mo-Billy, the heavenly Temple and the heavenly Altar.'

'I don't know what to say Alexander.'

'The fifth heaven will be difficult to see, so we will pass by it, Jetson.'

'What's wrong with the fifth heaven, Lorenzo?'

'There is nothing wrong, only that the light from the fifth heaven will blind your eye sight, Jetson.'

'Tell me then, what lies in the fifth heaven, Lorenzo.' I noticed that the carriage was brightening up.

'The fifth heaven contains the empyrean seat of God, along with its most Holly angels.'

Never had I seen such glorious light. My eyes began to burn from brightness. The entire carriage was swallowed by the light that stood brighter that the sun itself. I couldn't even see, Lorenzo.

Suddenly, like magic, the light went away and my eyes focused on, Alexander. I wiped the tears off my eyes because I was crying.

'We are now in the sixth heaven, Jetson Mo-Billy.' He said to me.

We found ourselves on a rocky road. The air was so clean, I took a deep breath. There's not a cloud in the night sky, only stars shining brighter than ever before.

The land itself was of many wonderful colors, with tress, and hills. I also saw a castle of enormous size. This is where the carriage is headed.

'It's here, Jetson, in the sixth heaven that the Guardian Angels of heaven and earth live.'

'Is this one of them, Alexander?' I asked.

'Yes,' replied he stopping in front of the castle.

The great castle door opened and a man of great prosperity and wisdom stepped out. He wore a red robe with sandals on his feet. He reminded me of an apostle.

'Greetings, Lorenzo Alexander, and to you, Jetson Mo-Billy, I've been expecting you,' he said.

Lorenzo and I stepped out of the carriage. Immediately I smelled the most fantastic cologne on this man it made my cologne worthless.

'How do you do sir,' I said shaking his hand.

'I am Zebul. Welcome to my house of peace.'

'Is this a castle, or is it a house?' I questioned.

'It can be both,' replied Zebul. 'Come. You all must be hungry,' he said as we all went inside together.

What I saw inside his house was unbelievable. The floors are of pearl white and the walls are of stone matching the color of the floor, and it had stained windows. One room was so large that a four bed-room house could fit there.

There were no torches, candles, or even electricity, and yet, there is light inside his house. I did not ask how this is done. I just kept looking around.

'I find your house incredibly interesting and charming.' I said as I followed him.   ·

In the next room stood a large oblong table. It was made of petri-fied stone even the chairs were petrified. The floor shined so bright that I could see myself.

'Sit, Jetson Mo-Billy,' said Zebul, sitting down himself.

I looked at him with ease. We said grace and we began to eat. I saw no maids, no butlers, or any kind of help, so I don't know how he kept his house very neat and clean. I looked at him a second time. This time he saw me doing it.

'Your curiosity overcomes me, Jetson Mo-Billy. What is it that you see in me?'

'You have no wings, sir Zebul.'

'What you say is wrong, Jetson Mo-Billy. I have wings on my feet and two pairs of wings on my back,' He replied.

'Why is it that I cannot see them, Sir Zebul?'

'You are a human spirit, Jetson Mo-Billy.'

I did not dare to ask him another question even though I felt as if he was reading my mind and he knew what my next question was. We finished our meals and walked outdoors next to our carriage.

'It was nice meeting you, sir Zebul.'

After saying what I had said, Zebul gave me a stare. I could not turn away from his staring; it had such power that it made me cry.

'Do you know why you are here, Jetson Mo-Billy?'

'Where is here?' I asked.

'You still don't know Jetson Mo-Billy, but remember my name, for I can help you any time of day or night, your time.'

'I will remember you, sir Zebul,' I said, getting into the carriage.

'I will come and talk to you later, Zebul.' Said Lorenzo.

'Stop by my house, Lorenzo Alexander,' he said watching us leave.

On our way, I turned around and saw Zebul standing in front of his castle. I turned and looked at Alexander with a question in mind.

'How many rooms are in that house,' I asked.

'I really can't say, but did you notice he had no furniture or bedrooms,' he said smiling.

'Why is that?'

'Angels do not rest and are never tired, among other things. You will learn this, Jetson, when your time comes,' said Lorenzo, reaching the seventh heaven.

'Look at the size of this tree, Lorenzo!' I exclaimed.

'This is the largest tree in the seventh heaven, Jetson. The tree tops touch the highest heaven, while the roots touch the lower regions. The leaves are souls waiting to be born,'

'Is this the Tree of Life, Alexander?"

'Exactly, jetson and the secrets of the souls are learned here.' He said going pass the great tree.

At long last I finally had the courage to ask Lorenzo Alexander a question that I wanted to know for a long time I turned and looked at him.

'Are you an angel?' I asked.

'No, but I'm learning. I have not yet gotten my wings,' he replied.

We reached the eighth heaven and I saw that it has been divided into sections each section has a treasure house.

'Do you know of the zodiac signs, Jetson?'

'Yes I do.'

'What you see here before you is the dwelling of the first six zodiac signs. The other six are in the ninth heaven,' said Alexander.

At an instant the carriage flew swiftly into nothingness. A space without time, darkness, light, or even stars. A feeling of not being born. I thought there was no such place as nothing, but there is.

'Enough of the heavens, Jetson, now we shall visit some of the planets,' said Alexander.

I could feel the pressure of the wind which meant this carriage is moving very fast. I blinked once and before I knew it we were on a planet with such fantastic sights to see.

'I don't suppose we have time to see these sights.' I said.

'No we don't, but I will tell you that this is the planet Venus, Jetson.'

'So what's on the planet Venus?'

'Angel school, Jetson,' replied Alexander, when all f a sudden the carriage disappeared from under us.

I didn't know what to expect from this or didn't have time to be afraid. I am falling like a rock and hit the ground hard on my back.

'Did you feel any pain, Jetson?' questioned Lorenzo, as he landed on his feet.

'No,' I answered.

'Do you know why you didn't feel any pain, Jetson?'

'Is it because I am spirit and not body, Lorenzo.'

'That is correct, Jetson.'

'The problem with this, Lorenzo, I do need to know how to fall right,' I said getting up from the ground.

'You will learn that when your time comes, Jetson.'

'If you say so, Lorenzo. Now that we are here, what do we do next?'

'Take my hand, jetson, and close your eyes,' I did as Alexander had asked me to do.

'Now what?'

'Open your eyes, Jetson,' I opened my eyes and I found myself looking at angel school. The walls were miles high and it stood miles wide. The spirits were friendly, all dressed in their clothing they were buried in.

'Can I see inside, Lorenzo?'

I can, but not you, Jetson.'

'Okay, I can understand that, Lorenzo,' I said as I was approached by a female spirit.

'Finally, you showed up,' she said standing in front of Lorenzo. 'I've been waiting and waiting for you.'

'I told you I had to do something Pamela.'

'Excuse me, but is Pamela your real name?' I asked her as I am curious to know.

'Yes,' she said looking at me, 'That is my earth name.'

'What is your spiritual name' I asked.

'I don't know yet,' answered Pamela.

Lorenzo Alexander, took hold of the woman's hand. Pamela, smiles at me, and Lorenzo looked at me as if he didn't know what to do.

'I have to take her to angel school, Jetson.'

'You are Jetson Mo-Billy?' questioned Pamela.

'Yes I am.'

'Everyone in angel school talks about you,' said Pamela.

'What are they saying about me?'

'They say you are a powerful organic man because you hold the keys to the doors of the supernatural. Is this true?'

'It can be. Yes,' I said.

'Aren't you afraid to have that much power, Jetson?'

'I only study its power, Pamela, not use it.'

Lorenzo Alexander is not worried about, Jetson Mo-Billy, after seeing an angel land on the ground. He felt happy walking toward him.

'You made it, Corat,' he said.

'Did I not say I wouldn't let you down Lorenzo,' said Corat, walking together.

'Jetson Mo-Billy, this is, Corat, he will take over where I left off,' said Lorenzo.

'How do you do, Corat,' I said.

'Come, Pamela, we must go,' said Alexander.

'Bye, Jetson,' said Pamela, walking away.

'Jetson Mo-Billy, it's up to me to take you to planet Jupiter.'

'Alright, angel Corat.'

'I ask of you, Jetson to take hold of my hand and close your eyes.'

In less than a minute we were on the planet Jupiter, standing on top of a mountain. I was watching spirits jump off the mountain with their wings, trying to fly, but they all hit the bottom.

'Do not feel sorry, Jetson Mo-belly, these spirits will try and keep trying until they've mastered the art of flying.'

'How did they get their wings, Corat?' I asked.

'They have earned them, Jetson Mo-Billy, as you will and everyone in your world.'

'I have seen enough of this, angel Corat,' I said touching his cold hand.

'I will now take you to planet Mars, Jetson Mo-Billy.'

I was amazed to see the wing span of Angel Corat and how his wings flap to the point of not being seen. In an instant we were on the planet Mars.

'What happens here on Mars, Corat?'

'This is where angels learn to do battle, Jetson.' He answered.

I stood standing and I don't see angels or legions anywhere though I do see mountains, hills, and desert soon after I saw angels flying while others were running, attacking each other with flaming swords.

'Are you sure they are only training, angel Corat?'

'To become an angel warrior, you must fight like an angel warrior, Jetson Mo-Billy.'

I don't get it, Corat. Why are these angel warriors training, when there is no war in the Heavenly kingdom.'

'The war between good and evil still exist, Jetson Mo-Billy, with mankind in the middle.'

'Good and evil I understand, but what does mankind have to do with it?'

'Do you know the answer to the question of why you are here, Jetson Mo-Billy?' asked Corat.

'No.'

'Then you must know the answer, Jetson. It's all about mankind,' he said walking away and I stood standing. 'Come, Jetson, we must go now.'

'Are you saying that these angels fight for us? Why?'

Angel Corat did not answer. We left the planet Mars and I found myself back to the island between heaven and hell. I followed angel Corat to a very large boulder near the river Lethe.

On top of this great boulder stood another angel. She was dressed in a light blue gown with colorful wings. She looked down at me saying to me.

'I am Dina, here to tell you a story.'

'Sit, Jetson Mo-Billy, and listen very carefully to this story,' said Corat.

'Before the earth was created, the Almighty made the heavens and the angels. Then he set forth to create the earth. While he was gone, there stood a rebellion among the heavens.

An act of war stood among the angels, the good overcome the evil. When the battle of the angels was over, there stood many vacant spots that needed to be replaced.

The Almighty decided that mankind shall take the places of the fallen angels, but must be tested on earth. You are all being watched to see if each and everyone is worthy.'

'Can that be true, Corat?' I asked.

'Tell him, Dina,' said Corat.

'Jetson Mo-Billy, look at me and tell me, why are you here?' she asked.

I looked at Angel Dina the way a child would look at her mother. It felt like I was being discipline for something I didn't do.

'I am here on earth to be tested, so that I may take the place of a fallen angel.'

'Now you know the secret of mankind,' said Corat.

'The fallen angels will stop at nothing to destroy mankind. They don't want anybody to take their places in heaven. They say, if they are going to the lake of fire, so is mankind,' said Dina.

'Go back to your living body, Jetson Mo-Billy, and remember all that we have showed you and told you,' said Corat.

'I Jetson Mo-Billy have spoken."

The chimes of a clock sounded out, showing six in the morning. Nelly got up from her chair stretching herself and yawning.

Jetson sat, and fell asleep, in his recliner; Jessica was nowhere to be seen. Nelly put on her coat and quietly made her way out of the house.

V

To the south of the city, on a hot muggy night, a black mass has just ended. Mitsy and her boyfriend, Stark, were on their way home. Mitsy was not feeling well with cold chills and a headache.

With her head bowed down resting upon her hands she is moaning. Suddenly a flash of lightning shot across the sky.

'Is it going to storm tonight?' Mitsy questioned looking at a full moon hiding behind the clouds.

"Heat lightning," answered Stark. He knew about her condition asking, "Are you getting worse?"

"I don't feel myself at all," replied Mitsy, shivering.

"Were almost home," said Stark, driving toward his apartment.

"Stark, this is not my home?"

"I know, but I'm going to take care of you, Mitsy. I'm not going to leave you by yourself," he said kissing her on the cheek.

"I'm so cold, Stark, keep me warm," she said kissing him with her cold lips.

It was only eleven o'clock at night when they entered into his apartment. Stark carried Mitsy inside noticing she had fallen asleep. He laid her on the sofa and kissed her on the forehead. At this time she awakens.

"Who are you?" she said in a male coarse voice, standing up on the sofa.

"What's the matter with you, Mitsy?' questioned Stark.

Mitsy stood standing on the sofa, looking around the room and she grinned. She looked at Stark with her dark spooky eyes and he was unable to speak.

"You are a human," she said falling to the floor unconscious.

Stark, ran to her and picked her up from the floor. "Mitsy! Wakeup, Mitsy!" he shouted shaking her.

Mitsy opened her eyes which was no longer dark, but normal. She continued to fee cold and Stark knew this by holding her hand. She felt weak as if something is attacking her body.

"Don't leave me," said she closing her eyes.

Stark laid her on the sofa and covered her with a blanket. He turned on the television and there was a woman talking about Walpurgis Night.

"That's right, I forgot, tonight is witch night. Walpurgis Night." He said looking at the wall clock.

"Witching hour starts in forty minutes from now," said he.

Stark sat on the couch listening to the television. He felt cold and the room was getting colder. He got up to see the temperature, but the lights failed to turn on. He tried other lights, but none of them turned on.

"Must be an electrical problem," he said, going back to his television program.

Forty five minutes later the television screen began to show frost. Stark got up and looked around the room. All glassware, windows, and water were frosted.

"What's going on here?" he said feeling chills throughout his body.

Stark walked to the door, but it didn't open. He picked up the phone to make a call, but he heard static. He tried to break a window, but the glass would not break.

Behind his back, on the sofa, Mitsy sat up. She turned her head and looked at Stark. She gave out an evil laughter that scared Stark to the floor.

He knew then that Mitsy wasn't herself anymore. A demon had taken over the body of Mitsy. Stark saw those darkened eyes without pupils. Her face was white, as if she has been dead for a month.

There stood a bad odor in the room, it had the smell of a dead animal. Mitsy stood on the sofa, casting a shadow on the wall. It wasn't her shadow at all; it was a shadow of a demon with wings of a bat.

"I'm not afraid of you," Stark said standing tall facing the demon. "I honor you! I know what you are! And I carry your mark!" he yelled showing the symbol to the demon.

"I enjoy those who carry my mark," said Mitsy in a low tone voice for me." "I want you to do something for me."

"What is it that you want me to do? And may I ask who in the hell are you?" questioned Stark.

"I am Bitu, and I want you to find a man called Jetson Mo-Billy. He has the keys to the doors of the supernatural and I want you to steal them from him."

"I will do what you ask, Bitu, but I do not know the man," said Stark, as he bowed before Mitsy.

"Mitsy knows Nelly, and Nelly met a woman named Jessica. It is she who knows Jetson Mo-Billy. Get those damn keys, Stark, and give it to your religious leader," said Bitu.

"I understand, Bitu," he said watching, Mitsy, fall back on the sofa.

Stark, stood standing and was astonished at what just had just happened. Five minutes after the possession, Mitsy, is awake and sat up. She rubs her eyes and combs back her hair.

"What happened to me?" she said looking at Stark.

"You don't remember anything?" questioned Stark, sitting on the sofa next to her.

"No," replied Mitsy.

"That's amazing."

"What did happened, Stark?"

"You were possessed by a demon spirit."

"What did I say?"

Stark, felt warm once more, the lights were on and the television was working. Stark, smiled at Mitsy, and kissed her on the cheek.

"I'll tell you in the morning," he said walking to his bedroom.

Early morning into the tenth day of Taurus, Jessica, walked to a donut shop, having a cup of coffee. She sat on a table watching television, yet her mind drifted away into deep thought. She acted like a woman under hypnosis.

"I, Jessica Sentena, have seen the power which Jetson Mo-Billy possesses. I have also seen the keys to the supernatural. I would do anything to get my hands on those keys. I would become very powerful."

"Excuse me, lady," said a man snapping his fingers at her.

Jessica comes out of her meditation. She is looking at a man in his early forties, sitting on the table with her having a cup of coffee.

"Yes?" she asked.

"I saw you at the camp ground last night and listened to your story about Jetson Mo-Billy. If the man is dead, whatever happened to all of his secrets?" he asked.

"Why do you want to know?" questioned Jessica, drinking from her cup.

"I'm pastor Fotley of Freedom religion. I am very interested in the works of Jetson Mo-Billy. It would be a great asset to my religion," he said smoking a cigar.

"Well, Mr. Fotley, I believe I can help you, but the works of Jetson Mo-Billy has to be bought, not given," said Jessica, biting into her donut.

"What do you have to sell?" questioned Fotley.

Jessica wiped her hands, "I have his notes, books, and the keys."

"How much are you asking?"

My price is high, Mr. Fotley, can you pay the price?"

"First, I want to see his work?"

"I can't do that until you pay my price, Mr. Fotley." "I can not pay your price until I see some proof."

"It would seem we do not trust each other Mr. Fotley."

"It would seem so, but here is my card. Show me some proof and I will pay your price," he said leaving her table, not cleaning after himself.

It's now eleven fifteen in the morning when Stark, walked in his pajamas and sat on a chair.

"It's about time you woke up," said Mitsy.

"I was up all night, watching over you," he said drinking a glass of water.

"What did I say last night?" Mitsy asked, sitting on a kitchen chair.

"The demon said that you have to see Nelly because she knows a woman name Jessica. This woman knows a man name Jetson Mo-Billy. We have to steal something important from him," he replied drinking a second glass of water. "Well that isn't so hard," Mitsy said getting up from her chair.

"Well are you going?" asked Stark.

"To see Nelly," replied Mitsy leaving.

"Me, I'm going back to bed," Stark said to himself making his way to the sofa.

On this kind of day Jessica would do her chores, but today she sits in the park watching the birds. A cup of coffee in her hand and her mind deep in thought.

"I, Jessica Sentena, must have those precious keys some way, somehow, I must find a way to take them away from Jetson Mo-Billy.

After I do this, is it worth it? To have all that power, or should I sell it to Fotley? I can't stand being poor anymore. I want the money so I can be rich. Yeah! Of that same day, during the afternoon hours, Nelly was at the laundry mat when she happen to see Mitsy walking inside toward her.

"I stopped by your house, but you weren't home, so I figured, being that it's Thursday, you would be here.'

"Now that you found me, what do you want to see me about, Mitsy?"

"About a guy."

"I know a lot of guys, Mitsy."

"Do you know a man name Jetson Mo-Billy?"

"I met him."

"What kind of man is he?" questioned Mitsy, watching government agents take a women away for not having the mark.

"I don't know, Mitsy. A man of mystery I guess. I only met him once," replied Nelly.

"I want to meet him Nelly, do you have his address?"

"Sure," answered Nelly, writing his address. At that very moment she stopped, giving Mitsy a suspicious look.

"Are you going to turn him in for not wearing the mark?"

"Does he have the mark?" asked Mitsy.

"I don't know, I only met him once, but you, Mitsy, are greedy and would do anything for money."

"I am not that greedy!"

"You turned in your own father for money," said Nelly giving her the address and walked away.

Mitsy felt embarrassed when Nelly had said that, and she followed close behind her pulling her arm. She looked at her eye to eye.

"Sometimes I think you don't like me, but I don't care and don't want to know why," she said leaving the laundry mat.

Late that afternoon Jetson sat by a table with a candle burning He was shuffling a deck of tarot cards, and he stared at the flame of the candle.

"A look ahead will tell me why I'm feeling uneasy." He said.

Jetson Mo-Billy laid the tarot cards on the table one at a time reading in what they say. He rubs his forehead with his hand and stands up.

"It's going to be an interesting night," he said walking to the phone.

Jetson made a phone call to Jessica, but the phone only rang. He hung up thinking for a moment. He then picked up the phone to make another call.

Nelly just arrived, coming from the laundry mat, and she could hear the phone ringing with a basket under her arm she ran to her house, and picked up the hone

"Hello," she said.

"Is this Nelly?"

"Yes it is and you sound like Jetson?"

"I am he and I'm wondering what are you doing tonight?"

"Not much of anything," she replied.

"I can't reach Jessica, so how would you like to come to my house for a few hours and join me in a cup of tea?"

"You must be lonely."

"I could use some company."

"Alright, Jetson, I'll stop by," Nelly said hanging up the phone.

Outside of Jetson's home, not far away from his twenty five acre property, he was being watched by Stark and Mitsy.

"I think the guy lives alone," Stark said looking through the binoculars.

"We shall soon see if he's alone," said Mitsy, making a call on her cell phone. She talks to the government agent's office, telling them that there's a man who does not wear a mark giving out his address.

"Are we doing this tonight?" asked Stark, looking at Mitsy.

"Yes, we are," she replied. "I want those keys, and you will find them for me while I'll take care of the guy."

"How did you know we wanted the keys? I never told you?" questioned Stark.

"A friend inside me tells me a lot of things."

"What do the keys look like, Mitsy?"

"You're looking for medallions with seals written on them," Mitsy said as she saw a car drive into the drive way.

A doorbell rang and a man opens the door." Are you Jetson Mo-Billy?"

"That's my name, and I know who you gentlemen are?" He asked looking at them with a straight face.

"We have reason to believe that you do not have the mark, may we see the mark?" one of the agents asked.

Jetson did not say a word, only showed his left hand to the agents, which had no mark, yet the two agents saw a mark on his hand.

"Satisfied," replied Jetson.

"We won't bother you, Jetson," said the agent leaving from his property.

"The man lives alone, Mitsy."

"That's just perfect, in a few hours we shall pay him a visit," she said, looking at the sunset.

"Can we eat now?" questioned Stark.

"Yes. I'm hungry too," replied Mitsy, giving Stark a hamburger.

"How about making love?" Stark asked looking at her with affection.

"Later," replied Mitsy, eating french fries.

Ten miles away Nelly finished washing her dishes and looked out the window to see the sun set as the night sky has come.

"I better get going if I'm going to see Jetson," she said to herself, putting on her coat on and walked out the door.

Under the night sky, Stark and Mitsy are at the house of Jetson Mo-Billy. Stark opened a window and they both entered quietly.

"Look for the keys," whispered Mitsy.

"Shhh," said Stark, looking around the room

Mitsy walked out of the room into the hallway that leads to the living room it's here that she saw Jetson sitting in his chair with his back facing her. Candles are lit everywhere in the room.

Mitsy picked up a vase and slowly made her way toward Jetson as quiet as she can be. She now stands behind the man, knocking him out with a vase

"Stark!" shouted Mitsy.

"What is it?" he asked seeing man in his chair out cold.

"The keys are on the table Stark."

Quickly, Stark hurried to the table and picked up the medallions. "Did he see you?"

"No, I got him from behind," replied Mitsy, taking books and notes, knocking over a lit candle.

The room suddenly catches on fire, spreading to the wall. It quickly grows upward to the ceiling and the smoke thickened making the two of them cough.

"Mitsy! Get out of here, I'll meet you at the car!" shouted Stark.

Outside Nelly entered the driveway, as she saw a lady running out of the house, across the lawn and toward the camp grounds.

Nelly stopped the car and got out of the car. She watched the lady run and she knew who she was. She then looked at the house which was aflame.

"Mitsy, what have you done?" questioned Nelly.

Coming out from the back of the house, Stark carried a sack coming out of the thick smoke. He ran into Jessica and the both of them were standing by the door, but she had a gun in her hand.

"I'll take that, if you don't mine."

"Sorry lady, but it's mine."

"Not anymore," said Jessica, shooting Stark dead. She also saw fire coming out of the window. She was only interested in one thing and she took the sack away from Stark, disappearing into the night.

Nelly ran into the house to find Jetson sitting in his chair. Fire was all around the room and the thick smoke made her cough.

"Jetson!" she shouted running up to him, finding him unconscious. The fire and heat is becoming intense as Nelly took a glass of water from a burning table and splashed it on Jetson's face.

Instantly he awakened and saw fire all around the room. He felt a little dizzy, but is able to move on his own power.

"We can't stay here!" shouted Jetson, coughing.

"Let's go!" shouted Nelly, as the both of them ran out of the house.

The two of them fell on the lawn and rested on the front lawn. They watched the house burn totality engulfed in flames.

"Are you alright?" questioned Nelly.

"Yeah. Thanks for saving my life," replied Jetson.

"What happened here?" she asked.

"I don't know," replied Jetson, catching his breath.

Nelly looked down the road side and saw a car go by that she recognize. She turned to Jetson and he looked at her.

"All of my works, gone up in smoke" he said, getting up from the lawn.

"You can stay at my place, Jetson."

"Thanks for inviting me to stay, Nelly," he said walking toward her car.

Mitsy arrived at the apartment of Stark. Although he was not with her she was very angry. She did not have the keys; she paced the floor, broke a mirror, and left the room in a rage of anger.

This is a busy night for Jessica, who now has the keys. She looked at the medallions, plated in silver, each in their own sacred pouches. The seal were inscribed in bronze.

"Excellent," said Jessica, picking up the phone and made a call.

The phone rang four times before a female voice is heard. "Freedom Religion, may I help you?"

"Is Fotley there?"

"Yes he is?"

"May I talk to him?"

"One moment please."

Jessica made herself a cup of coffee and sat down to relax after what she had done tonight. She then heard a male voice on the phone.

"Fotley speaking"

"Are you still interested in the keys?"

"As I said before, Jessica, I want to see them first"

"I will show one of them to you. If it meets to your satisfaction, I will name my price."

"Fine. I will see you at the donut shop tomorrow morning," Fotley said as he hung up the phone.

"It's now two fifteen in the morning. Nelly has Jetson in her apartment giving aid to the wound on Jetson's head.

"It's not too bad," said Nelly, putting a band-aid on the wound.

"I have a headache."

"I have some aspirin, Jetson," replied Nelly hearing a knock on the door. "Who is it?"

"Somebody who wants to see Jetson Mo-Billy."

"He's not here, Mitsy!" shouted Nelly recognizing her voice.

The door is locked with three locks, yet it opened with such force that it brought Jetson and Nelly on their feet, Mitsy entered the room.

"You are not what you seemed to be," said Nelly.

"You, I don't want to talk to," said Mitsy pushing her to the wall.

Nelly found herself held to the wall, unable to move. "She's not herself Jetson!"

"He already knows that," said Mitsy, looking at him.

"Who are you?" Jetson asked, staring at her.

A cold wind blew about the room, making the wall paper fall off the wall. The voice of a female changed to a low baritone voice.

"We've met once before, Jetson Mo-Billy, and I told you I would find you."

"Bitu," Jetson said, with strong voice.

Bitu laughed so loudly that mirrors cracked, and glasses shattered. Mitsy's body rose upward, until her head was touching the ceiling.

"Do you want to challenge me?" asked Jetson.

"No."

"What are you doing here, Bitu?"

"Where are they, Jetson?"

"Where is what?"

"I want the keys, Jetson."

"They are burned up in the house fire."

"I don't believe you, Jetson"

"Go away, Bitu, before I get angry with you."

"Alright, Jetson Mo-Billy, I'll go, but I'll be back to challenge your faith," said Bitu, as the body of Mitsy floated out of the apartment.

Nelly fell off the wall and ran outside, but Mitsy was nowhere to be seen. She then walked back inside, closing the door.

"Why didn't you fight the demon?" asked Nelly, facing Jetson.

"I'm in no mood to fight a demon," replied Jetson as he sat down.

"Ahab has to know about this," said Nelly.

"Who is Ahab?"

"That's Mitsy's Father," replied Nelly, lying on the couch.

"Right now, let's get some sleep, what's left of the night," said Jetson, lying down on the floor

The clock is at three twenty in the morning. Time meant nothing to Fotley, who was sitting in his private room at his house, with a computer before him.

With a speaker attached to his computer, he was talking to his friend in Canada. Fotley is looking at a plan on his computer screen.

"Yes, I believe it will work." He said

"If everything goes according to plan, we will have about two million in gold, but I don't know how we are going to bring it into America," said a male voice on the speaker.

"Get yourself a cargo ship, then you will melt the gold down, Noel. When you have achieved in liquefying the gold, you will then seek out a room on the cargo ship. Paint that entire room in gold, Noel."

"Yes, that may work, Fotley"

"Of course it will work. Once the gold has hardened you paint over it and put cargo into it. Nobody will ever know."

"Fotley, you're a genius," said Noel laughing.

"When do you plan to do this, Noel?"

"Four days from now, Fotley."

"Good, that will give me plenty of time," having a thought in mind. "Call me, Noel, when you cross the American border."

"We'll keep in touch, Fotley," he said shutting off the computer. Fotley yawned and walked out of his room exhausted.

Late the next morning, Jessica waited inside the donut shop. She looked at the wall clock and became agitated. She has waited long enough and decided to leave. Jessica got up from the table, seeing Fotley enter the shop.

The man buys a cup of coffee and walked toward Jessica sitting down on her table and yawned. He looked like a man who slept in his clothing.

"You're over an hour late," said Jessica.

"I've been up late."

"Look at yourself, you're a mess," Jessica said.

"I said I was up all night, I didn't get enough sleep, I'm still tired and I'm here," said Fotley, drinking coffee.

"Do you still want to see the keys or shall I leave," said Jessica.

"Show it to me," Fotley said yawning.

Jessica passed a pouch to Fotley. The man opened the pouch and held a medallion in his hand. Fotley looked at it carefully and put the medallion back into the pouch.

"Is this all you got?"

"I have more," Jessica answered drinking a second cup of coffee.

"How much are you asking?"

"Two hundred and fifty thousand per key."

"Your price is high Jessica."

"Power is priceless, Fotley, can you pay it?"

"I will pay you in gold, Jessica."

"When?"

"A week from now, Jessica, I will call you."

"No Fotley, I will call you a week from today," she said taking her pouch away from Fotley and left.

"A very tempered woman," said Fotley yawning.

VI

WALKING THROUGH THE RUINS of a burned down house, Jetson,
tried to find the keys, yet he found nothing except grief.

"Everything, gone up in smoke, Nelly, nothing left of my work."

"Including the keys, Jetson?" questioned Nelly, finding a rosary
among the ashes.

"No trace of them," replied Jetson as he walked up to Nelly.

"Well at least something got saved," she said showing Jetson a
rosary.

That afternoon Fotley made his way to the pier where a ship from
Canada is docked. Noel smoked his pipe standing on the deck of the
ship.

"You are here in America which tells me that you had no problem
getting here," said Fotley walking toward him.

"I only had one problem and that was getting rid of my crew,"
Noel said smiling.

"Well, where is it?"

"Follow me Fotley," replied Noel, walking together below deck.

They came to a room that has empty crates and barrels. The floor
had the look of fresh paint as Fotley picked up a crowbar. He scraped

the floor with the crowbar and underneath the paint stood a floor of gold.

"Magnificent Noel," said Fotley.

"What do we do now?"

"We melt the gold and take it off the ship," Fotley said with a smile.

"I will do that later, but first let us go to an American bar and have us a drink," said Noel.

Okay, Noel, let us do that," said Fotley as they both walked out of the room.

On this same day, somewhere in the city, Nelly, was driving with a friend inside. She knows a friend in need of a friend, driving up to a house.

"Who lives here?" asked Jetson.

"A friend of mine whom you will stay with," replied Nelly, getting out of the car.

"Does he knows that I'm staying here?"

"How do you know it's a he, Jetson?"

"Well, you won't let me stay with you so it wouldn't be another female."

"Do you remember a few nights ago we met a girl who was possessed by a demon?" questioned Nelly, as she walked up to the door and knocked.

"Don't remind me," answered Jetson.

"The man who lives here is her father."

"Suppose the girl lives here, Nelly?"

"Then, I get to see you fight the demon, Jetson," as the door opened.

"It's good to see you, Nelly," said Ahab as they hug each other.

Jetson remained standing outside while the two of them hugged each other. It was then that Jetson sees the mark on the man's hand.

"I want you to meet, Jetson Mo-Billy," said Nelly.

Both stared at each other at the way they were dressed, not saying a word to each other, until Ahab shook his hand.

"I've heard of you, people say you are a man of mystery," said Ahab.

"What do you say?"

"The same. I am Ahab."

"It's nice to meet you, Ahab," uttered Jetson, entering his house. "Do you have a daughter named Mitsy?"

"Yes I do. Why?"

"Does she live here?"

"Her things are still here, but I haven't seen her since she betrayed me."

"I've met her once before," said Jetson.

"Are you still looking for a roommate, Ahab?" questioned Nelly.

"Have you found one, Nelly?"

"You're looking at him."

"Are you looking for a place to stay, Jetson?" asked Ahab.

"I'm only staying here until my house is rebuilt and I will pay you rent," said Jetson.

"You can stay here, for now," said Ahab.

"Thanks," said Jetson.

"Do you know where Mitsy is Ahab?" questioned Nelly walking around the room.

"I have no idea, Nelly."

"I have to find her."

"What has she done now, Nelly?"

"Her boyfriend Stark has been killed and I'm wondering how she is feeling," replied Nelly, walking toward the door.

"Nelly, if you find her, let me know I'd like to help," said Jetson.

"Don't worry, I have you in mind," she said leaving.

"That daughter of mine, I just don't know what is wrong with her. Sometimes I think she's possessed."

"Maybe she is possessed," Jetson said looking around the room.

"What do you mean?"

"I don't know yet, but something other than your daughter is inside of her,"

"Let me show you to your room, Jetson," said Ahab, walking up the stairs.

Two days left of Taurus and Gemini begins. All this time Nelly search and failed to locate Mitsy, even though she waited at Starks's apartment.

Else where a phone rings at the office of Fotley. It rang for times before it could be answered by a man who is busy in his office.

"Freedom Religion, the pastor is in."

"Richie Rich on the line," said a male voice.

"Hold please," Fotley said switching to his private line. "Do you have it done, Noel?"

"All done, Fotley, we have more than five hundred one ounce gold bars."

"That is very good, Noel. Do you know what to do now?"

"Yes, I do" he replied hanging up.

With a thought in mind he dials a phone number. He hears the tone of the phone ringing and then the sound of a female voice.

"Hello."

"It's been over a week, Jessica, I've been waiting and waiting for your call," he said.

"I didn't think you were interested, Fotley. I still have the keys, do you have my payment?"

"Come to my church tonight, Jessica and bring the keys with you."

"Is around midnight alright, Fotley?"

"Sure, you can stay and listen to my mass, Jessica," he said hanging up.

A few hours later, Fotley got dressed in his suit and tie. He made his way to the kitchen, looking at his wife with a smile.

"Things are going to change around here, my dear." said he.

"Tell me how?" questioned Mary Rose.

I'm going to get you a maid, this house will become a mansion, and my church will be a real church, and you will be more beautiful then ever before," he replied kissing her neck on the.

"It must be nice to dream." said Mary Rose.

"You doubt me, my dear, well, you just wait for what's going to happen in a few weeks," Fotley said walking outdoors toward his church.

During the evening hours, Noel arrived in a truck. Fotley joined him and the both of them unloaded wooden cases putting them in the back of his church. There stood twenty five cases in all.

Fotley opened a case and he held a one ounce bar of gold. Noel brings out a bottle of whiskey and stands in front Fotley.

"Very well done, an excellent job, Noel."

"I had no trouble at all, Fotley," he said taking a drink of whiskey and passed the bottle to Fotley.

"This is to you, Noel," taking a drink.

"What do you want me to do now?" asked Noel.

"You rest me friend. Your going to be my assassin," replied Fotley, patting him on the back.

"I'm already your assassin, Fotley."

"Come Noel, you must be hungry," Fotley said walking out of the barn like church.

Late at night, a blackmass was being held. Fotley performed his mass in his barn. There stood less than twenty members, with Fotley leading the blackmass.

A few minutes after midnight, Jessica arrived at the church. She carried with her a notebook, making her way to the church. Once inside, she sat in the back row of seats and listened to Fotley.

Fifteen minutes into the mass, Jessica got a headache, both of her legs began to cramp, and she felt sick, very uncomfortable. Looking around she saw a women staring at her.

This woman had the look of evil on her face, and she sat across from her wearing a purple dress. She looked like a witch from hell.

After the blackmass was over, Jessica waited until everyone had left. She then walked up to the woman, rubbing her legs to ease the cramps.

"Take your spell off of me."

"Why should I?" the woman asked staring at her.

"Because I did nothing to you and I don't know you." replied Jessica, as the woman smiled.

"Let me introduce myself," she said standing up. "I am Mitsy, and you killed my boyfriend, Stark."

"I don't know your boyfriend?" questioned Jessica.

"Oh yes, but you do. You killed him on the night the house burned down. You took away my love and left me with nothing, but hate."

At that very moment, Jessica remembered the house fire, and the man she met at the door. She also remembered killing him, and taking the keys away from him.

At that very moment, Jessica remembered this house killing him, and taking the keys from him.

"How do you know I am the woman?"

"I can see right through you. I know you are her," replied Mitsy.

"You are not that powerful," Jessica retorted.

"Try me," Mitsy said, staring at her.

Jessica didn't say a word, but she slowly backed away. The spell has been taken off and she never took her eyes off Mitsy.

"You are here to see Fotley. You also have what I wanted, but I'll let you see him. Afterwards, Jessica leave this city. Run and hide because I will find you no matter where you are, and when that happens your time is up."

At the back of the church Noel and Fotley each had a bag of gold. Both bags totaled five millions in gold. Hearing the sound of footsteps, Fotley saw Jessica coming toward him.

"Come in, Come in," Fotley said, entering the office together.

"Here are the keys," she said putting a notebook on his desk.

"A drink?" said Fotley, holding a bottle of liquor.

"After the deal," she said.

"Yes" he replied.

Fotley sat down in his chair and opened the notebook. He observed each and every key carefully. Jessica stood standing watching his every move not saying a word.

"At long last I have them all," said Fotley, with, such greed.

"Where's my payment?" Jessica asked.

"Give it to her, Noel," answer Fotley, as he pulled two hags out and set them next to her.

Jessica unties the string and opened the bag. She smiled as she held a single bar of gold in her hand. At this time she reties the strings around the bag.

"I will now have that drink with you, Fotley."

"By all means, Jessica," he said pouring two shot glasses. "Here's to us."

Jessica picked up the shot glass and drank it in one swallow. She then smashed her shot glass on the concrete floor.

"Well, I gotta go, Fotley," said Jessica, trying to move a bag of gold.

"You need help with that, lady?" asked Noel, picking up two bags of gold.

"Thanks," replied Jessica, heading out.

Fotley poured himself another drink, looking at each key. The door opened and Mitsy walked into his office being seen by Fotley.

"Your not invited here." retorted Fotley.

"Did Jessica give you the keys?" she asked.

"My goodness, Mitsy, you seem to know everything that goes on around hear," said Fotley, watching Noel come into his office quietly behind her."Do you realize what you have in your possession, Fotley?" Mitsy asked walking toward him.

"I know what I have, Mitsy."

"Do you even know how to use the keys, Fotley?" she asked once more as her voice began to change.

"Who am I talking to?" he questioned knowing that it was no longer Mitsy.

"You know who I am and what I am, ask me for my name?" it said.

Mitsy, who is no longer herself, reached to a table and sits down on a chair. Only her head turns around and she looked at Noel.

"Go away, Noel, unless you want to see my display of power."

Not saying a word, Noel smelled the foul odor and the voice of a female that turned into something monstrous. He saw her head turned around once more and he walked outdoors as he is told.

"What shall I call you?" asked Fotley.

"I am Bitu, and I will teach you the ways of the keys on those medallions, Fotley. You will become very strong powerful man, but you must serve me."

"I already know how to use the keys, Bitu," said Fotley putting a cigarette into his mouth as Bitu lights it with his thumb.

"Books only tell you very little, but the real secret of the keys are with me," Bitu said staring at Fotley.

"If I allow you to teach me what will you want in return?"

Misty's complexion began to change to an evil facial feature. Bitu smiled as he slowly stood up looking at Fotley.

"I want all of your people to serve me and only me."

"What about Mitsy? Will she be as powerful as I?" questioned Fotley.

"Mitsy is mine, you need not to worry about her." replied Bitu.

Fotley paused for a long moment, walking out of his office to the altar of his church. Bitu follows close behind, until a decision was made.

"Teach me, Bitu."

"Be here, same place, same time, Fotley," Bitu said walking away from the church.

Five minutes had passed when Noel returned to the church. He looked around the room and the lady is not seen. He smoked a cigar as he looked at Fotley.

"Did you make a deal with the devil?" he asked.

"Did you see her leave?" asked Fotley.

"I didn't see anybody," replied Noel, pouring himself a cup of coffee.

A new day into Gemini brings Jetson Mo-Billy out to his property watching his burned down house get torn down. He then saw a woman standing not far from him in which he recognized her. Jetson walked toward her with a smile on his face.

"Hello stranger, where have you been?"

"I just got back from vacation, Jetson, when I heard what happened to your house," answered Jessica telling a lie to a man she once helped.

"I lost everything, Jessica."

"What started the fire?"

"I don't know. It's under investigation, Jessica."

"I'm really sorry you lost all your work, Jetson."

"In a way I'm glade it got burned, Jessica, and didn't go to the wrong hands," he said as they left the area together.

In the middle of the afternoon, Mary Rose was setting up the church. The altar table was set with dark red candles. The chairs were straightened and the altar bible was put in its place.

"Mary Rose," said a strong male voice in the dark. Hearing her name called she walked toward the light switch to turn it on.

"You need not to do that, Mary Rose," as she stopped and saw the candles light themselves, incense burners were flaming, and two buckets of water were aflame, giving light to the room.

"I'm not afraid of you."

"I did not ask you to be afraid, Mary Rose." It said.

Mary Rose stared at the darkness and she saw that the male voice came from Mitsy. She stared at Mitsy and her faith was erased with evil. Her soul was overcome with hate, and her attitude changed for the worse.

"I know what you are, but I don't know who you are, Tell me your name and I will obey your every command," said Mary Rose, kneeling to Mitsy, kissing her hand.

"I am Bitu, be my spy, Mary Rose, I want you to tell me everything that your husband does behind my back and keep an eye on Noel.

"As you wish, Bitu, my master," she said standing up.

"Talk to me. Mary Rose, through the looking glass, I will hear you."

"I will do so, master," watching Mitsy disappear into the darkness. Everything that stood lit suddenly went out, and the church remained the same as it was.

It is now in the hour of Mars in the night of Gemini. Fotley stood in his church, dressed in a black robe with a witch's pentagram on the back. Drinking whiskey and having the notebook of keys on the altar table, he waits.

Incense was burning as he looked at his watch. Soon, Fotley notices a change and feels an evil presence in the room. Mitsy walked through the door.

Her skin looked as if it has been coated with wax. Her hair was coiled like she had been through an electric shock, eyes were empty white, and when she spoke, smoke poured out of her mouth.

"I hope this is to your looking, Bitu," said Fotley drinking his whiskey.

Bitu, kept quite as he walked up to the altar to where Fotley is standing. He stared at him and took the book of medallions and looked at the seals.

"Before you start any of these rituals, you must be prepared. Your mind shall be emptied of thoughts, thinking of nothing, but the devil himself.

Your soul shall be filled with hate, and your body washed with the blood of a serpent. Can you remember that?" questioned Bitu.

"Yes. I won't forget," Fotley said.

At that very moment Mitsy slapped him in the face twice. Fotley fell to the floor by the hit in the face of a demon. He gets up rubbing his cheek.

"You will speak only when you're spoken to! Understand!" shouted Bitu.

Fotley didn't say a word, but only nodded his head. Bitu looked at the first seal of the first medallion along with Fotley.

"Seal number one gives you the power to read minds. Draw it with your hand one hour before sunrise. When in use, make sure it touches the left side of your body and listen to what others think.

Seal number two gives you the power of command. With this seal, you control others at will. Draw this seal on a full moon. You must meditate on that person's name of whom you wish to control. Do not try to control two at once, you are not that powerful.

Seal number three gives you the power to change organic matter. You can become any animal you wish, except a dove. This seal must be worn when you meditate on that animal of which you wish to become. It is done on a moonless night, and you only have five hours in which you remain that animal.

Seal number four gives you the power of invisibility. On odd hours of time, day, or night, read the seal and carry it with you when you wish to be invisible.

Seal number five is a protection key," said Bitu being interrupted

"I don't need that," said Fotley, specking out of turn.

Mitsy looked at him with anger in her eyes. Fotley knew what he had done, speaking out of turn. He kept quite afterword's.

"What will you do when another with such a power challenge you?" Bitu asked.

"I will be very powerful by then, I will destroy him or her," replied Fotley.

"What if he has a protection seal and you do not. Who would win?"

"Are you telling me I will lose against them?"

Bitu lays the seal on the table and pass it to Fotley, where he picked it up and looked at it. Bitu only stood still, staring at him.

"Carry it at all times, Fotley."

"So I shall."

"Seal number six you do not want."

"Why not?"

"You're speaking out of turn, Fotley," Bitu said becoming irritated.

"Seal number six is against my kind, it's no use to you," he said crushing the medallion with its bare hands.

"Seal number seven is what you are going to use during your church service."

"What dose it do?"

"Listen to me!" yelled Mitsy, pounding her fist on the table. Fotley fell to the floor and the table broke in half.

"This seal is for calling out the evil. Mitsy will be your victim. You, Fotley, will call out my name and I shall possess Mitsy. Everyone will see how powerful you have become." Fotley got up from the floor. "Well Fotley! Say something!"

"I like it, Bitu."

"I will show you how to set it up Fotley, tomorrow," said Bitu, standing up and walked toward the door. "I will see you tomorrow, Fotley, right here."

"I'll be waiting, Bitu," he said watching Mitsy go through the door.

Two hours later the sun has rising. Fotley slept throughout the daytime hours. Mary Rose changed her house by putting up charms and a circular mirror. She had learned the ways of making potions and casting spells.

It's now mid afternoon under cloudy skies. Ahab talked on the phone while Jetson asked.

"Who are you talking to?"

"My friend Nelly, she's on her way down hear," Ahab said as he saw a shadow in the kitchen. He walked to the kitchen and saw Mitsy sitting in a chair.

"How on earth did you get in hear?" he asked.

"It's not hard when you learn the ways of black magic, dad."

"Evil magic, Mitsy."

"Are you talking to yourself Ahab? Questioned Jetson, entering the kitchen.

"Meet my daughter, Mitsy," said Ahab.

Both looked surprisingly and realized they knew each other. Jetson showed very little fear with in himself. Mitsy kept silent and gave him a dirty look with her eyes.

"I believe we met before," Jetson said watching her eyes changed from normal to deep red.

"Why don't you tell me who you are?"

"I am Mitsy."

"No your not, tell me again who you are?" asked Jetson, walking towards her.

At that very moment Mitsy pushed Jetson to the floor and Ahab over a chair. She made her way to the door, greeted by Nelly.

"Mitsy!" Nelly exclaimed as she grabbed her.

"Let me go!" she cried out as herself.

Nelly held on tight Mitsy tried to stepped out door, but Nelly kept pushing her back inside. Nelly began to scream fighting Misty.

"Don't let her go, Nelly!" Jetson shouted running up to her.

There is a struggle and all three fall to the floor. They roll Mitsy to the floor with Nelly and Jetson on top her. There is kicking, biting, and screaming and all of a sudden they find themselves on the floor.

"Where is she? Where did she go?" questioned Nelly, knowing that Mitsy simply vanished before them.

"I thought demons don't get powerful during the day?" questioned Ahab.

"They don't, but your daughter has something that I thought was destroyed in the fire." answered Jetson, as he got up from the floor.

"She has the keys," Nelly said as Ahab helped her up.

"We have to find her," said Jetson, heading back to his room.

"At least I know my daughter is still alive," Ahab said.

"What was she doing here?" asked Nelly.

"She didn't say the moment I introduced her to Jetson everything went crazy."

"Ahab, your daughter is possessed with evil," said Nelly walking toward the kitchen.

"I had a feeling that something was wrong with my daughter," Ahab said as he followed Nelly to the kitchen.

Another night has come. Fotley waited in his church. A door opened itself and Mitsy stood by the doorway. She spoke with the voice of a demon.

"Follow me, Fotley."

Fotley walked down from the altar and toward the doorway. He came out of the barn and followed behind Mitsy under the night sky.

"May I speak, Bitu?"

"What do you wish to say, Fotley?"

"Where are we going?"

"A trip to the Wicked Fields," replied Bitu, getting into Fotley's car.

Fotley got into the driver seat and turns on the engine. He then looked at Mitsy as she stood still like a statue, not a single part of her body moved.

"Which way do I go, Bitu?"

"Go west and stay on that heading until you see something unusual. You shall stop there and call on me." answered Bitu.

Fotley kept silent and did as he was told to do. He drove westward to wherever lies ahead. His mind was overcome with thoughts as he looked down at Mitsy.

"I wonder if she is asleep or meditating," he said to himself.

There was no radio to listen to, and Mitsy was not in the mood of talking to him, so his thoughts continued to overcome his mind.

"I'm looking down the road and see nothing unusual. The stars are bright, the moon is full, and everything looks the same. What am I suppose to see?"

Lighting a cigarette and feeling tense he noticed that the black top road has changed to gravel. An hour later farms disappeared and soon he was driving through empty fields.

Far ahead of him he saw what looked like a black cloud rising with lighting bolts within it. The cloud grew rapidly in size as Fotley began to talk to himself.

"It looks like a storm yet it doesn't act like a storm," he said getting closer to it. "What the hell is this?" as he saw that the black cloud was rotating like a tornado. He stopped the car finding himself in a pasture.

"We are here, Fotley," said Bitu, looking at him covered in sweat. "You should fear the strange and unusual, Fotley," said Bitu getting out of the car.

"Is this the Wicked Fields?"

"Yes, Fotley, it is and hear you will find everything you need to make potions, spells, and every kind of evil thing." He said walking on the trail made of ashes.

"You will come here only at night," Bitu instructed as he came upon a rock. "This is what I was looking for, pick it up Fotley."

Lifting the thirteen pound rock, Fotley took a closer look at it. The rock itself had no value; it was just a worthless rock.

"This is an ore rock."

"Put the rock in my hand, Fotley," said Bitu, receiving the rock in Mitsy's hand.

Mitsy placed her other hand on the rock and stared at it. Fotley watched with amazement as the rock began to change into a dagger.

"Will I learn this?"

"In due time," replied Bitu, giving the dagger to Fotley. "With this dagger you shall draw two diagrams, one is for Mitsy and the other is for me, which you will conjure up."

"I will do as you say, Bitu."

"Come, Fotley, let us get back to your car," said the demon heading out of the Wicked Fields.

"I didn't even know the Wicked Fields existed, Bitu."

"You will draw the diagrams tonight, Fotley in your church," said Bitu as he reached the car.

"I understand."

"Tomorrow night everything must be consecrated before your member arrives," Bitu said as Fotley drives and listens. "Your members must see the power that you have, Fotley. Then watch yourself grow rapidly. I will see through Mitsy's eyes in everything that you do."

"I will not fail you, Bitu," he said arriving at his church. Bitu and Fotley walked together toward the church, but when Fotley entered the church Mitsy had disappeared. Five candles lit themselves and he knew what he had to do. Throughout the long hours of the night he worked.

It's six in the morning of a new day, when Fotley walked into his house tired and sleepy. Mary Rose was awake drinking a cup of coffee.

"Did you do all that had to be done?" she asked.

"All that it needs is to be consecrated," replied Fotley, walking to his bedroom.

"I can do that," said Mary Rose, pouring a second cup of coffee.

That afternoon, Jetson Mo-Billy came out of his room with a pad of paper. He passed the pad to Ahab, who is watching television.

"Take a look at this?"

Ahab took the pad and looked at a few drawings on each page. He showed concerned at what he was seen, although he did not know what it meant.

"Are these the seals you thought were burned?" he asked.

"Yes, but they are in the hands of your daughter," replied Jetson pacing the room. "Each seal has one magical power and I'm only concerned with one seal."

"Which seal is that?" Ahab asked.

"The seal of conjuration," answered Jetson. "If she uses that seal, all hell will be upon us."

"If my daughter has all these seals, then I hope Nelly finds her real quick," Ahab said giving the pad back to Jetson.

At long last evening hours approached in which Mary Rose had made a cauldron a mixture she consecrated the diagrams, the room, the tools, and herself.

Fotley entered the barn with a cup of coffee in his hand. He saw his wife putting the remaining mixture into a bottle. He knew then that everything had been consecrated.

"Everything is all set for tonight," said Mary Rose.

"Bitu will be pleased," said he kissing Mary Rose on the check. "Come my dear for I need to be prepared," said Fotley walking out of the church.

A clear evening and a beautiful sunset, draw Nelly to the cemmentary, hoping to find Mitsy, she saw a woman in black standing by a grave. At long last her search has come to an end.

She stopped her car and she got out. With her eyes focus on her she walked toward the lady in black. A cold wind blew as she approached Mitsy from behind.

"Stop where you are, Nelly," said Mitsy in her own voice.

"Your getting to powerful, Mitsy."

"She will die for this," said she, looking at Nelly.

"Who's going to die, Mitsy?"

"Jessica, she killed my boyfriend."

"Listen to yourself Mitsy, you don't sound like my friend anymore," Nelly said coming closer to her.

"Don't touch me, Nelly."

"What happened to you, Mitsy? Are the keys making you this way? If it is, give them back to Jetson."

Mitsy began to laugh and looked at Nelly as if she wanted to kill her. A laughter of insanity giving Nelly a scare of not trusting her.

"All this time you thought I had the keys!"

"Well, don't you?"

"Stark had the keys when Jessica killed him and she took the keys. At this time the keys has been sold to a church where I am now."

"Don't do this, Mitsy, you're not that kind of person. Jetson said the keys are very dangerous."

"I tried, Nelly, but I can't stop myself from doing it, and it's already too late for me," as she runs through the cemmentary.

"I will find you, Mitsy! And I will help you!" Nelly cried out going back to her car.

Tonight is the night, like no other night. Fotley is in his purple robe, and smelled like the walking dead. He walked to his church and stood in front of the altar. He kneeled to a portrait of the devil and faced the group.

"Good evening to you all," said Fotley, clapping his hands and the candles lit themselves.

"Tonight, all of you will witness the power of our lord through me!" shouted Fotley.

At this time, Mary Rose and Mitsy came to the altar. The both of them sat in their chairs. Mary Rose stood calm and silent, but Mitsy was restless and frighten.

"What all of you will witness tonight shall not be discussed outside this church," said Fotley.

It began with the foul smelling incense. Fotley fell to his knees under heavy meditation. Mary Rose brought forth a bowl of animal blood. She dipped the dagger into the blood and drew a five pointed star on the palm of Mitsy's hands. On her forehead Mary Rose drew and upside down cross. Mitsy felt cold throughout her entire body, dressed in her dark red robe, Mary Rose began to wash her feet in animal blood.

At this time Fotley stood up, listening to a chant which Mary Rose was saying. He brought Mitsy to the first pentagram, placing her inside. Mitsy herself was in a trans, hearing Fotley recite a prayer other than his own language.

Fotley then walked to the altar, where Mary Rose placed on him the seal of conjuration. Fotley walked to the second pentagram shouting.

"Behold the gates of hell shall be opened!"

A fire burns fiercely within the circle. He tossed the blood of a dead animal, ashes of a dead corpse, and hair from Mitsy.

With his hands held high, he shouted out the demon name Bitu more than once, and entire church was filled with an evil presence.

Fotley picked up a bowl that contained a mixture of ashes from a black cat and human blood. After reciting his chant, the mixture was thrown into the circle. A mushroom of black smoke rose, fire ignited, and a monstrous figure appeared. It stood eleven feet tall.

"Behold it has come!" Fotley yelled out.

The group went down on their knees crying out his name. There were others who began to show homage to the demon.

"Hail to the dark angel, Bitu, demon of the dark regions!" the group stood up and began to clap their hands.

"I say onto you Bitu! Take Misty and Misty let Bitu come inside you. The one call Mitsy lies in the circle. She is yours to possess."

At this time, Mary Rose swept away a part of the circle with a witch's broom. The group continued to repeat the chant.

Mitsy stood inside the broken circle, allowing the demon to enter. Her lovely body vanished into the blackness of the demon. Her screams were heard, but her body couldn't be seen. Bitu has consumed a living body and her soul was stained with evil.

Finally, the shadow of Bitu faded into the body of Misty. She stood with darkened eyes, bursting into flames, yet she did not burn, only the robe did.

Mitsy fell to her knees laughing like a crazy woman. When the fire burned itself out, Mary Rose covered her with a blanket of the dead and took her away.

Fotley looked at his group like a madman in hell. His entire small group did not know what to say, but only kept quite.

"This mass has now ended. There's a bowl at the door. As you leave purify yourselves with the oil in it. Believe in what you have seen and go about your evil ways."

Mary Rose and Mitsy were sitting in the kitchen with darkness all around. Fotley entered the room with much pride.

"How did I do, Bitu?"

"You have done well, Fotley. My congratulations to you."

"Damn, was I good!"

"Our work is not yet done Fotley, come," Bitu said, walking outside.

"Put these away, my dear," Fotley said, giving Mary Rose the seals. He then followed Mitsy outdoors.

The both of them got into the car and Fotley drove. They didn't go far, only a five mile drive. Bitu saw a near by church.

"Stop here," he said as Fotley drove into the parking lot. "This Sunday you are going to interfere with this church service by taking over."

"How will I do that, Bitu?"

"I will teach you what to say and you will challenge that minister in faith. The people of this church will belong to you."

"Your command is mine to obey," said Fotley, driving out of the parking lot heading home.

With the sun rising, Nelly stopped by Ahab's house and she hurried up to the door. Inside Ahab and Jetson waited for her arrival.

"What is so important?" asked Ahab.

"I found Mitsy."

"Fine! Let's go and get her, Nelly," said Jetson.

"We can't."

"Why not, Nelly?" questioned Ahab.

She's under control of a demon and under the power of her church."

"Is it that same church Stark went to?" asked Ahab.

"I suppose so."

"Do you know where the church is, Nelly?" questioned Jetson.

"Yeah, I know where it is."

"Let's take a drive to that church and see what were up against," Jetson said walking out with Nelly and Ahab.

Away from his friend, deep within the city, a man walked into a hotel room where he has been staying for several days. Living on the third floor, Mitsy appeared in a black outfit and knocked on the door. The door opened and their stood a man.

"You must be Noel."

"You're that possessed lady," he replied.

"You do know who I am?"

"Go away, I do not have time for you," Noel said shutting the door.

"I want to talk to you. Don't shut me out Mr." said Mitsy, making the door open itself.

Noel walked backwards until he reached a chair. He then sat down having much fear within himself like he never felt before. Mitsy stepped inside the room.

"Since I can't stop you, what is it that you want?"

"I'm about to make you rich," replied Mitsy, standing in front of him, looking like a zombie.

"I only work for Fotley and nobody else."

Mitsy doesn't pay any attention to what he said. Instead she grabs Noel by his shirt and lifts him off the chair and floor.

"Listen to me in what I tell you."

"Alright," said Noel having a hard time to swallow.

"Do you remember the day you, Noel, helped a woman with two sacks of gold. That woman's name is Jessica?"

"Yes, I do recall that," answered Noel.

"If you wish to be rich, that gold can be your, because Jessica is going to die."

"When?" asked Noel, as he became interested, having the look of greed on his face.

"I will call you, Noel," setting him down the floor. "But even better than that, fifty miles from where she will be killed is a forgotten burial ground with a treasure to be found."

"You want me to find this treasure?" he asked.

Not answering his question, Mitsy puts her hand into her pocket and pulls out a strange looking root. She placed the root on the table.

"This will help you, Noel," Mitsy said.

"What is it?"

"It's a wonder root and it will find your treasure."

"What is this treasure?"

"A book, Noel, look for a book of Demonology." replied she. "Find it, and you yourself will become powerful, perhaps even more than Fotley," said Mitsy, walking out of the room and the door closed by it self.

It became a warm humid evening as a car drove down the country road. It slowed down turning into a private driveway.

"This is where Mitsy goes to church," said Nelly.

"It's just an old barn?" questioned Ahab.

"Nobody seems to be home," said Jetson.

"This is where your keys would be, Jetson." said Nelly.

"When do they have their services?" asked Jetson

"Midnight, Friday's," replied Nelly.

"We have to be here next Friday to catch Mitsy and my keys," Jetson said.

"Let's get out of here, Nelly, before we get caught," said Ahab, driving out of the driveway.

Two days pass. Sunday is here and Fotley is dressed in a black gown, a purple tassel across his chest, and a smile as he looked at the clock.

"I am as powerful as a saint," he said.

He looked at himself in the mirror, putting on his black hood splashing foul smelling oil on himself. He walked out of the house to his car and drove toward the church.

Mass service was already in progress in the church when Fotley arrived. He saw Mitsy standing in the parking lot. She walked up to the car as Fotley stepped out.

"Do you know what to do?"

"Step by step, Bitu."

"That's my man; let us damn this church, Fotley."

Inside the church the Rabbi turned to his people, ready to begin his sermon. All of a sudden the doors burst open and a blast of hot wind blew through the church."It would seem we have visitors."

"No! You do not have visitors, Rabbi. I have come to challenge your faith," said Fotley walking slowly down the aisle.

"My faith can not be fought with."

"We shall soon see, Rabbi," said Mitsy.

"Yes," replied the man.

Fotley saw a man with a broken leg, which had a cast. He stopped near him." You got hurt two days ago?" he questioned."Yes" replied the man.

Fotley touched Mitsy's hand and then touched the man's leg. He concentrates, whispering a chant and looked at the man with a smile.

"You will no longer need a cast, because you will be able to walk."

Fotley walked down the aisle and stopped next to a middle aged woman. Both looked at each other and Fotley spoke to her.

"You are dying of cancer?" he asked.

"Doctors say I only have six months of live," said she coughing.

Fotley, once more, grabbed Mitsy's hand and touched the lady on her back. After five minutes he looked at the lady.

"Go to the doctor and tell him that you will smoke as much as you want, as many times as you want. You no longer have cancer."

Upon hearing this, the lady stood up, took a deep breath and let it out without coughing. She took Fotley's hand and shook it.

"How can I ever repay you?" she asked

"Come to my church on Friday at midnight," said Fotley, making his way up to the Rabbi.

"May I take over your sermon Rabbi?"

"No! You may not! This is my church!"

"How can you say something to your own people when you can't even speak," Fotley said taking his power of speech.

Mitsy took hold of the Rabbi and they both sat down on some chairs by the altar. Fotley stood by the podium looking at the people. He pointed his finger and candles lit themselves. He clapped and the lights went dim in the church.

"I'm here to tell you false information. What you read in this book," holding a bible in his hand. "It's nothing more than diaries written by men who thought the name Jesus is the son of God. Well, he's nothing but a man like myself and as well as you all.

The men called Jesus was a great magician. I myself am a great magician, as he turned water into wine, I can turn wine into blood. Jesus raises the dead; I cure a woman from cancer. Jesus made the blind to see, I made a man walk. Magic, that's all it is, magic.

Do you really believe that Jesus died for your sins? I do not think so. Do you all pray to a god who does not help you? The Devil did more for us than God ever did.

God made us to suffer in many ways, you call that being saved? God never did anything for me, but the Devil gave me a hell of a lot more than I asked.

It was he who helped us out of suffering, and he will grant each and every one of you people anything you desire. All he asked is that you worship him as you worshiped God who ignores you.

I challenge the faith of this damn Rabbi that if his church still stands by next week Sunday, he can laugh at my face. If his church does not stand by next Sunday, you people will join my church."Fotley stepped back from the podium "This mass has now ended, may all of you be damned." He looked at the Rabbi pointing at him "Prepare yourself for battle Rabbi," said Fotley, walking down the aisle with Mitsy behind him.

Everyone stood silent as the two of them left the church. At this time people got up from their pews and began to leave.

"My mass has not yet ended!" Pleaded the Rabbi, who can now speak.

"It is for me," said a voice in the crowd.

"Come back! That man is a false prophet!" pleaded the Rabbi.

"If he's so evil, why did he make me walk?" said the man who once was lame and now he walks.

"I will wait to see what happens next week, Rabbi," said the lady who once had cancer.

Driving away from the church of the Rabbi and heading toward his own church, Fotley felt good about himself as he drove.

"You haven't said a word about the sermon, Bitu?"

"What is there to say, Fotley it's the following week that I'm looking forward to. That's the real test for you."

"Do you think we can defeat that Rabbi, Bitu?"

"Not we, you Fotley. The Rabbi is weak in his faith, I can sense his fear, and you will defeat him."

Arriving at his church, Mitsy stepped out of the car and she spoke to him.

"Go to your house, Fotley, and bring Mary Rose to the church."

"As you say, Bitu," he said walking toward the house.

Mitsy walked to the church under the night sky. Going inside, she sat on the chair. With a wave of her left hand the incense began to burn.

The door opened and Fotley with his wife entered the church. They saw Mitsy sitting on the altar chair which was about five feet from the floor.

"We are present, Bitu," said Fotley.

"Sit before me and listen to me, for I will tell you what's to come. In a short while, the mark which you wear now will change from a picture to a number.

The beast will kill anyone and everyone who doesn't wear his mark. When all this is done, then the Anti- Christ will be at hand."

"Will the Anti- Christ be a man or a woman, Bitu?" asked Fotley.

"Why don't you asked Mitsy that question, my beautiful Mitsy, she knows who the Anti- Christ is."

Fotley and his wife, Mary Rose, went down on their knees to the floor. The chair which Mitsy was sitting on came down to the floor.

"I'm no longer in need of you, Fotley, but Mary rose will remain here with me."

"As you say, Bitu," Fotley said, leaving the church.

"Come, Mary Rose," said Bitu, walking toward the table that Mary Rose had set up. The table had a red cloth, one candle, and one burning incense.

Sitting down in their chairs, Mitsy touched the crystal ball, which also stood on the table. She moved her hand clockwise.

"Do you have the conjuration seal?"

"Yes, I do" replied Mary Rose, setting the seal on the table.

"Watch, Mary Rose, and learn the magic in its most evil ways."

The crystal ball brightened while the two ladies gazed into the ball. Soon an image appeared within the ball itself.

Mitsy became herself in her own natural voice. Bitu had left her body and Mary Rose knew that she was with Mitsy herself.

"I said it before, Jessica, you can not hide from me, and my vengeance shall be fulfilled."

A hundred miles away, where she once lived, Jessica was on her way to make a new life for herself. Driving on Beaver Cliff Road, on the darkest hours of the night, she only thought about the gold which was in the rear of her trunk. She thought about how and when to spend it.

With the radio on and the car window down, Jessica felt good about herself in her new found riches. She looked at the rear view mirror and saw an evil eye looking at her which frighten her. She stopped and rubbed her eyes, and saw nothing in the mirror.

Jessica continued to drive on a lonely and quite road. The radio went into static, the car began to feel cold, and the car windows were starting to fog up. Later, Jessica felt uncomfortable as if something or someone was in the car with her.

In the middle of her front windshield, a small red dot appeared, but whatever the reason, the dot got bigger and bigger. Jessica couldn't see through the redness of the dot which is now covering the entire windshield. Its redness stood bright giving off heat.

Jessica put on the brakes, but the brakes failed. She took her foot off the gas pedals, yet the car gained speed. The doors couldn't open the woman screamed as the heat became intense. The steering wheel melted, the dashboard caught fire, and entire inside of the car burst into flames before crashing into a tree.

"I am now satisfied," said Mitsy watching all that has happened in her crystal ball.

"Very impressive, Mitsy" said Mary Rose.

"When you become as powerful as I am, Mary Rose, nothing will be able to stop you," she said yawning. "Right now I'm very tired," said Mitsy, getting up from the table.

"I have a room in my house, Mitsy, if you want to spend the night here."

"I will do that, Mary Rose, thank you," she said walking out of the church together and toward the house.

Early next morning, Noel is in the shower when he heard his cell phone ring. Not coming out of his shower he reached for his cell phone.

"It's me," he said.

"There's a car accident at Beaver Cliff Road. It you want the gold; go their now before the police get there. Remember what I told you about the lost treasure," said a baritone voice of Bitu.

"I'm on my way," said Noel hanging up.

Today is the day for preparation to battle demons. Nelly and Ahab sat on the sofa, while Jetson spread incense in every room of the house. Each one lit a candle and recited a prayer.

At this time, Jetson walked to the kitchen to look at a boiling pot of water mixed with herbs. He entered the living room.

"Who wants to go first?" he asked.

"I'll go," replied Ahab.

"Take your candle and set it in the washroom and light your incense," said Jetson.

"This is what Alexander did to me," Nelly said.

"I do remember him," said Ahab, making his way to the washroom.

Jetson poured a pot of herbs into a tub of water. With his right hand, he stirs the water, while he recited a prayer form the bible.

"You can now take a bath, Ahab."

"I'll start another pot of herbal water," Nelly said filling the pot.

Jetson set the table with three chairs. On this table stood holy powder, a large white candle, and fragrance oil.

"I'll go next, Jetson."

"Alright, Nelly," said Jetson as he noticed Ahab had cone out of the washroom. "Is the pot boiling?"

"Its ready to go," replied Nelly.

"What do I do now?" Ahab asked.

"Sit here and wait for me," Jetson answered, preparing the bath water for Nelly.

"Is it ready?"

"You're all set, Nelly," replied Jetson.

"I have my candle and my incense," Nelly said entering the washroom.

"Alright! While she is taking a bath, you put holy powder on yourself from head to toe.

"What about the oil, Jetson?" asked Ahab.

"Put that on after the powder and meditate for one hour on your knees."

"Do I do it now Jetson?"

"You can if you want, or you can wait for the rest of use."

"I believe I will wait," Ahab said, relaxing in his chair

By the time, Jetson and Nelly were ready; they see Ahab asleep in the chair. He was snoring as the two looked at each other.

"What shall we do?" asked Nelly.

"Put some oil on him," replied Jetson.

Nelly picked up a small bowl of oil from the table. She then splashed oil on the face of Ahab, which awakened him quite sudden.

"We will now meditate for an hour, we will not be bothered by any disturbances made in this house," Jetson said, remaining quite along with Nelly and Ahab.

For four days, this had to be done; there must not be any temptation among them, not even swearing. Their souls had to be pure and faithful.

It is now Saturday, the eve of battle. Fotley, Mary Rose, and Mitsy made their way into the Wicked Fields. Each held a burning torch as Mitsy led the way. They come to a waterhole and with the voice of Bitu, she speaks profoundly.

"I stand here, Fotley stands in front of me, and Mary Rose will stand to the left."

Mitsy turned to Marry Rose and gave her the seal of future events. Mary Rose put the seal around her neck and looked at Mitsy.

"Do your work, Mary Rose."

Mary Rose bow to Mitsy and goes down on her knees with her eyes close, concentrating. Fotley and Mitsy stood still watching Mary Rose at work.

"Strengthen me oh spirit of darkness, I ask of thee to let us see the Rabbi whom we challenge. By the power of this seal, show me the living soul of the Rabbi?" she opened her eyes staring down at the waterhole, "Behold!"

The three of them saw an image upon the waterhole; they see the Rabbi sitting down in his church reading the Bible.

"Look at the man who reads from the book of good, for he is weak in faith. He reads only to save himself from battle." Mitsy smiled with such hate, "You did well Mary Rose, but stay here and watch all that is to happen."

Fotley and Mitsy go up a hill and stop at the top. They look down and see an open field. Fotley knew what had to be done.

"It is here where you will do your work, Fotley."

"As you say, Bitu," he said going down the hill, carrying two pouches and a wand.

He reached the bottom of the hill and looked up seeing Bitu. With the wand in his left hand he drew the sign of the devil. He began to talk in language of witches, writing out a demon name within the devil sign.

Fotley then made the sign of a cross upside down. With the first pouch, he held it upward with both hands, and he spoke.

"The herb of power to open your doors," said Fotley spreading the herb over the devil sign.

With the second pouch, Fotley held it high once more with both hands, facing the full moon he spoke his words of enchantment.

"With this herb, I gave it to thee for nourishment. Rise, come forth into this world," he said spreading the herb upon the devil sign.

Fotley then walked up the hill joining Bitu. He stands next to him looking down at the bottom of the hill. Bitu turned to look at him.

"Don't stop now," he said.

Fotley stood standing in front of the devil sign, holding the wand in his left hand he raises both hands high and shouted out.

"Angles from the underworld! Angels of darkness! I summon thee to rise with all your power! Awaken thee and do my bidden, to the Westside," pausing for a moment.

"The first church that you encounter must be destroyed! Do my task and let it be done!"

There stood silence, a cold chill surrounded the Wicked Fields making Fotley shiver. He felt the ground tremble under his feet and a roaring sound could be heard.

The ground cracked at the bottom of the hill with sulfur rising from within. Before long, the ground at the bottom of the hill caved in with a flying demon rising upward into the night sky heading westward.

Bitu shouted like a mad animal, putting an arm around Fotley's shoulder. The man himself smiled at what he had just done.

"I've taught you well."

"Thank you, Bitu," said he with a smile.

"Come, let us join Mary Rose and see into the waterhole,? said Bitu, walking toward the waterhole.

It's now five minuets pass the midnight hour and the Rabbi knew this by looking at his watch. He then smiled as he tossed the Bible into his brief case.

"I don't need God's help when fighting false prophet," he said to himself walking out of his church with the brief case. At that instant, a strong wind blew so sudden pushing the Rabbi against the door. He saw a great sized demon flapping its wings, the strong wind knocked over the church steeple.

The Rabbi screamed and ran back into his church. The great powerful demon made a fist and pounded the roof of the church forcing it to cave in. with its fiery eyes, it set the church in a roaring blaze.

All that has happen was being observed by three people at the waterhole. Mitsy stands up watching the demon go away.

"Let us go, your work is done hear," said Bitu, leading the way out of the Wicked Fields.

The following morning, a police car and a fire engine were present with many people astonished to see their church destroyed. A body was taken out of the ruins, which turned out to be the Rabbi.

Mary Rose walked among the crowd, passing out flyers to attend their church. "Come to our church, come to our church."

"Will the man who challenge our Rabbi be there?" said a woman

"Yes he will," replied Mary Rose.

"I'll be there," she said walking away.

Some where among the crowd, Nelly met Mary Rose, receiving a flyer, but Mary Rose felt the strength of her faith.

"My goodness, you have strong faith, it should be taken."

"Are you challenging me?" questioned Nelly.

"No, but if you come to our mass, I know someone who would like to feel the power of your faith," replied Mary Rose, passing her by.

"Wait!" Nelly cried out, walking up to her. "Do you know what happen here?"

"A prediction came true; the power of one church overcame the power of another. A demon like thing killed the rabbi and destroyed its church."

"How do you know it's a demon? Have you seen it?" asked Nelly

"I believe in what I see."

"A demon doesn't just come; it's conjured up and commanded to do what the master tells it to do. Do you know such a person?" questioned Nelly

"Come to our church and see for your self," replied Mary Rose walking away.

At Nelly's apartment, Jetson gave Ahab a pack- sack. Both men were putting items into the pack- sack ready to do battle with the forces of evil.

"A half of gallon of Holy water, a pint of Holy oil, three crosses, three protection medallion, one Bible, two crucifix, and incense."

"I have the matches, Jetson," said Ahab, putting the matches into his shirt pocket.

"We are all set," Jetson said hearing the door opened.

"I'm back!"

"What time is it Nelly?" asked Jetson.

With her coat on Nelly made her way toward Jetson. She put her purse on the couch and looked at her wrist watch.

"It's after four."

"That's enough time for us to eat out," replied Jetson.

The three of them left her apartment to a near by restaurant, they find a table and seat themselves. Looking at the menus, they gave their orders to the waitress.

While waiting to be served, they heard the sound of footsteps, yet they see no one. A voice came from behind Ahab.

"Good evening, father of mine."

Ahab turned around to see Mitsy standing behind him. She was dressed in black wearing a devil's medallion and she even had an upside down cross.

"I can not stand to see my daughter with the devil, you even allowed yourself to be possessed, but being that I'm your father I will fight the evil out of you," he said.

"Let us help you, Mitsy," said Nelly.

"It's too late for that, Nelly. I know what's going to happen tonight."

"Who told you, Mitsy?" asked Nelly.

"The seals, you read our minds," said Jetson.

"It's amazing what a person can do with the power of the seals. Look at yourselves you can't even defeat me. I even know who the Anti- Christ is."

"Who is the Anti- Christ, Mitsy?"

"If you had lived with me, father, I would tell you, but I can't."

"Is your soul and body that evil, Mitsy?" questioned Nelly.

"I'm here to warn you, Nelly and you, father, don't come tonight. I don't want to see you hurt."

"It's you who's going to get hurt, Nelly," said Jetson.

"You, Jetson, we are expecting," said Mitsy, walking away from them into nothingness.

"Did you see that?" questioned Nelly, being surprised.

"The power of invisibility," said Jetson softly.

"I can't help my daughter now; she's to far gone from being a Christian."

"Not really, Ahab, there's always a chance in getting her back," Jetson said as they received their food

"I'm not giving up. I want my friend back," said Nelly.

"The only thing I want to know from Mitsy is, who is the Anti-Christ and where?" questioned Jetson, eating his meal.

The sun is setting; the time has come, but not the hour. Jetson, Ahab, and Nelly are on their way to do battle. The war of the angles are about to begin.

Nightfall has come and the hour of battle is at hand. They watch the barn, waiting for everyone to leave before the battle begins.

"This night is in our favor," said Jetson.

"Why?" asked Ahab.

"No moon," replied Jetson.

"People are leaving," said Nelly.

"We are being expected, so this is no surprise to them," said Jetson.

"So what do we do, just walk into their church?" questioned Ahab.

"That's the idea," said Jetson, making his way toward the church.

Nelly and Ahab put on their protection medallions and meet up with Jetson. They all got closer to the church; Nelly saw a demon on top of the barn.

"You guys see what I see?" she asked.

"I see nothing," answered Ahab.

"What do you see, Nelly?" asked Jetson.

"There's a demon on top of the barn, hiding in the darkness," said she as they stopped walking.

"You have good eyes, Nelly," said Jetson, pulling out a pouch from his pocket. Inside the pouch came forth a stone. "I call my friend, Lorenzo Alexzander! Send forth an angle to do battle with this here demon!"

"That's an angel stone, am I right?"

"Yes, it is, Nelly," replied Jetson, hearing a voice behind all three of them.

"Long time no see, Nelly."

"Lorenzo Alexander!" she gasped.

"You looked good Ahab, for your age," Lorenzo said surrounded with radiant light.

"Are you an angel, Lorenzo?" asked Nelly.

"I'm a cadet." He replied.

"I need your help, Alexander," said Jetson.

"Tell me what's happening?"

"There's a demon on top of that barn, can you get rid of it?"

Lorenzo paused for a moment looking at the barn. He saw the wings of that demon flapping over the roof. He then looked at Jetson.

"His name is Kunospaston, and the angle Iameth will be more than happy to know he's on earth. I will go tell him."

"Lorenzo! Will you come to my dreams," asked Nelly.

"I am very busy, but when I have a chance, I will come," he replied fading away.

"Jetson, I would like an angel stone for myself."

"Remind me when this is over, Nelly."

"Look!" Ahab cried out, pointing upward to the southern sky.

They see streaks of lighting and the angel Iameth appeared with a flaming sword. He immediately attacked Kunospaston. Both fought on top of the roof, first with swords then hand to hand combat. Kunospaston flew upward chased by Iameth.

"Now is our chance," said Jetson running toward the barn entrance.

Inside the church, Fotley sat in a chair in front of the altar with Mary Rose behind him. Both were watching the entrance way.

"Welcome, Jetson Mo- Billy and guest. We've been expecting you," said Fotley.

"So, now I am here and you have something that is mine," Jetson said, walking down the aisle.

"You must be talking about the keys?"

"You know what, I want Fotley," replied Jetson, standing in front of the altar.

"I don't have them, Jetson, but there they are," he said pointing to a concrete wall which the keys have been embedded.

A door behind the closed, whereby Mitsy stood by the doorway. Them noise of the door made Nelly turn around and see her friend.

"Mitsy!" she called out.

"I told you not to come, Nelly, but you didn't listen to me, now you're going to get hurt."

"I have come to saved you, Mitsy."

"Nobody can save me, Nelly," said Mitsy as her voice changed. "It is you who is going to need to be saved."

"We meet again, Bitu."

"Yes, indeed we have, Jetson Mo- Billy, and this time I will have your soul."

"That remains to be seen, Bitu."

A wink of her right eye and Ahab went crashing into the chairs up against the wall. A wink of her left eye, and a force pulled Nelly to the bookcases.

"Those medallions you're wearing keep evil spirits away. I'm a fallen angel," said Bitu.

"I have something for a fallen angel," said Jetson but was unable to move a single muscle of his body.

Ahab got up from the floor and attacked Fotley, knocking over the altar table. Mary Rose set out to help Fotley, as she is fought down by Nelly spilling her evil brew.

Mitsy saw everything that was going on as she knelt down and knocked on the floor. After three knocks she got up with her arm held high shouting.

"I command you falling angels of darkness to rise and do battle!"

At this time Jetson cried out even though he could not speak well or move and part of his body he managed to talk.

"Angels of the Lord! Legions of Michael! Angel's warriors! Come Zebul on this very hour and do battle with us!"

Demons came from out of the floor and some came through the walls. They were hideous, coming in all shapes and sizes. For every demon that appeared an angel appeared with their flaming sword.

Mitsy quickly made her way to the door. Jetson was free from the spell and chased Mitsy. He catches her and both of them break the door down.

Mitsy and Bitu are separated. An angel appeared to fight Bitu. Nelly went after Mitsy, and Jetson entered the church to help out Ahab.

Outside the church, Mitsy broke free from the grips of Nelly. A rainstorm has turned into a storm of hail. The ground trembled and exploded in a mushroom of fire, knocking Nelly to the ground.

A demon of an enormous size arose from within the fire. It opened up its great powerful wings as flames raised high in the sky.

"Come to me, my child, and I will see to it no harm will come to you."

"Don't do it, Mitsy!" shouted Nelly, watching her friend got taken by the monstrous size demon. It disappeared in an explosion of fire and smoke.

The fight continued inside the barn. Jetson held the keys in his hands getting jumped by Fotley. The concrete broke releasing the keys. In a struggle, Jetson kicked it away Fotley.

Quickly, Jetson picked up the keys, but was taken down by Fotley. It's then that Nelly entered the barn seeing them fight.

"Destroy the keys!" Jetson shouted.

Nelly picked them up and saw a pot of boiling mixture of herbs. She tossed the keys into the hot pot, hearing her name called out.

Mary Rose stood holding the head of Ahab in her left hand. The head of Ahab called out to Nelly a second time and Nelly screamed.

"Ahab!" as she saw a horrifying sight,

"I have defeated him as I will with you!" Mary Rose shouted, dropping the head of Ahab on the floor.

A loud roaring sound ends the battle with the hot pot spewing the mixture over its top. Electrical bolts came forth, starting fires every-where in the church.

Everybody ran out in their own way, just as the barn exploded into a ball of fire and sparks. Nothing remained standing, only the stars in the night sky could be seen.

"The keys are gone forever," said Jetson.

"Ahab is with God, bless his soul," Nelly said getting up from the ground. "Let's go home, I'm tired."

"Yes, so am I," getting up and walked with Nelly.

VII

WHEN YOU'RE ALONE, YOUR mind becomes your companion. It talks to you and you talk back to it. What I say is my way of thinking, my name is not important, but I am a greedy man and I am an assassin.

I'm driving on Beaver Cliff road in these early morning hours in the thick fog. I'm on this road because I'm told by a lady named Mitsy that I would find gold.

It didn't take me long to find a wrecked car, and yes she told me the truth, I found gold. If I was an honest man, I would take back to Fotley. But I am not that kind of man, so I will keep this gold for myself.

I should leave town and not return, but I keep going down Beaver Cliff road. Mitsy told me that there's a lost treasure somewhere around here.

I remember Mitsy saying that I need to find the forgotten cemetery, even though I don't know where it is I say, forget the treasure and just go.

I stopped at a rest area overlooking a lake. The fog cleared and the sky was dark, I lit myself a cigar and I saw lightning in the distance toward the lake.

I'm the only one here watching the storm intensify. I looked down below the rail, a long way down about a thousand foot drop. I remember something that Mitsy gave me. I put my hand into my coat pocket and I pulled out the Wonder Root. I did exactly as Mitsy had told me. I placed the root in the palm of my left hand. I moved my hand from right to left watching the Wonder Root to see what would happen.

I don't believe in the supernatural, but seeing is believing. I noticed that the Wonder Root is moving around in circles on my hand. It's telling me that I should go East instead of South.

I got into my car and headed south until I saw a road to the East. I turned onto this road to the East. I turned onto this road in which the pavement became gravel.

I drove a few miles and up ahead I saw a dead end. I was surrounded by tall trees and a swamp. I got out of my car and looked around holding the Wonder Root in my hand. The root told where to go. I walked beyond the trees, into the grassy swap. My new shoes were ruined, and my dress pants were wet up to my knees. However, I found the cemetery within the swamp.

Only a few gravestones were standing, the cemetery itself was surrounded by rotted trees, swamp grass, and tall weeds. Where is the book of Demonology could be hidden? I thought to myself.

I wondered through the cemetery, I touched the largest gravestone and it fell into the grassy swamp. I watched the stone get swallowed, but from that very spot, a fog rose into the air.

Like I said before, I don't believe in the supernatural, ghost, gods, or strange things. But when I saw something that I couldn't explain, then it becomes believing.

This fog that I saw took the shape of a woman figure. It was so frightening to me that it sent chills down my spine.

"You come for the book?" questioned the ghost lady.

"Yes," I replied, looking at her with fear in my eyes.

She pointed to a grave talking as if she had lost her voice. Her ghostly figure only showed half of her body.

"Take the gravestone," said the ghost lady as she disappeared from my sight, leaving nothing except a skull.

I was already too scared to say anything and I didn't care to see anything else, so I picked up the gravestone, ran out of the swamp, to my car, and out of that area as fast as I could.

I was covered in sweat, my mouth was dry, and I needed to relax. I remember passing a bar, so I decided to stop there for a drink to calm down my nerves.

It didn't take me long to reach the bar. I went inside, sat on a stool and ordered my drink. I could feel myself calming down, but also I felt like I was being watched. I ordered a second drink seeing a well dressed man stepped in front of me.

"Are you still working for Fotley?" he asked.

I looked and I am surprise. "Well I'll be dammed, Ceepot."

"Long time no see, Noel."

"It's been awhile, Ceepot," I said shaking his hand.

"Come and join us at the table, Noel" said Ceepot.

I took my drink and followed him to the table in which another man is sitting down. He did not look very friendly to me.

"This is Mr. Taylor, a government agent," said Ceepot.

"Mr. Taylor you don't look so good."

"What do you mean?" asked Mr. Taylor.

"From the look of those eyes you haven't slept well," replied Noel.

"Just having trouble sleeping, that's all." said Mr. Taylor.

Noel consumed his drink and looked at Ceepot at how he was dressed in uniform with medals on him. He looked very good for himself.

"What are you? The last time I remember, you were only a sergeant in the armed forces."

"I'm a General now," answered Ceepot.

"The General tells me that you worked for Fotley."

"Part time, Mr. Taylor," Noel said, smoking a cigar.

"Do you know what happened to Fotley?" asked Mr. Taylor

"No. I don't keep up with the news," answered Noel.

"Fotley's church and all his works were destroyed by fire started by an arsonist. What do you think of that?" asked Mr. Taylor.

"I think. Fotley, will be looking for me."

"I agree Noel, but what I'd like to know, is what ever happened to the gold that he had?" questioned Ceepot.

"What makes you think he had gold?"

"Rumors," replied Mr. Taylor as they stared at each other.

"Did, Fotley, have gold?" questioned Ceepot.

"Why don't you ask him?" answered Noel.

"Why don't you think, Fotley, is still alive?" questioned Ceepot

"Mr. Taylor seems to think so, isn't that right?" asked Noel

"I'll find him," he replied smoking a crooked pipe.

Still smoking his cigar Noel took a drink and looked at Ceepot as he himself took a drink from a bottle which he had.

"What about you, Ceepot? What are you doing here?"

I'm here on government business." He replied.

"What kind of business? asked Noel.

"The kind of business like the mark that you don't have on yourself, Noel."

Mr. Taylor smiled at Noel, "Don't worry; we aren't going to arrest you because the mark is changing to a number."

"When that happens, Noel, you'd better have the mark," said Ceepot.

"Failure to wear this mark, Noel, means I get to shoot you on the spot no questions asked," said Mr. Taylor with a smile, pulling out his gun from its holster.

"Tell me more about this number? Is it any different than the mark we have now?" questioned Noel as he ordered more drinks.

"Six months from now all currency will end in America, and everyone living in America will be given a number. This number will be attached to their social security number. It will buy, sell, and trade anything and everything Noel," said Ceepot still smoking.

"Are you saying that if I don't have this number, I can not buy, sell, or trade, in fact I could get killed?"

"Yes, Noel, and I am looking forward to that. It will be like hunting, and the government won't call it murder," said Mr. Taylor

"I might as well leave America and never come back."

"It wouldn't make and difference, Noel, sooner or later all nations will be doing this," said Ceepot.

Noel poured himself a drink, put out his cigar, and drank from his glass. He is confused in what he has been told.

"I still don't understand how this is going to work?"

"The number will have color codes. The high class will be red, the middle class will be blue, and the lower class will be green. All this will be placed in a powerful computer," said Ceepot.

Mr. Taylor drank from his bottle and sat it on the table getting Noel's attention. He looked at Noel with a mean look.

"I think you should be labeled in the lower class."

"I'm starting to dislike you Mr. Taylor."

Ceepot continued "A low class person works forty hours, instead of receiving a payroll check his forty hours will computed. In one month, this person would have 160 hours; in one year 1920 hours will be computed."

"Then what?" asked Noel.

"Since this person carries hours, he or she will be able to pay, buy, sell or trade anything and everything using their hours of work. The computer will deduct seconds, minutes, or hours from their hours worked. Time is money Noel," replied Ceepot.

"So, all this person has to do is to show the number under the computer and the computer does the rest."

"That is correct, Noel," said Ceepot

"What is this number, Mr. Taylor?" asked Noel, Mr. Taylor looked at Ceepot. "Should I tell him?"

"Why not it's no secret," answered Ceepot.

"The number is six, six, six."

"People say that is the mark of the beast Mr. Taylor," exclaimed Noel.

"Do you believe that?"

"I'm not religious, but I would be force to wear this mark or I lose everything?" asked Noel.

"Everything that you own including your life," said Mr. Taylor.

"When is this going to happen?"

"In six months, Noel, and in ten months every person throughout the world shall carry the mark," replied Mr. Taylor.

"Would you kill women and children, Mr. Taylor, if they didn't have the mark?"

"Sure, I would."

"You're nothing but a goddamn murderer, said Noel, finishing his drink getting up from the chair.

"Six months from now, Noel, I'll be looking for you, just to see if you have the mark," said Mr. Taylor.

Noel gave Mr. Taylor a dirty look without saying a word. He exit the bar headed toward his car where he sees a woman sitting in the front seat of his car. Noel opened the car door.

"Leave the book there and get out of the car," he said.

"Be not afraid of me, Noel," she said in a strong male voice.

"I'm not afraid of you, Bitch," said he, with anger in his voice.

"Come in and join me, Noel," said the lady, forcing the man into the car by something unknown.

"You're not a lady."

"I am Murmur, Listen to what I say. You will go to the north side of the city and look for a place of worship called Angel of Lights. It is there that you will find Fotley," she said stepping out of the car and walked away.

Ceepot walked out of the bar and watched Noel drive away. A lady walked toward Ceepot and stand next to him, looking at each other.

"Do you see that man driving away?" asked the lady.

"What about him?" questioned Ceepot.

"He has gold in the trunk of this car, something to think about," the lady said walking away.

Somewhere at the north side of the city, a van drove around the neighborhood as if it was lost. By evening the van stopped in a parking lot. Twelve people came out from the van. Among the twelve, Fotley lead them to a building that looked like a hospital.

Inside, the guest wondered around the lobby looking at statues of demons, satanic books, and a shop of ritual items for sale.

Fotley entered a room that looked much like a church of Satan. It stood in darkness, and there stood a cross upside down. He also saw a man in a purple robe liting black candles.

Walking down the aisle toward the altar, Fotley approached the man from behind as he turned around facing him.

"I saw your sign saying that the Angel of Lights feed the hungry."

"Yes, the Angel of lights stands by that, only if you attend our services."

"May I ask you who you are?"

"I am Father Oune, and this is the church of evil doings,"

"I am Fotley, master of the Black Arts, a leader of the occultist."

"Welcome to my church, Fotley."

"I have my company of many who are hungry, and yes, we will attend your services, just to see how you perform."

Oune walked up close, looking at Fotley eye to eye. He shook his hand and saw a pentagram on the palm and felt the coldness of his body.

"Do you find me interesting?" questioned Fotley.

"My people, including myself, have been receiving messages from the unknown. The evil spirits say that a man would come and join us. I believe that you are that man."

"Maybe I am, maybe I'm not Oune."

"If you are that man, I have much to learn from you, Fotley," said Oune, walking toward the lobby.

"What makes you think I'm that man?"

"The evil spirits also say that this man knows secrets of the Black Arts, Fotley."

Fotley smiled to himself. "I would like to know who the evil spirits are; they seem to know me very well."

"Bring your company to the cafeteria, Fotley, there is enough food for all of them," Oune said leading the way down the stairs.

From out of the ashes of a burn down house a new house is made. Outside the city limits, Jetson lit a candle in his new house.

"What's the candle for?" asked Nelly.

"In the memory of Ahab a good man, a good Christian," replied Jetson.

"Did you forget someone else?" questioned Nelly, lighting another candle.

"Who did I forget, Nelly?"

"This is for Lorenzo Alexander, for helping us."

When finished praying to their dearly departed, Jetson walked out of the praying room with Nelly close behind him. From the praying room to the dining room they walked.

"Is this for me?" asked Jetson spotting a cup of coffee on the table.

"Yes it is," replied Nelly, picking up the newspaper.

"Have you seen the paper yet?"

"No." she answered.

"Do you know what the government is going to do to us people?" asked Jetson.

"Tell me?" questioned Nelly.

"They are going to change the mark to a number and put it next to our social security number."

"I'm not surprised, Jetson."

"According to the paper, everybody is going to wear it, it's a must, and if you don't have it the agents will have the privilege of killing you on public streets."

"That is terrible, Jetson."

"This is becoming very serious, Nelly," he said.

"What kind of number are they going to use?" asked Nelly.

"It didn't say."

"Six, six, six."

"Paper doesn't say that?" questioned Jetson.

"No, but the Bible does."

"Suppose your right? What are the people going to do? The mark of the beast will be here in the next six months."

"I don't know. I guess people will panic."

"Let me show you something," said Jetson, writing the number 666 on a pad. "Each six is referred to hours, which means that every six hours something has to be done. The first six hours begins at midnight.

If we add the three sixes together we get eighteen. We now take that number and let it be one plus eight which equals nine. By remembering that all evil ways is done backwards that would mean the Anti-Christ will make himself known to the world on 8-1-09 at about 6:00 pm."

"How do you know all this?" asked Nelly

"I did a lot of research with the help of the angels, Nelly," he replied finishing his cup of coffee.

Nelly felt fear all over herself after being told of what is to come. She got up from the table and looked out the window.

"I wish you didn't tell me that, Jetson?"

"Why?"

"In six months everyone in the United States will carry that number not knowing what it really stands for. It's very frightening to me," replied Nelly.

"The Christians know what it means, but what's more frightening is who will control the world when the number is out? I'm sure it's not the president, in fact the president will be taking orders from it."

Nelly stopped looking out the window and turned around looking at Jetson holding an empty cup. She had many thoughts in her mind.

"That's a good question. Who could it be?"

"Prophecy has it, Nelly, that the Anti-Christ can not come as man, can not come as animal, but as a thing of beauty."

"That can be many things, Jetson."

"That's right, so somewhere in this world the Anti-Christ is walking among us."

"I hope I'm dead before all this happens," said Nelly walking toward the living room.

Jetson took the newspaper and followed Nelly into the living room seeing her sit on the sofa. He brings the newspaper to her.

"You are forgetting why you are here."

"I am here because the angels are fighting over me so that I can go to heaven."

"That is correct, always remember that," said Jetson. Leaving her alone in the room.

Nightfall has come, a blackmass is being held. It's done by Oune with Fotley observing the mass. Already, he's displeased in what he is seeing. A small audience in a big church.

Looking around, Fotley saw a man standing in the lobby waving his hands. Fotley got up and quietly excused himself as he made his way to the lobby.

"I saw what was left of your church, Fotley, and I'm very sorry about the death of your wife."

"Her soul is now with the devil, but I must avenge her death," he said hugging the man. "Noel, it's good to see you again. How did you find me?"

"Someone told me where you were," replied Noel as he is quite concerned. "Tell me, Fotley, whatever happened to the gold?"

"Buried in the ruins," he answered.

"I brought you something for you, something useful," Noel said giving the book to Fotley.

The man's eyes grew large looking at the title "The Book Of Demonology. This book was said to be lost forever.

How did you get it?" asked Fotley, smelling the book.

"Never mind how I got it, can you use it?" questioned Noel.

"With this I can avenge the death of my wife and become master of darkness."

"Fine, then you keep it."

"With pleasure, Noel. Now what can I do for you?"

"I don't know yet, but I'll think of something. I'm going back to my hotel, if you need me, call me."

"I'm sure I will," said Fotley heading back to mass.

Noel left the church and looked at his watch. It's four in the morning, so he stopped by a bar for a few hours. By seven in the morning he drove to his hotel.

He arrived at his hotel room. Two men also got out of their cars and walked to Noel's car. One of the men broke open the trunk, and found the gold.

"Put the gold in my car, Metcalf."

"What about, Noel?"

"I'll take care of him myself, "said Ceepot.

"Do you want me along?"

"No, just wait for me in the car," replied Ceepot as he walked toward the hotel.

At his hotel room, Noel was taking a shower, unaware that Ceepot had forced himself into the room. He quietly walked and hears the shower on which he entered the room. Ceepot pulled out his gun with a silencer and saw Noel come out of the shower.

The first shot went through the towel striking Noel in the chest. Ceepot opened the shower room door and fired a second shot into Noel's head. The man fell backwards into the wet tube.

"So long old friend," said Ceepot leaving the room.

Outside the hotel, Metcalf was in the driver seat waiting by the hotel entrance. Ceepot stepped out of the hotel to the car. He opened the door and got inside the car as they drove away.

"Got all the gold?"

"In the truck," replied Metcalf. "Noel is out of the way?"

"Noel is asleep and won't wake up anymore," answered Ceepot with a smile.

The hours of the afternoon of a new day brought Fotley to the Church of Lights. He stood alone in front of a demon statue and knelt before it.

Fotley opened the *Book of Demonology*. Looking through the pages of the book he found the page he was looking for and started at the statue.

"Hear me, Bitu! Do my bidding!"

"He can not help you," said a voice in the dark.

"Bitu, is my teacher, is he angry with me?" asked Fotley.

"No, but Bitu, is behind the gates of hell and can not help you at this time," said the voice of a female.

The church itself stood in bitter coldness with the smell of evil in the air. Fotley was shivering from the cold that surrounded him.

"Who are you?" questioned he walking around the church.

"I am known to you as Helcat, and I will assist you," she said appearing in front of the alter.

Fotley saw the female demon and walked toward the altar. Her long stringy hair changed colors in the mood that she was in. Her rough skin felt like a man who was covered with acne.

The brightness of her long stringy hair that touched the floor blinded the eyes of Fotley. He could not see the nakedness of her body.

"What is it that you want me to do, Fotley?" she asked smiling with her rotted teeth and bad breath.

"I want you to go pay a visit to Jetson Mo-Billy and let him know that I am still alive. The battle continues between me and him."

"Do you have a dollar bill, Fotley?"

The man pulled out a dollar bill from his wallet.

"Here you are, Helcat," he said giving her the dollar.

Helcat took the dollar bill and she folds it in such way that it formed a pentagram. She then put it in her mouth and began to chew.

"Wait here," said Helcat disappearing before Fotley.

That same afternoon Jetson stood in the house of Ahab packing up his belongings so that he could take them to his new house.

The sun was shining brightly through the windows, but Jetson noticed that it was getting darker then usual. Jetson stopped packing and looked around the rooms of the house as it got darker and darker.

At this time footsteps were heard coming down the stairs. Jetson walked toward the stairway and saw a shadow standing in the stairs in the dark.

"Who is there?"

"It is me Jetson!"

"Fotley!" he shouted.

"Yes, it's me you asshole, and I'm still alive you son-of-a-bitch. You did not kill me the first time, Jetson, so our fight continues."

"Bring on your demons, Fotley."

"Beware of me, Jetson, this time I will strike first," he warned walking back upstairs into the darkness. Then the darkness faded away.

At the Church of Lights, Fotley stood at the front of the altar meditating when Helcat appeared before him. Spitting out the dollar bill.

"Did you do as I asked?" questioned Fotley.

"It is done," replied Helcat, pacing the altar floor.

"Your name will be remembered in the blackmass,"said Fotley, watching her walk back and forth.

"I want souls," she said stomping on the floor.

"You shall have it, all in good time, Helcat."

"I want one now starting with yours," said she looking at him.

"Bitu already has my soul. I can not give what I do not have," said Fotley.

The female demon faced Fotley and grabbed him by the shoulders, lifting him into the air. Fotley showed no fear, but her ugly breath made him sick.

"If you ever need me, call me, I'm in the book," and saw no sight of Helcat. He then walked to the back of the church and saw Oune.

"That was amazing what I just saw."

"What did you see, Oune?"

"I saw you floating up in the air, I would like to learn that Fotley."

"You didn't see any demon?"

"No, just you," he said taking the book away from Fotley. "Is this your book of shadows?" asked Oune.

"Take a look at the title," replied Fotley.

Oune looks at the cover of the book and reads the title. "The *Book of Demonology*, I heard about this book. It could make you Master of Evil."

"How would you like to learn from it?" asked Fotley.

"Hell yes. I would love it," answered Oune excited walking out of the church together.

That evening Nelly entered her apartment finding candles and incense burning. She did not know what to think, taking her coat off.

"What's going on?" she asked.

"Fotley is still alive, he came to me in spirit form," replied Jetson.

"I had a feeling we hadn't seen the last of him," said Nelly as she sat down.

"He said the battle isn't over yet," Jetson said looking through his notes.

"He can't be that powerful? We destroyed the keys, unless he's getting power from somewhere else."

"I don't know, Nelly, but if he's still alive then I believe Mitsy is too."

"Of course, Jetson, Mitsy disappeared during the battle, which means she has returned," said Nelly thinking about it.

"The problem is that he knows where we are and we don't know where he is," said Jetson.

"What do we do about that?"

"We wait until he makes his move, Nelly."

"No. we don't have to wait, Jetson."

"What do you have in mind?"

"We do the cards," she said walking toward her bedroom.

In the night of a full moon at the church of lights, a crowed gathered inside. Oune walked to the altar and turned to the people.

"My fellow servants, tonight I will not perform the mass of Satan. Tonight, Fotley, a high priest, will take the altar and perform a ritual that I or any of you have never seen done," said he walking to the chair.

At this time Fotley walked up to the altar table. With him he had the book of Demonology as he set the book on the altar.

"I ask you all, fellow servants, to be silent and meditate as I perform this ritual."

"I do not know you or your works!" shouted a voice in the crowd.

Upon hearing this Fotley stepped down from the altar and walked up to the crowed. He raised his voice at them. He stood fearful and bold.

"On this night! All of you will know who I am! And what I am! Oune, your priest, will soon be as powerful as I am! He will be able to turn candles on without matches!" as Fotley snapped his fingers and the candles lit themselves.

"Anything that Oune says will happen as I will watch it happen. Light the incense!" he demanded as the incense did light themselves. Fotley clapped his hands and a burner lit up under a cast iron pot. People were astonished in what they have seen.

"All this and more Oune will learn from me!" he said putting on a black robe.

Fotley returned to the altar table. He picked up a glass jug from the floor. He holds the jug in his hand showing it to the people.

"This is urine of a pig and goat," he said pouring it into the cast iron pot. "Head of bat, tail of rat, and eye of blind dog," said he tossing it into the pot. The crowd listened and stood quiet.

"Roots of Hembane, powder of Anise, and bark of a dead oak," said he tossing it into the pot. Fotley stirred then raised his hands into the air and put out the lights.

The church stood in semi- darkness as Fotley brought a large square mirror and place it in the front of the pot. With a strong voice he called out.

"Let the world of the unknown meet the world of the organic! Come back to me, Mitsy! Follow the odor! It will bring you back to the organic world! I, Fotley, command you, Mitsy, to come forth!" he repeated the chant a second time in another language.

Within the church of lights a breeze blew about, turning into a strong gust of wind. It began to blow objects from within the church. A roaring sound was soon heard. It got louder, and the church itself rocked like an earthquake. The group in the church did not know what to think or didn't have time to be afraid. They were all astounded.

"Now is the time! Be here! And now!" Fotley yelled out suddenly, without, warning, the mirror image vanished and burst into a thousand pieces as well as a mushroom of black smoke.

Everything stood silent, nobody moved, and when the thick black smoke cleared, Mitsy stood among everyone. She was dressed in rags and her skin was as white as a ghost.

Fotley took a red robe and put it on her. She walked slowly to the front of the altar facing the group. The group held onto their noses for Mitsy had a bad smell.

"I am Mitsy, queen of the night."

The group clapped their hands and cheered. They got up from their seats and walked up to Mitsy, kissing her hand or knelt to her. Whatever the people asked for, Mitsy gave to them.

"What you did here tonight, Fotley, people will now come and fill my church."

"This is only the beginning, Oune, in what you will learn."

"I can't wait for you to teach me all this and more Fotley," said Oune, watching Mitsy walk to the altar.

Mitsy kissed the floor and turned to the group. Her skin color was returning to normal, although she felt weak from hunger.

"Can anyone tell me if night and dark is one of the same things?"

"Yes, it is the same thing," replied a voice in the group.

"Are you sure about that?" questioned Mitsy in her own natural voice.

A woman stood up. "Then you tell us, Mitsy. Is there a difference between night and dark?" she asked sitting down.

"Right now, at this time, its night and what do we see?" asked Mitsy, pacing the altar.

A man spoke. "We see the stars, moon, houses, and trees, almost everything the eye can see."

"That is correct. We see everything exactly the same as we see it in the light of day,"

At this time Mitsy stopped pacing. "Now then, let us see what's in the dark?"

With a waved of her hands from east to west. Mitsy had all the lights, including the candles, went out within the church. It became extremely dark that people couldn't see each other.

"We see nothing," said a man.

"It's like being blind," said a woman.

The lights go on and the people see Mitsy with her hands held high. She walked up to the people looking at them.

"You all just witness darkness. Which is more frightening, night or dark?"

"That's hard to say," said a lady.

"Imagine this. A shadow was cast in the night when the moon was out. There is no shadow in the dark. Night follows time, darkness does not. The devil would rather hide in the dark than in the night.

In total darkness you can't see your hand in front of you. A noise is heard, but you don't know where it came from, you don't even know if it's a man or beast. All you know is that it's here with you in the dark.

You walk slowly in circles with fear in your mind, trying to feel your hands, but there's nothing to touch, not even the ground you're standing on.

Let your nose smell of something evil. It can see you, but you can't see it. The smell tells you that something is with you in the dark.

Now I ask of you? Tell me if night can be the same thing as darkness," said Mitsy hearing nothing, but silence. "There's no such thing as night in hell. Darkness conquers all," she said walking away from the altar, and sat next to Onue.

Fotley walked up to the altar and faced the people. "Know, my fellow servants, in what I have done bringing Mitsy, queen of darkness, here in this church. Spread the word among your friends and all around for this mass is now ended. Go and do bad things, so let it be," he said walking way from the altar.

People stood up and left the church while others kissed Fotley's hand as he stood at the altar. He watched everyone leave the church. At this time Fotley stepped up to Mitsy.

"I'm very impressed in what you know since your disappearance."

Mitsy turned to the man next to her. "No need to tell me who you are, Oune. I know all about you."

"Welcome back, Mitsy," Fotley said hugging each other.

"It's good to be back, and I'm starving."

"I suppose you are and we have some unfinished business to attend to," said Fotley.

"Yes, we do," said Mitsy walking together. "Come, Oune, you must learn from Fotley," she said walking toward a dark room.

It's now in the fifteenth day of Virgo, somewhere in America. An occult shop is about to open its doors. Anna, a woman engaged to be married, was putting money into a cash register. A woman all alone in the shop like any other day, but today something strange began to occur, that made her believed in supernatural.

While counting the money Anna began to smell smoke. She looked around her shop and saw smoke from the back of the shop. She quickly walked toward it.

Looking for something burning, she saw no fire, but the smoke came out of a mirror which hung on the wall. It startled her. "What in the hell is this?" she said talking to herself, witnessing a vision from within the mirror.

What she saw was a man standing on a hill with his back on Anna. Smoke covered the sky turning day into night. A raging fire burned upon an ocean and the screams of people burning alive echoed into her ears. There's fear on her face as she covered her ears.

"No! Stop it!" shouted Anna, when all of a sudden she heard a knock at the door.

The vision was gone, she only saw herself in the mirror. What happened that day, she could not explain, but it bothered her all day long.

That afternoon, Nelly was hard at work as a clerk in a supermarket, when she was approached by another woman. Her voice sounded familiar.

"I'm back Nelly."

"Mitsy," she said watching her walk by.

"Follow me, Nelly."

"I can't. I'm working."

"Don't worry, Nelly, nobody will ever notice you're gone."

With that in mind, Nelly left her work station and followed Mitsy to the backroom of the supermarket without being seen by her employees.

"Are you really Mitsy or a demon inside her?"

"What does your faith tell you, Nelly, am I a demon or am I Mitsy?"

"You're a demon."

"You are wise, Nelly."

"Are you here to challenge me?"

I'm here to cast a spell on you, Nelly, but first I want to tell you more about the mark."

"I don't want to hear it," said Nelly walking out of the back room.

To her amazement, Nelly saw everyone standing still like statues within the supermarket. Mitsy comes out behind her.

"They are really moving, Nelly, only you cant tell."

"What did you do, Mitsy?"

"I pulled you out of their time zone. They can not see you, Nelly."

"Why did you do that?"

"Because I want you to hear what I have to say."

"You must be very powerful demon to do all this, so say what you have to say."

"What Jetson told you about the mark of the beast is only half true. You already know what the mark of the beast is."

"It's six, six, six," said Nelly.

"You already know how it's going to control the human race."

"Yes, I do, Mitsy."

"And you already know the date of the coming of the Anti- Christ."

"That is correct, so what else is there to know?" questioned Nelly.

Both ladies began to walk around the supermarket."Lets break up the sixes Nelly. The first six is equal to one plus five, the second six is equal to three plus three, and the third six is equal to four plus two.

By doing this you know the age of the Anti- Christ. It came forth into this world on the six month of the year; on the six day of the week in the year nineteen hundred sixty seven. The devil himself baptized it.

The first six, Nelly, tells you that at the age of fifteen, the devils taught it their powers. At the age of thirty three with the power of hell it became very important and popular person, loved by many. When it reaches the age of forty two it will have the power over the world, a leader among leaders."

"That won't happen until the eleventh day of Leo two thousand nine."

"Now you know everything about the mark, Nelly."

"And I still won't wear it."

"That's up to you, Nelly, but I will seek you out and will be able to kill you."

"That is if I don't find you first, Mitsy," she said walking away from her.

At this time Nelly forgot to say something, she stopped and turned to look at her, "I want to talk to Mitsy herself?"

By then it was too late. Nelly returned to her normal time zone. Nelly walked to her place of work hearing a voice in her ears.

"I put this spell on you, Nelly, that if you ever challenge demons, the earth shall open beneath you and swallow you whole, so let it be done."

"I have to talk to Jetson about this," sighed Nelly.

On this same, cloudy day, Jetson was at a place where he fought Fotley. Looking among the ruins for clues or items that belonged to Fotley.

He needed theses in order to make the cards work in locating Fotley. All he found was ashes and burnt down remains.

Jetson returned to his car and drives away from the area going westward with his radio on. Country western music was playing on the radio until static came about.

Jetson played with the dials until a voice that he recognized came forth. The voice of Fotley came on. "A spirit can not undo what has already been done. Instead it feels what the body feels, what has already happened.

A man without a soul is a man without love. A man without love is said to be full of hate. A change within himself.

A hateful man has no peace; he hates his friends, family, and himself. To hate is to be lonely, to be lonely is to give up."

Jetson turned the dials, changed stations, even turned the radio off, but it continued to speak with the voice of Fotley.

"He who gives up is a body without spirit. A body without spirit is a body possessed by evil. The evil makes the body do what you don't want to do. A great loss to your spirit, a great loss of faith, and a great loss to your God. Your doomed, Jetson, the laws of death are at hand, what must be done will be done with affection. In reality death is an end, but in spirit your death is never an end, only to suffer."

The radio went static and Jetson saw Fotley standing by the shoulder of the road. He stretched his hand bringing forth a large green fire across the road. The car in which Jetson was in went through the flames.

Jetson stopped the car and got out of the car just in time to see it explode. He looked at Fotley who was now walking toward him.

"Let our fight continue, Jetson!"

"I'm not yet prepared, Fotley!"

"Then I have you were I want you!" as he walked right through the flames toward Jetson.

"If I ever needed help. Now is the time, Lorenzo."

"He can not hear you, Fotley, not even the angels can help you, because I put a curse on this area."

Quickly, Jetson pulled out a protection medallion from his pocket, but the medallion flew out of his hand. He knew he was helpless.

"Did you lose something, Jetson?" questioned Fotley holding a medallion in his hand.

"What made you so powerful in the light of day?" asked Jetson facing him.

"I have something better than keys, I now have the Book of Demonology," replied Fotley.

"That's not possible; the Book of Demonology has been lost for centuries, said Jetson.

"You are powerless, Jetson, you can not fight me, I have you in my power, so now I ask you, come with me to the Wicked Fields. A place you must see."

"I would refuse this, Fotley, but I can't stop myself because of your power over me," walking together into the Wicked Fields.

Walking side by side, Jetson saw trees letting off a horrible order, poisonous plants, and a thick mist that changed color of human skin.

"This place doesn't exist, Fotley."

"Its part of hell, Jetson," he said reaching a clearing.

At this time, vines grabbed Jetson's ankles and wrist. He's then pulled to a dead oak tree, where by he's tide down.

"You have me now, Fotley, so go ahead, and get rid of me," said Jetson. To turn you into a zombie, my personal servant willing to obey my every command."

"I'm goint to turn you into a zombie, my personal slave willing to obey my every command."

"Why you miserable, good for nothing jackass!" retorted Jetson feeling the ground shake.

The oak tree fell to the ground, yet Jetson was facing upward looking at Fotley. The man only smiled at him with an evil look in his eyes.

"Are you comfortable?"

"Kiss my ass, Fotley."

"I love it when you swear."

Soon little creature like demons began to come out from the roots of the oak tree. Jetson saw them run on top of his body.

"Your pets, Fotley?"

"As a matter of fact, yes, they are and the first thing their going to do is strip you down, Jetson," as the little demons began to rip his shirt and jeans.

From out of the Wicked Fields come forth, Oune, carrying a basket of herbs. He sees Fotley and a bunch of little demons upon a man.

"I found what you asked for, Fotley."

"Bring it here, Oune."

The man walked up to Fotley with the basket containing leaves and flowers. By this time the little demons had vanished leaving Jetson naked.

"Is this the man giving you trouble, Fotley?"

"This man is more evil than you are, you should keep away from him, said Jetson.

"I want you to meet my apprentice, Oune," said Fotley giving back the basket to him. "You may now proceed."

"Yes, teacher," he said putting the leaves and flowers into a small pot. Fotley stirred the pot until he got a liquid substance. He then walked up to Jetson, looking at him.

"For a person who should be afraid of what is about to happen to him, you sure are calm."

"Why should I be afraid of you, my faith with God is very powerful, you can't hurt my spirit, all your doing is hurting my body and that, Fotley, is what angers God."

"I'm sure my God is very proud of me," Fotley said brushing the liquid mixture on Jetson's body.

"What is this stuff?"

"This mixture is what I need to control you, Jetson," replied Fotley passing the pot to Oune. He then picked up a large and sharp like claw.

"This is what makes the work of the devil so gratifying," Fotley cut the skin of Jetson's body at several places, yet no blood was shed. What happened was the liquid mixture ran into the wounds of the body.

"I feel no pain, I feel no pain," Jetson said not felling anything.

"This mixture isn't suppose to hurt you, Jetson, it only gives me power over you," said Fotley.

"I'm still myself, I haven't changed, and you failed, Fotley!"

"Are you sure about that, Jetson?" he asked with a smile on his face. "Allow me to control you."

"What are you going to say to me, Fotley?"

"I want you to rise from that tree, break the vines, Jetson, and stand before me."

Without any hesitation, Jetson couldn't stop himself from breaking free. No matter how hard he tried he had no control of himself. He stood up facing Fotley.

"You son- of- a- bitch."

"Your body is mine to command, you eyes will be my eyes, what you see I will see. What you hear I will hear. Where ever you go, what ever you're doing, I will know you're every move," said Fotley laughing hard.

VIII

Twenty days into scorpio, somewhere in another state, after Anna received her first vision, she became amuse of what she had just seen. She brings the mirror to her house. It's been several days since her last vision and she had forgotten all about it.

Today Anna is cleaning house when all of a sudden she hears screams of a woman. Dropping in what she is doing, she hurries to her bedroom and saw a vision in the mirror.

With in the mirror she saw a woman running for her life. Anna also saw a shadow of a man and a demon chasing this woman. She also saw the number six, six, six, appeared in the mirror. What all this meant she did not understand as the vision fades away.

"I don't get it," said Anna to herself walking out of her bedroom scratching her head.

On this Scorpio day of Friday the thirteen, is a special day. It's a day of preparation for a feast that is to be held tonight. Everyone from Oune's group and Fotley's group were excited.

The woman prepared food in many different varieties, yet no salt was used, no bread, no water, and herbs were used in place of seasoning. Nothing sweet was made in which drinks had to be bitter.

The men prepared the land where the feast is to be held on the beach front. This private land belonged to Oune, which the group had purified. Tables were set up; a large stain bowl filled with unclean water is set for baptizing.

Two large pile of wood was made to create a bon- fire. Pentagrams were being drawn throughout the beach grounds. There's even a flag on a pole with the sign of the devil.

With the arrival of sunset, everybody knew it is time for them to prepare in their own way. They had to be dirty, they had to look ugly, and they had to act cruel.

The women wore thin see through gowns, some were even topless. Their gown had to be red, purple, green, gray, black or blue. They put heavy make- up on themselves covering their natural beauty. It's clear that the women did not want to look upon as ladies, but as creatures of the night. They had done their hair in a cruel and unusual manner not to be reckoned with.

The men wore old and dirty suits while others wore just plain shorts and tie. They rub their bodies with pig fat splash themselves with foul smelling cologne which they had made.

By nightfall the bon- fires were lit up and the feast has begun. Foods were set on the dirty table and music is being played back- wards. At this feast nobody is having a good time, they don't want it. Everyone had to be in a bad mood.

New members were being baptized as others were doing blackmagic. On this night Fotley showed Oune how to conjure demons to join this feast.

A feast in the honor of Jetson, a Sabbath night for Friday the thirteen, and a feast to all who came to join. Everything is going well according to Fotley.

Among the entree ceremony stood a man that looked like or a werewolf. He was being watched by others in the party. No one knew who he was or how he got here. They ignored him, although he behaved in a peculiar manner, but on the hour where demons worked best he walked to the sand dune showing the people a fantastic sight.

On top of the sand dune stood a lady of power. She stood straight and tall, dressed in a blood red gown of silk, dark shoes, dark scarf, and known as queen of the night. Surrounded by darkness of night, a strong wind blew about her lightning streaks behind her. She looks down upon the people attending the Sabbath.

"The queen! It's the queen of the night!" shouted Oune.

A cold wind blew upon them bringing out their fear. They showed homage to her. A true queen of evil, queen of witches, princess of darkness, and a terror that was here and now.

Before long the queen mingled with the people below. The feast continues and Fotley met the queen. He brought to her a drink.

"You made quite an entrance, your highness, but I want to know who you really are?"

"I am Mitsy."

"Mitsy, you are not, I know Mitsy very well," said Fotley, presenting the queen with a distasteful food.

"I am Helcat."

"That's much better, your highness," said Fotley eating together. "I have something of interest to show you, your highness. Come with me." Fotley led her to a man tied to a pole. "Do you know him?"

Helcat smiled with saliva dripping out of her mouth. "If it isn't my most hateful person, Jetson."

"I will not participate at this feast!"

"Shut up Jetson! I can make him do anything. What do you want him to do, your highness, he's under my power."

Helcat, in the body of Mitsy, walked around Jetson. Her eyes were dark and her breath had a foul smell. She laughed at him.

"Fotley may control you, but I want your soul."

"You can't have it, Helcat, no matter how hard you may try."

"We shall see, Jetson Mo- Billy," she said walking up to Fotley. "Has he been baptized?"

"No, your highness," replied Fotley.

"Let me see your power over him."

Fotley bowed to her and walked up to Jetson. "You will break free from those ropes and walk toward Oune. You shall be baptized and after that you will dance around the bon- fire taking your garments off until you are naked."

"I will not do that." said Jetson.

"Oh, yes you will, Jetson," said Fotley looking at him face to face. "Do my will that I have asked."

Jetson could feel a force take over him. He tired to resist, but he could not stop in what he is doing. Everybody watched him dance around the bon- fire, stripping himself of his clothing until he stood naked, he stood before Oune and he baptized him.

"Can I control him as well, Fotley?"

"By all means, Helcat."

The woman called out to him. "Come here, Jetson Mo- Billy, you ugly looking thing!" people laughed. "Come to me you fool! Kneel to me! And kiss my feet!"

Jetson slowly walked up to Mitsy, even though he tried to resist. He approached Mitsy, queen of evil, possessed by Helcat.

"May the Lord Christ see in what I am doing and all of you be doomed."

"Yes, let your Lord see what you're doing, Jetson, then he can cast you out as your servant," laughed Helcat. "Do as I asked, Jetson," she said as the man knelt before her.

It's the morning of a new day. The sunrise was more beautiful than ever before. Nelly was awaken by the sound of her alarm clock. She got up, made coffee, and combed her hair. She sat in the kitchen looking at her newspaper. She began to make herself a cup of coffee when she heard the door open.

Jetson staggered on the kitchen floor. His body was covered in mud and bruises. It's as if he has been through a tortured chamber.

"Jesus, Mary, Joseph, what happen to you?" questioned Nelly.

"Don't touch me," said Jetson crawling onto a chair. He's all na-ked except that he found a torn blanket and tied it around his waist. Nelly stared at Jetson, unable to speak. "Turn away from me and do not let me look at you," he said sitting on the chair. Taking a deep breath he relaxed with his eyes closed. "I have been dirty and stained by the forces of evil. They have complete control over me. Fotley and Mitsy did this to me," said Jetson showing tears of anger.

"I should have known that," Nelly said.

"I need your help."

"What do you want me to do?"

"I want you to prepare a holy bath, Nelly."

"I'll start it right now, Jetson," walking out of the kitchen.

Jetson grabbed a dish towel and blindfolded himself. By doing this he knew that Fotley was also blind. He talks to himself.

"If I can not see, you can not see, Fotley," said Jetson, feeling the table with his hands touching a box of Kleenex. He then stuffed his ears. "What I can not hear, you can not hear, Fotley."

In the meantime Nelly had set the bath water and was boiling herbs. Oils had already been added to the water and the pot of herbs is brought to a boil.

"It will be ready in a few minutes, Jetson," as Nelly did not hear a single word from the man because he could not hear her.

Instead, Jetson wrote notes to Nelly and Nelly followed his every instructions. Fasting tea was being made at which time Jetson removed one ear plug.

"I want you to know Nelly that Fotley and Mitsy have another man working with them. His name is Oune, beware of him. They also have the book of Demonology."

"Have you seen this book, Jetson?" asked Nelly being concerned.

"Yes, I have, and it's making them more powerful than ever before."

"Your holy bath water is ready, Jetson," said Nelly taking his hand and leading him to the washroom.

"I also want you to put in the bathroom a mixture of garlic powder, cloves, bay leaves, and anise in the washroom. Light a candle for me, Nelly."

"I can do that for you," said Nelly, leaving the washroom.

Jetson put one leg into the holy bath water. He could feel a burning sensation within himself as he relaxed his body into the tub of water.

In the kitchen, Nelly began to prepare the mixture. She could hear the screams and the moan of Jetson. There's banging against the walls, crashing on the floors, and sounds as if another person in the washroom.

Nelly made her way to the washroom to listen, but everything had come to dead silence. She turned around when suddenly, the washroom door shattered, knocking Nelly to the floor. She screamed and saw a demon with a sword wrestling and angel warrior. They rolled on the floor and the demon freed himself running through the wall, out of the house.

The angel picked up his sword and looked at Nelly. "Woman, the man called Jetson is free," it said flying upward through the ceiling.

Nelly got up from the floor, ran to the washroom and saw Jetson lying in the water peacefully and clam. They looked at each other.

"Did you see it, Nelly?"

"Yeah, I saw it," she replied.

"You did it, Nelly, you broke the spell that was on me."

"It had to be a powerful spell, because I saw an angel chase that demon away, Jetson."

"Do you know who that angel was?"

"No I do not, Jetson."

"I must thank that angel, Nelly," washing himself as Nelly left the room.

In the hours of the afternoon, Fotley took Oune down the road in a pick up truck. Oune did not know where he was going until he arrived at Fotley's property. "What I'm going to show you must be kept secret, no one must know about this." Fotley said.

"I understand," said Oune, getting out of the truck.

"Today I found out that my friend Noel has been found dead in his hotel room. I need you to trust me and help me move this treasure from my place to your place," Fotley said digging through the ruins.

It didn't take long when Oune pulled out four metal boxes out of the ground. Oune wipes the sweat off his face with a handkerchief.

"Open it and share my secret," said Fotley, watching Oune open one box.

"This treasure must be very important to you," said Oune, opening the lid. "Gold," he added with a smile.

"When my church burnt down, no one knew about my gold. Jetson was here yesterday and did not find it. Do you have a secret place to hide our gold, Oune?"

"I sure do," he answered loading the metal boxes onto the truck.

Hundreds of miles away, in another state, Anna had just received another vision. She walked to the kitchen where her mother stood and sat down staring at the wall.

"Are you alright, Anna?" asked her mother.

"Mother, I just had vision." She replied

"Tell me about it," said a sweet, overweight lady, with gray hair.

"I saw fire, explosions', smoke, and heard the screams of people dying."

"That's the second time you had a vision of war, Anna."

"No mother, not war, but massive destruction is going to happen somewhere."

"If that's what it is to be then may God help them, Anna," pausing for a moment. "Maybe we should say a rosary."

"Mother, what if it happens where we are?"

"Then may God help us, Anna."

The young lady looked at the clock, finished her coffee, got up and kissed her mother on the cheek. She then walked toward the door.

"Time for me to go back to the store," said Anna, walking outdoors.

The light of day came to an end and night came forth with all its mysteries. Mitsy found Fotley at the Angel of lights. She approached him with anger.

"Did you know that Nelly helped Jetson in breaking your spell?"

"Are you telling me that I have no control over Jetson?" said Fotley.

"That's exactly what I'm telling you," replied Mitsy.

"Damn that woman!" Fotley yelled out. "I gotta start all over again by capturing Jetson once more.

"I'll take care of Nelly," said Mitsy, walking away.

Daylight hours turned into evening as Jetson slept the entire day. Everything becomes night and Jetson awoke as he walked out of the bedroom.

"I feel like I've been blessed."

"I'm glade you're feeling better," said Nelly watching television.

Jetson sat on the couch, "I know Fotley and his gang are coming after us."

"Do you have a plan?" asked Nelly.

"Yes, but right now lets eat," replied Jetson.

"I'm way ahead of you, I ordered a pizza."

"Your always one step ahead of me, Nelly."

"So, how do we stop Fotley?"

"We don't we go after Mitsy," replied Jetson.

"How?" questioned Nelly, hearing a knock on the door.

"Who could that be?" Jetson asked.

"That's our pizza." answered Nelly, getting money from Jetson. Receiving the pizza Nelly paid the man.

"After we are done eating we need to go shopping," said Jetson.

"What are we shopping for?"

"A mirror, Nelly, a wooden mirror big enough to see your whole body," answered Jetson, taking a bite of pizza.

It's night of the fog mixing with darkness. Evil thoughts play with the mind of Oune. He sat in his office listening to himself as if someone is with him.

"I am a greedy man and the more I think about the gold the greedier I become. I see Fotley and Mitsy working their evil ways, which gives me a chance to set my trap. I do not wish to share with Fotley, so I must do away with him."

During the hours of the night, Oune remained in his office until a knock comes to his door. He turned around to see a young lady.

"I am here, Oune."

"Thank you for coming, Christina."

"What do you want me to do?"

"I want you to sit down on this chair, Christina, and look at me," replied Oune.

The sweet and innocent eighteen year old, Christina, sat down on the chair and looked into Oune's eyes Oune had her hypnotized.

"I want you to follow me." He said.

"I will follow you," she said softly.

Oune left his office and made his way to the hidden vault where the gold laied on the floor. The young lady followed Oune entering the vault.

"You will now go down on your hands and knees," said Oune.

Christina did as she was told as Oune tore her clothing. With a silver chalice and a brush he began to put slave on her body. Each time he recited the evil spell over and over again until the body of Christina was covered with slave.

"You will remain in this room, you will guard this gold. By Satan's command you will become a blood sucking she-wolf" Oune said.

Christina is no longer herself, she was in a deep sleep but her body began to change. Oune concentrated very hard transforming Christina into an animal.

"Smell me she- wolf, know who I am, for if anyone other than me enters this room you will kill them and feast upon it," he said.

Oune put his hand into his pocket and pulls out a pouch. Inside the pouch he took out a charm and places it around the animal, at which time it disappeared.

"Sleep and do not awake until you smell your prey," said Oune leaving the vault.

A new day in Scorpio and Jetson did not find a mirror last night, but he did find one today at a flea market. A large hexagon mirror.

Once the mirror was at the house, Jetson began to carve on to the wood four symbolic signs, two on top, and two at the bottom.

He then washed the mirror with Hyssop and let the air dry the wetness. The wood had to be rubbed with oil to make it shine.

Jetson waited for the sun to be at its brightest hour. At this time the mirror was placed facing the sun receiving the full rays. He had to be careful not to cast his image on the mirror.

By midafternoon, Jetson covered the mirror with a purple silk cloth. He took the mirror to a dark room, which he prepared earlier. He lit incenses so that the room was filled with smoke. At this time he drew on the mirror itself the sign of Necronomicon. In all, it took two days to create the "Mirror of Chance."

It is evening somewhere in the northern states; Anna was about to close her shop for today when a man entered at the last minute.

"I am closing!" Anna called out.

The man walked around the aisle in an overcoat, a hat, and a walking stick. He walked toward her as she stood at the counter.

"May I help you?" she asked.

"No, you can't but I can help you, Anna." The man replied.

"If you're trying to be funny then I have to ask you to leave."

"I know Anna, that you are having visions by a mirror. I also know that you and your mother are faithful Christians that is why you don't carry the mark."

"Who are you?" she asked.

"If I told you, who I was, would you believe me, Anna?"

"Maybe," she replied smelling a fragrance of a flower.

"I am John Leonard?"

"Saint John Leonard?" questioned Anna.

"Of course."

"I don't believe it?"

"I told you that you wouldn't."

Anna felt his clothing and touched his hands. The man only looked at her with a smile and walked to the back room.

"You're real. How can you be John Leonard?"

"Come with me, Anna, I have something to show you, and I have something to teach you."

Anna did not know what to think, she stood in confusion, but she followed Saint John Leonard to the back room to listen and learn.

It's morning of a new day in Scorpio. Jetson comes by to visit Nelly at her apartment. He knocks on the door and heard a voice.

"I know it's you, Jetson, so come on in."

By the sound of her voice, Jetson felt that something is wrong. He opened the door and entered the room finding Nelly sitting on the sofa with a headache.

"You don't look so good," he said.

"I've been having nightmares the past two day, I think Mitsy is up to something," said Nelly.

"Let her come, Nelly, she's going to challenge you. What she doesn't know is that it will take place at my house," said Jetson giving aspirin to Nelly and takes her out of her apartment.

Unknown to them all this time they were being watched through a crystal ball. At this time the crystal ball faded out.

"It would seem that they have something for us," said Fotley.

"A trap for us," Mitsy said.

"When you get Nelly out of the way, let me know. Then I can deal with Jetson."

"Do not worry, Fotley," said Mitsy looking at him with such dark eyes. "Nelly will be out of your way,"

Jetson arrived at his house and entered the house with Nelly. They walked into a room where there stood a mirror leaning on the wall with a purple cloth.

"How are you feeling?" asked Jetson.

"Much better," she replied.

"Good."

"Is this the mirror you were talking about?" questioned Nelly.

"Yes, and don't touch it. The mirror will work if we can bring Mitsy to this room," answered Jetson.

"What happens then?"

"The purple cloth comes off, the image of Mitsy is then captured within the mirror, and she will be drawn into the mirror, Nelly," replied Jetson.

"Is that it?"

"No, not really, because once Mitsy is inside the mirror, you will paint the mirror with spray paint. If all goes well, Mitsy is gone forever." replied Jetson.

"Where will you be when all this happens?" asked Nelly sitting down."I will leave my house so that Mitsy will know you're alone. I will get into my car and park on the street. I will then return to my house through a window and make my way to the mirror," replied Jetson.

"So, I would have to keep Mitsy in this room at all times?" she asked.

"Yes, Nelly," answered Jetson.

"I suppose I can do that."

"The only thing that can go wrong, Nelly is if Fotley comes with her," said Jetson making a pot of coffee.

At Washington D.C. of those same hours of the afternoon, a meeting had just been finished within the white house. Politicians, top officials, and important men make their way to a room in another part of the house. Among the group is Taylor and Ceepot walking together.

"Where are you going to put your numbers?" asked Ceepot.

"On my hand," replied Taylor smoking a pipe. "What about you?"

"I don't know yet. I could have it like the president has his," Ceepot said.

"On the forehead?"

"Yeah. It looked good on the president, but I don't know about myself," said Ceepot.

Both men stood in line with the others, waiting for their turn to get the number six, six, six on themselves. Taylor blew smoke from his pipe.

"Let me see now, after everyone here in the white house get their mark, then it will spread among the congressmen, senators, governors, and mayors. One month later, all service men in the armed forces will be marked. A month after that, all prisoners serving time in prison will get the number, and after all that is done, every man, woman, and child throughout America will get the number."

"Christians aren't go to like this, I know them." said Ceepot.

"Who cares what they think. I'm going to enjoy killing them; it'll be like hunting deer said Taylor.

"I would rather keep some alive and make slaves out of them," Ceepot said laughing.

It's the end of the afternoon hours and evening was setting in. all this time, Nelly was trying to take a nap, but couldn't sleep at Jetson's house. She sat up on the bed, only to find an angel looking at her."Who might you be?" asked Nelly.

"My name is not important. I am only a messenger, so listen in what I tell you."

"Speak, my angel friend," said Nelly.

"Once your mission is complete, you are to leave this state and go far away to the northern states. You keep going until you hear your name and then you know it is your place of stay."

"I hear and obey. Peace be with you my angel friend, said Nelly watching the angel fade away in the brightness of light.

"There's coffee on the stove if you want some," Jetson said seeing her sitting on the bed.

"Alright," she said yawning looking at the wall clock showing six fifteen.

At about the same time, not far away, Misty walked to the altar dressed in black. She opened a window, spoke to herself, and faced the altar.

"Tonight is the night and the hour is right for me. I shall capture Nelly making her my slave." Mitsy looked into her crystal ball and saw Jetson leave his house. "At last I have you alone," she said going down on her hands and knees transforming herself into a black cat. Once she has become a cat she jumped out the open window.

Inside the house of Jetson, Nelly was restless since she got up from bed. She paced back and forth, holding a cup of coffee in her hand. She turned to the television, but did not watch it. She looked out the window and the phone rang.

"Hello," said Nelly, listening. "No, he's not here, but I'll take a message," she said hearing a knock at the door. "Okay I'll tell him that. Bye," said Nelly hanging up the phone. She then made her way to the door and opened the front door seeing nothing except a black cat, which entered the house.

"Come back here!" she called out chasing the cat.

The cat ran into the bedroom, under the bed as Nelly chased it. She got down on her knees to look under the bed. The black cat jumped on top of the bed watching her.

"Where did that cat go now," Nelly said sitting up on her knees. It was then she saw the cat face to face.

"Boo!" said the cat frightening Nelly to the floor. The cat jumped off the bed and made its way to the couch.

Nelly got up from the floor and heard the laughter of a woman. She walked out of the bedroom, to living room and saw Mitsy sitting on the couch.

"Think that's funny?"

"You should have seen yourself, Nelly," said Mitsy laughing.

Nelly felt upset as she walked up to Mitsy and stood standing looking down at her.

"Why don't you transform yourself into a pig so that I can laugh?"

"Are you insulting me, Nelly?"

"Do you want some coffee?"

"Answer my question?"

"No. I want you to feel the way I felt, Mitsy. Now answer my question."

"I prefer alcohol or wine," replied Mitsy.

"Are you yourself? Or am I talking to someone else?"

"I am both," answered Mitsy, receiving her drink.

"My voice is myself, but my eyes and body is someone else."

"I know that you are not here to see me, Mitsy, but you are here to fight me," Nelly said standing in front of the purple cloth.

"You are so right, Nelly, and this time I will have you." She said standing up from the couch and walked toward Nelly.

"You can not have me, how many times have you tried and failed," said Nelly.

Mitsy made a sudden stop near Nelly and stared at her. At this time Nelly felt very uncomfortable the way she was being stared at.

"You have a trap for me," said Mitsy.

Nelly didn't say a word. She quickly grabbed Misty by her arm and pulled her into the open mirror, at which time Jetson came in to take the purple cloth off the mirror.

The force of the mirror took Mitsy inside, but the woman fought back. Only half of her body was inside the mirror while the other half fought to get out.

Jetson and Nelly stood at a distance watching Mitsy. Both were certain that the mirror would take Mitsy inside, yet the room shook like an earthquake.

"You can not fight the force! You lost!" shouted Nelly.

"I can never be beaten!" cried out Mitsy. "By the power of hell, give me the strength of twenty demons!" she pleaded.

"No I will not let this happen!" Jetson shouted, seeing that Mitsy had gotten out.

"I'm free!"

At once Jetson ran toward Mitsy and the both of them had fallen back into the mirror. Mitsy fought Jetson trying to get out of the mirror.

"Paint it!" shouted Jetson.

Nelly quickly grabbed the spray cans and began to paint the mirror watching Jetson holding Mitsy down.

Her strength was too much for Jetson and pulled herself free.

"What about you!"

"Forget me, Nelly!" shouted Jetson, wrestling Mitsy down.

"The angels be with you, Jetson!" She shouted painting the mirror while hearing the voice of Mitsy.

"Hear me woman! I curse you that you will be lonely. Your heart and soul will shrink to nothing. Loneliness will swallow you whole and not I or your angels or anyone in your world will ever know about you!"

Nelly covered the last open spot of the mirror; she fell on her knees in tears. Soon after, a flower never seen before fell in front of her.

She turned around only to see Lorenzo Alexander comforting her. Nelly wiped her tears off her face and smiled.

"Have no fear, Nelly, Jetson will be alright and the curse on you can be broken," said he.

"I'm glade to hear that, Alexander."

"You must leave, Nelly, right now, don't wait," he said disappearing from sight.

Nelly got up from the floor and hurried out of the house without any of her belongings. She got into her car and drove out of town as she was told to do.

Its midnight hour at the Angel of Lights, Oune and Fotley are conducting mass when all of a sudden a foul odor of smoke arose from the floor. People coughed and others held their noses. The smoke thickened, the lights went out, and a display of electricity was seen.

"What does this mean?" questioned Oune.

Fotley stood silent and meditated, and then he said in a soft voice. "Mitsy is dead," turning to Oune. "Finish this mass," he said as he walked away from the altar.

The smoke was so thick, and the odor was so strong that the people began to leave. The church service had to be cancelled.

Oune stood all alone in his church, sitting down on his altar chair listening to voices within the smoke. One sounded like the voice of Mitsy.

"Into the world comes forth a mark, a number that would control humanity. A number of the beast that would decide the faithful ones from the unfaithful ones. To those who bore not the number become slaves, or hunted down like animals to be killed. These people will have no money, no credit, no house, no jobs, or anything the world has to offer. To the eyes of the world these people must die. He who bears this number shall live like kings. All shall be rich, happy, and willing to take anything and everything from those who bear not the number. Let it be known that the Anti- Christ shall be praised upon," said the voice echoing the church.

IX

SAGITTARIUS BROUGHT STORMS AND the cold weather, but this is nothing new for the people of Minnesota. Raquel, mother of Anna, enters the store to find her daughter reciting a poem to herself She listens to Anna, not saying a word.

"One deceives another, an evil desire to rule over others. Taken by greed and selfishness an act of aspiration which turned to ambition by which sin the angels fell.

One who envies for power takes it without any hesitation. Once on the throne the lust of power becomes overwhelming of being a god. The true aspiration of angels which turned to ambition by which sin did they fell."

"Where did you learn that?" asked Raquel.

"Mother!" becoming emotional, "You scared me, I didn't know you were behind me."

"Where did you learn that poem, Anna?" repeating the questioned.

"Saint John Leonard taught it to me, Mother."

"Saint who?"

"Saint John Leonard, Mother."

"Oh, Anna, you've been working too hard" taking her coat off.

"He came and told me a lot of things, Mother."

"What kind of things, Anna?" helping her clean up.

"He told me the secrets of a human soul. He told me what my visions met and he also told me about a lady that I'm going to meet."

"Did he also tell you that you are late in closing the store, Anna?"

"Is that why you're here, Mother?"

"Yes, to help you, Anna."

"Alright, Mother." She replied locking the door and the both of them leave through the back way.

It was in the tenth day of Sagittarius that Fotley found the house of Jetson, four days after the disappearance of Mitsy. Fotley enters the house as he walked from one room to another. He saw Helcat standing next to a mirror.

"What do you want from me now?" Fotley asked.

"See this mirror?" questioned Helcat looking very ugly.

"Yeah," replied Fotley as he saw paint cans on the floor and the mirror painted.

"This is where Mitsy died, however so did Jetson. If you want to avenge the death of Mitsy you must seek out, Nelly."

"Where is Nelly now?" Fotley asked.

"She's no longer in this state, but somewhere in the northern states," Helcat replied.

"I will find her," Fotley said with an angry tone of voice leaving the house of Jetson.

At the church of the Angel of Lights a noise was being heard. Oune stood in his office hearing his name being called. He gets up, walked out of his office to the lobby. There Oune sees an agent with two soldiers standing in the lobby.

"Are you Oune?" asked the agent.

"I am."

The agent walked up to Oune. "I am Agent Bane and I'm here to let you know that this church is under the power of the government."

Oune doesn't say a word except to walk back to his office being followed by Bane. Oune cleared his desk of his worked and looked at Bane.

"This church does not belong to any organization, you can not consider it a church," said Oune.

"You do worship?"

"Yes."

"Then it is a church," said Bane.

"Exactly what does the government want to do with a church?" asked Oune, sitting down in his chair feeling disappointed.

"That is not my concern, but you will continue to do your normal religious duties until you hear from us," answered Bane setting a paper on his desk.

"What is this?"

"You must sign it in order to keep this church running. If you refuse to sign it this church will be closed down," replied Bane.

Oune felt aggravated in signing the paper, but he done what had to be done. He then tossed the paper back to Bane.

"Whatever happened to the power of the church?"

"After the death of two great religious leaders the power of the church is being taken over," said Bane.

"Do you know who is going to control all this religious power?" asked Oune.

"No, I don't, but in my opinion I believe there's going to be one order church, one rules all," replied Bane.

"Sounds like the power of the antichrist," said Oune having a thought in mind. "I wonder what's happening to the churches of Rome."

"Haven't you heard the news?"

"What news?" questioned Oune.

"The churches of Rome are being burned down for refusing to sign the paper. Looters are stealing the gold, I wish I was there," replied Bane leaving the office.

News of what was happening to the churches reached the ears of Anna and her mother. Both were at home watching the news on television. It's shocking and disturbing to see the churches of Rome in flames.

"Are we going to church this Sunday, Anna?"

"No, mother," she replied turning the television off.

"What are we going to do?"

"If the churches are being controlled by the government we won't go. Instead we are going to have church right here at our house, Mother."

"That would work, we can read from our bibles," said Raquel.

"We'll have candles and incense burning, that's about all we need," Anna said.

"What about blessed water?" asked Raquel

"Forget about it. Let's use olive oil in its place," answered Anna hearing a bell ring. She peeked out the window and opened the door.

"Greetings, my love," said Ramon, giving Anna a passionate kiss.

"Did you see what happened to the power of the church, Ramon?" asked Raquel.

"Yes, I saw it on T.V"

"What do you think about that?" asked Anna.

"I think it's sad, but did you see the diplomat?"

"No. What about him?" questioned Anna.

"He had the number six, six, six, on his forehead," replied Ramon.

"It's started, Anna, and it will be on us real soon."

"Saint John Leonard told me this would happen, Mother," she said staring at Ramon.

"If that day comes, are you two going to wear the mark?"

"Are you, Ramon?" questioned Anna.

"Would you go to church, Ramon?" questioned Raquel.

"Sure, I'll go to church."

"This Sunday?" asked Raquel.

"I know its being taken over by the government, but I'll still go to church."

"Would you come to our church, Ramon?" asked Anna.

"Sure, I would go." he answered.

"Here, at our house, Ramon."

"You're having church at your own house, Anna?"

"Sure," responded Anna.

"I don't know," said Ramon being doubtful. "What's wrong with going to your church?"

"The word of god will be erased from our church, Ramon. The government will take that away from us," replied Anna.

"How do you know that?"

"Believe me, Ramon, I know," answered Anna.

"I have to hear it, to believe it."

"Come on, Ramon," Anna said taking his hand and walked out the door.

It's that time of day that turned to night. In the state of California, Fotley stopped by the angel of lights. He entered and saw Oune in his office.

"Where have you been all day, Fotley?" asked Oune seeing each other.

"I know what happened to Mitsy," he said in a disturbing mood.

"Where is that lady?" asked Oune.

"She's been killed and I know who did it. I have to leave here if I want to get her," replied Fotley sitting on the chair.

"I'm sure you will find that woman who killed Mitsy can get even with her," said Oune.

"I'm taking to gold with me."

"The gold will be fine here, Fotley."

"I don't plan on coming back, Oune."

"Well then, do want your gold now?"

"Not now, I'll let you know, Oune," replied Fotley walking out of the office.

Oune paused for a moment, watching Fotley leave the church. Having a thought in mind, he picked up the phone making a call.

"Is this Rodney?"

"Yeah, it's me."

"I need to see you, come to my office tonight say about eleven," said Oune.

"A job for me?"

"Yeah," answered Oune.

"See you at eleven," said Rodney hanging up.

A good night sleep never existed for agent Taylor, not since he condemned Lorenzo Alexander. He sat in a recliner having a nightmare in the days of when he was a general.

A man decorated with medals, standing straight and tall, respected in every way. He stood next to a prisoner tied in chains, Lorenzo Alexander, a man of power.

General Taylor beat and tortured the man with a whip as well as with his hands. Alexander withstood the pain calling out his angels. A bolt of lightning killed general Hemkock and a curse fell upon Taylor.

"Leave me alone! Get out of my head!" shouted Taylor bothered by the ringing in his ears.

Agent Bane entered the room with a bottle of whiskey. He looked at General Taylor, not as a general, but a man heading for disaster. Taylor wipes the sweat off his face as Bane sets the whiskey on the coffee table.

"I can't take this much longer," Taylor said taking a drink from the bottle.

"You have to find someone with magical powers," said Bane.

"Why?"

"What do you mean, why?" questioned Bane, looking at the man. "I was there, Taylor, I saw what, Lorenzo, did to you. There is a curse on you, and right now, you are cracking up. Looking at yourself in the mirror, the curse is going to kill you, Taylor."

"Go away, Bane, leave me alone, let me think," Taylor said trying to stand up staggering to the floor like a drunken slob.

"I know someone that can help you, Taylor," said Bane.

"Get out!"

Not saying another word, Bane walked up to the door. He turned around to see Taylor crawl up to his recliner. It was a sad sight.

"Remember, we have a meeting at the Pentagon in the morning. That's if you can make it," he said walking out the door.

"Fuck the meeting!" Taylor cried out. "Lorenzo! You son-of-a-bitch! I'm fucked!" he yelled drinking from the bottle of whiskey.

"Do you want to end of the curse, Taylor?" asked a voice.

Upon hearing this Taylor opened his eyes and saw Lorenzo leaning on the dresser with a smile on his face. Taylor showed anger on his face.

"It's you." He said.

"Do you want to suffer even more, Taylor?"

"Take it off Lorenzo, I want to sleep, take it off now!"

"Kill yourself, Taylor, and the curse is broken."

"No! That's what you want me to do."

"You can't last much longer, Taylor, look at yourself, you're a mess, you're going insane, and you're hearing a buzzing sound in your ear."

"Shut up, Lorenzo! Or I will kill you!"

"You can't kill me, I'm already dead Taylor, but I'm doing a good job haunting you."

Taylor screamed like and insane man attacking Alexander, knocking over furniture, fighting his own shadow, hurting himself, and Lorenzo stood to watch.

At the Pentagon, Bane waited at the door for Taylor, but he never showed up for the meeting. Bane entered the room and sat with Ceepot.

A very important government official stepped forward to the podium. He looked at a room with agents and high ranking officers.

"We are gathered here this morning to talk about changes and setting goals to the churches of America," He said. "We will do away with the ordered of the churches. There will be a one order church throughout the entire world. Whatever happens to other countries will also happen here in America.

Those who run the church will be able to conduct mass one time a month, the remaining of the days are for government purposes. Those people who conduct masses will become caretakers of the church. This book will be rewritten," he said holding the Bible in the air. "I will let you know more information about this book at a later date.

Gentlemen, it's in these churches that we will give out the mark. People will be told to come into these churches and each one will receive the mark. Those who refuse will be punished."

At this time everyone stood up from their chairs and began to clap their hands and cheered. A few minutes later everyone sat down in their chairs.

"Are there any questions?"

"How will America receive information for this new world church?" asked an agent.

"We will receive information by satellite and then we send it to the churches, where people will see and hear what they have to say."

"Where is this signal coming from?"

"That's strictly confidential."

"How many leaders will run this new world church?" asked another agent.

"One."

"Is this the antichrist?" Bane asked.

"I cannot say and I do not know."

"Is there an antichrist?" asked Ceepot.

"No such person exists," as the room remained silent "no more questions gentlemen," looking around the room. "What we discussed will take effect on Monday of this coming week," he said walking away from the podium."

"This meeting has now ended," said a Senator.

Ceepot stood up and turned to the man next to him who also stood up. They looked at each other and smiled at each other.

"Agent Bane."

"General Ceepot," he said shaking hands.

"Where is Taylor?"

"He did not show and I'm going over to see him. You wanna come, Ceepot?"

"No, I'm heading to the airport," said Ceepot.

"Where are you going?" asked Bane

"Out of America and into Iran," replied Ceepot.

"Have a nice trip and watch yourself over there," said Bane, leaving the room.

Bane got into his car and left the Pentagon Building to the hotel where Taylor was staying. He knew something must have happened since he left him alone. He was concerned about him since he did not show up to the meeting.

Bane knocked on the door, but Taylor did not answer. Bane forced the door open and saw a mess in the room as if he was fighting with someone.

"Taylor!" shouted Bane making his way to the bathroom which had a light on. Bane stopped at the doorway seeing a gruesome sight. A man's leg stood inside the toilet bowl, in the bath tub stood the body of Taylor. A butcher knife laid on the bathroom floor, blood on the walls, sink, toilet bowl, and bath tub. It made Bane sick as he ran out of the hotel room.

Afternoon hours in the state of California, Rodney met his wife in a restaurant. She had already ordered food for the both of them.

"What did Oune have to say?"

"We got a job to do, honey," he answered kissing her on the cheek.

"Any killing involved?" Penny asked.

"No, just stealing a book," replied Rodney as he began to eat.

"What kind of book?"

"A very old book," he answered.

"What's the title of the book?"

"It's called *The Book of Demonology*" he replied as he sipped a glass of water.

"Did you say *The Book of Demonology*?"

"Yes, I did," answered Rodney.

"I have never seen that book, but I heard about it," said Penny, sipping her coffee.

"We are going to steal that book tonight and bring it to Oune," said Rodney.

"Why bring it to Oune?" questioned Penny.

"What do you mean?"

"If it is the true *Book of Demonology*, I know some people who would pay cash for the book," replied Penny.

"Yeah, that would be better than just giving it to Oune, unless Oune is willing to pay for the book," said Rodney

"Well it's time for me to go," Penny said looking at her watch.

"I'll take care of the bill," said Rodney.

"I'll see you at home," said Penny, giving a kiss to her husband.

At the Angel of Lights, Fotley had brought a pick-up truck as he parked it in the parking lot. He entered the church to the office where he found Oune.

"I'll be leaving tonight," said Fotley.

"You want your gold?"asked Oune.

"I'll pick it up about ten," he replied.

"I'll be here at ten waiting for you," said Oune.

"My people will stay here with you, tell them that I'm on a mission," said Fotley.

"Will you be leaving from here?" Oune asked.

"That's my plan," answered Fotley, walking out of the office.

Somewhere in Minnesota, Anna and Ramon entered a fast food restaurant. They received their order and sat down. It was evening on that day and they had plans for tonight.

"Movie starts in forty five minutes, so we got time to kill," said Ramon.

Anna sat down taking a bite of her hamburger, two tables ahead of her, sat a lady this lady becomes familiar to Anna as she stared at her.

"What's the matter?" questioned Ramon, looking behind him seeing a lady eating alone.

"Oh my god, I don't believe this," said Anna in astonishment

"What's wrong?" asked Ramon.

"There's a lady here that I saw in my vision," replied Anna.

"It's only coincidence," said Ramon.

"There's only one way to find out," said Anna walking toward her table.

The woman drank her coffee hearing her name called out. "Are you Nelly?"

At once the lady dropped her cup of coffee on the table. The woman looked at the lady standing in front of her.

"My journey is over," she replied.

"You are that lady in my vision," Anna said.

"May I asked for your name and what I did in your vision?" asked Nelly, looking at Anna with a friendly face.

"I see you running from something or someone, and my name is Anna. I'm supposed to learn from you and you are to learn from me."

"In that case, let me find a place to stay," said Nelly as Ramon stands next to Anna.

"If you're looking for a place, my father owns apartments and he has rooms for rent," said Ramon giving Nelly a business card.

"Thank you, I will call your father and check it out," Nelly said with a smile.

"Here's my number, call me when you find a place."

"Let's go, Anna, before we miss our movie," said Ramon leaving Nelly alone.

Nelly remained silent watching Ramon and Anna walked to their car. She drank her coffee and looked at the business card

"Angles of god, what will happen next?" Nelly sighed.

Darkness fell in California. A car is parked on the side of the street watching Fotley put two suitcases and a large thick book in the front seat of his truck.

"There he goes," said Penny.

"Follow him," Rodney said as Penny drove.

The truck drove around the corner and into a gas station. Penny stopped at the side of the street watching him put gas into his truck.

"He did not lock the doors," said Penny.

"This is it then," said Rodney getting out of the car. "Keep the car running, I'll be back," he said walking toward the truck.

Unknown to Fotley that the man is coming he went to pay for the gas, giving Rodney his chance. The man broke the passenger window, grabbed the book, took the truck keys, and ran toward the car being seen by Fotley.

"Hey! Mother Fucker!" he shouted as the car took off at a high rate of speed. Fotley ran to his truck and realized that he couldn't chase them because the keys to the truck were missing.

Penny and Rodney laughed together as Rodney held the truck keys in his hand. He then threw the truck keys out the window.

"We did it!" shouted Penny.

"Yeah, we did," said Rodney tossing the book in the back seat.

The spirits of the book has been mistreated. Therefore the book remained in the back seat with its cover opened and the pages turning about.

"Sometimes I am so good at what I do," said Rodney lighting a cigar.

"Check out the book, Rodney? See if it is *The Book of Demonology*."

"Alright my dear, Penny," he said turning around seeing a figure sitting in the back seat.

The figure itself had a black robe, a black hood, and its face could not be seen. It held a sickle in its right hand.

"Damn! Mr. Death!" Rodney cried out.

At that very moment, Penny screamed in pain as the sickle snagged into her shoulder. She lost control of the car and crashed into a tree. After the crash a storm of electricity came upon the car and it burst into flames.

Oune stood in the lobby looking at the clock, which showed five minutes after ten He then saw a truck parking and Fotley stepped out coming into the church angry.

"What's the matter with you?" questioned Oune.

"My book of Demonology has been stolen!" retorted Fotley swearing.

"Let me find your book and I'll send it to you," said Oune calmly.

"Yeah, I suppose you're right that would work," Fotley said being himself once again.

"Do you want your gold?" asked Oune.

"That's why I'm here," replied Fotley walking together down the stairs.

Both men stood facing a wall at which time Oune pressed a secret panel on the wall and it opened. Both men looked at each other giving each other an avarice look.

Oune enters the room and carried out one box of gold. Fotley entered the room picking up his box of gold and he got attacked by a voracious beast.

With a box of gold in his hands Fotley falls to the floor. He could not see the beast, but his clothing was being torn to shreds, he could also feel the bites of the beast.

"Oune! What the hell is this!" he shouted, screaming in horror, but his screams could not be heard in a sound proof room.

Oune kept silent watching Fotley be torn apart. A leg flew out of the room, staining the hall with blood. The beast made a meal out of Fotley, devouring him grossly.

"Your gold is now my gold," said Oune with a smile

"Feast on him my pet, leave no trace of him," he said kicking the leg of Fotley back into the room and closed the wall.

A cold rainy night in the state of Minnesota Ramon brings Anna home from their date. Anna ran to her home and walked inside to hear her mother's voice.

"Anna! You have a telephone call" Raquel called out.

"Thank you mother!"She shouted picking up the phone.

"Hello," she answered taking off her coat.

"Is this Anna?"

"Yes, it is, who am I talking to?"

"Nelly. The lady you met this evening."

"I remember."

"I just wanted to let you know I have an apartment and you can come and visit me."

"I will do that, Nelly," said Anna writing down her addresses and phone number.

"Now that you have my address, come and let us learn from each other, Anna. I have to go now."

"Good-bye, Nelly," hanging up.

Anna prepared herself for bed; she walked to her mother's bedroom to check on her. She was fast asleep as Anna lit a candle that her mother forgot. Anna walked to her own bedroom and lit a candle for herself. Anna was about to pray when she noticed no reflection in the mirror.

"What are you going to show me now?" she said talking to herself.

Before long the continent of America was shown in the mirror. Anna watched the continent split into three parts and a face of a man appeared in the mirror.

"Have no fear of me, Anna, I am only a messenger. "What you have seen is soon to come, but if you go to the Seven Hills, there you will be saved. If you leave the continent, make sure you are about a hundred miles away. Watch the signs, Anna, and know that the wrath of god is not far away," said the man fading away.

"Seven Hills, I don't know" what the Seven Hills are? I don't even know where they are. One thing for sure, I know that some of the signs have already come," Anna said getting into bed.

It's the last day of Sagittarius and the beginning of Capricorn. Nelly was sitting down drinking coffee and looking in the newspaper for a job. A knock came to the door.

"Is that you, Anna?" she asked.

"It is."

"Come right in," said Nelly as Anna walked inside.

"It's a cold day," Anna said.

"Have some coffee," said Nelly, as Nelly made herself a cup.

"What are you doing?" asked Anna.

"Looking for a job," Nelly replied.

"You don't have to do that, you can work for me. I run a mystic shop and I could use another person," said Anna.

"Well, thank you."

"We can start as soon as we finish our coffees," said Anna sitting down with her. "Can I ask you a question?"

"Ask away."

"In my vision, Nelly, I saw you running, but I also saw a book. Is that why they are after you? Did you steal that book from them?"

Nelly put away her newspaper, and made a second cup of coffee. She then looked at Anna with a concern look on her face.

"I don't know if I should tell you? They might come after you?"

"Do you have the book with you, Nelly?"

"No, Anna. I was running away from that evil book." Anna felt disappointed.

"It's an evil book, not the book I thought it was."

"Cheer up Anna. What kind of book are you looking for?" asked Nelly.

"I heard a story from Saint John Leonard about another book that got stolen from heaven and fell to earth. Let me tell it to you, Nelly."

"Do you have time?"

"We've got plenty of time," said Anna making a second cup of coffee Nelly takes a bite from her donut and listened to Anna.

"Ten thousand years ago, there came to the world a book which no man can look upon. Its contents foretold the secrets of the heavens, stars, planets, the magic of good and evil, and names of mortals who did not appear in the book."

"It sounds like you're talking about the Book of Life?"

"Let me finish, Nelly," said Anna continuing her story. "The book cover is of sparkling gold, its pages are of metallic, and every word is a work of art. The book gave off a perfume of sweet smelling odor that if we breathe it, then it could change our youth. Demons call it the Book of good and evil, but the angels call it the *Book of Life*. It came to be that his book got lost somewhere on earth, the angels must find this book before man discovers it. The time has come for the angels to come down to earth in search of this book."

At this time Nelly got up and pours hot water so that she could make another cup of coffee. Anna kept quiet watching her.

"I'm listening," said Nelly.

"In the darkest part of hell, an army of demons are celebrating, for it was they who cast the book out on heaven down to earth. It was a plan well executed that the angels never knew how it happened. Satan has done many evil deeds, but this is the greatest of them all, he admires himself for a splendid job. He sits on his throne watching his demons celebrate.

At long last he stood and spoke loudly. 'Our work isn't yet completed! I want the book in my hands, and I want it now! I say unto you, my loyal ones, go and spread the word of the book to the mortals! Whoever knows that whereabouts of the book, I will grant them anything they ask. Go before the angels find the book.'

So it became known on the twenty second hour of the night. Every witch, sorcerer, and people who was evil knew about the book and its rewards.

On the seventh hour of a new day, the angels had arrived on earth having the form of holy men. They walked on the road seeing a man on a bicycle.

'We are in need of your help.'

'We are looking for a book with a cover like gold. Have you seen such a book?'

'No, father, I have not, but if you go to the library I'm sure you'll find it there,' the man said, leaving with a suspicious mind.

Of all the people in the land, it's a hermit who found the book. He held it in his hands and sat in his resting place. He opened the book so that he may read it, but when his eyes saw the first word, his body began to tremble. The hermit couldn't stop himself from trembling, but he could be sure the book was no longer in his hands.

By the sixteenth hour of time, a young lady known for her evil ways took a walk in the forest collecting herbs for her special brew. She came upon a tree to take its bark, but in doing so, she discovered the book embedded into the tree. How proud she was to find the book for the demons. Eager to tell the demons of her find, she chopped the tree, releasing the book, smelling sweet perfume. At once her youth began to fade away with every minute that went by. All of her youth had gone from young to old. She can no longer walk or talk, and the book was no longer in her possession.

In the twentieth hour, a black mass was being conducted. A couple was about to be married in the sight of Satan. The man spoke proudly, 'we have found the book which you seek master.'

'Where?' questioned the voice of Satan.

'It lies where souls are laid to rest.'

At once Satan shouted out, 'go my loyal subjects! Fetch me the book!'

'What about my reward? I want what is mine,' said the man with a demanding voice.

'And you shall have it,' retorted Satan spitting on him. A fire of high intensity burnt the man into nothingness.

'Foolish mortal, you should never trust the master of great lies, now you belong to me'

The bride-to-be wept, walking out of the church in sadness. Twenty one and a half hour had gone by, when the bride to be encountered the holy men.

'Woman we are in need of your help?' said one, noticing that the woman did not hear him. She only stood with her head down.

'Woman, why do you weep' he asked.

'I lost my loved one because of a book,' she replied.

'Where is the book now?'

'Why does everybody want that book?' she asked wiping the tears off her face

'If you wish for your loved one to be saved, we need that book.'

'I supposed that's the least I can do for him,' she replied at the holy men. 'You can find that book at the closest cemetery,' said she.

It's now the twenty forth hour. Satan walked among the cemetery in search of the book. With a face of madness, he located the book, buried into the ground covered with moss. Putting his hands into the ground he pulled out the book. He laughed insanely holding the book in his hands the sky unleashed bolts of lightning and a roar of thunder.

'It's mine at last!' Satan cried out.

A cold wind blew about the trees, and Satan looked into the wind seing four holy men standing before him. He knew who they were and why they were here.

'Give us the *Book of Life*, oh Satan,' said one holy man.

'The book belongs to me.' He replied.

'It belongs to God.'

'I will fight you for it.'

'Must we use force, oh Satan.

'Force I will use and my army will be at my side, you don't stand a chance against us.'

'You dare to challenge us, oh Satan,' a holy man said, for there came a great light upon them. Satan looked upward into the sky and saw thousands of angels looking down on him and his army.

'Someday I shall have my revenge,' said Satan tossing the book toward the holy men.

"Go in peace, oh Satan.'

'Damn you all!' he yelled out returning to the land where he is king."

"That is a very interesting story Anna. I would say the *Book of Life* is more powerful that the *Book of Demonology*," said Nelly.

"Tell me about the Book of Demonology Nelly? It must be a very evil book if you were running from it"

'If I tell you don't go looking for it, Anna, It's a very dangerous book."

"Don't worry Nelly; I just want to know about it."

"Legend says that the *Book of Demonology* is really a Book of Shadows that belongs to Satan. In it has spells, curses, names of demons, conjurations, stories of what demons did to mortals, and many other evil things. They say the book can kill and will destroy your Christian faith."

"Oh my goodness look at the time," said Anna." We better get going so that I can show you my store," she said as they leave the apartment.

X

SUNDAY, IN THE MONTH of Capricorn, at the angel of Lights, Oune was amazed to see over a hundred people in church. He never had that many when he conducted mass.

Oune sat in his altar chair watching a large screen that hung on the ceiling. All that he could see and hear was a voice with a thin line talking, no picture, was ever seen.

A loud and powerful voice was heard, Agents stood by the doors making sure no one left. What is happening to the Angel of Lights was happening all over the world, in every church, of every kind.

"Two months from now, all of you will come to this church and receive your new mark. The old mark will be erased. This new mark will help you in business, education, employment, the things you buy or sell, and so many other ways. I warn those who do not wear the mark, that on the third week of the second month, if you still do not have the mark, you will be shot without question.

The whole world will see great miracles happening to our planet, and many of you will be frighten by it. But know this, the miracles that you see happening are done by me. You should know I am in what you say I am. Please, do wear the mark if you wish to be saved."

At this time, Oune walked to the front of the altar holding a Bible in his hand. He held it high so everyone could see it. He then hears a voice once more.

"The book that you see before you is old fashioned, it shall be discarded along with every other Bible If you are found with these Bibles, you will be heavily penalized."

Oune dropped the Bible to the floor and picked up a new bible and held it high. Once more he hears the voice talking.

"This will be our new Bible. In the pages of this Bible I have eliminated the Book of Revelations. I have also changed the name of Jesus to a magician since that's all he was. The word of God has changed to gods. Every person will receive this new Bible in about a week from now. So I say onto you, my brothers and sisters, this meeting is now ended. Go in peace." People began to leave the church while others gathered around talking among each other.

At the same time of day, church service was also being held at the house of Anna. The Star of David was drawn and placed on the table with two crosses. Each person attending the service and had their own astrology candle. In the center of the star stood a white lit candle.

Beginning with Raquel, she would purify herself with olive oil, lit her astrology candle, and place it inside the Star of David. Anna would be next, followed by Ramon. Each would recite a prayer, read a portion of the bible, and meditate. It lasted one hour and all was done until next week.

"I did what you asked me to do, Anna," said Ramon placing a map of the United States on the table.

"This is great,' said Anna looking at the map. "I'm going to show you what I saw in my vision. There's going to be volcanoes, earthquakes, tidal waves, explosions, and many people dying."

"Sounds like the end of the world,' said Raquel.

"No, mother it's the wrath of God"

"Maybe, Anna is trying to tell us that a great nation is going to fall apart," Ramon said eating a cookie.

"In my vision, an angel told me when the seven causes are complete, the seven signs will begin. From out of heavenly skies came a Great King of terror. It will bring forth great devastation upon

American empire. The super power from the great American empire could not stop the Great king of terror. There was fear and panic among the people.

So great is the quake that it could be felt on the other side of the world. So great of an impact that America cracked into three parts.

Continents near America suffered tremendously, but when they saw what happened to America they knew the great American Empire had fallen."

"It sounds frightening, Anna," said Raquel.

"The first crack began at the Mississippi river. The earthquake separated the land masses of what was once the Mississippi river.

Florida collided with Cuba and that state sunk into the ocean leaving nothing, but islands. Half of Cuba also sunk and tidal waves destroyed the rest of Cuba.

Michigan, Indiana, Illinois, Missouri, Arkansas, and Louisiana will face the Atlantic Ocean. All of these states would be flooded with tidal waves.

Ontario will sink into the ocean. The Canadian coast will be facing tidal waves, the thumb of Michigan will crack and sink, the Great Lakes will disappear.

The second Crack began in California and will travel into New Mexico, Arizona, and into Texas. The land mass will separate bringing the Pacific Ocean into the Gulf of Mexico.

Mexico will break away from South America, tidal waves will hit the lands, and the quake will awaken volcanoes," said Anna.

"You saw this happen in your vision?" asked Ramon.

"Yes," replied Anna.

"My god how can we be saved," said Raquel frighten.

"The angel said in order to be saved we must go to the Seven Hills."

"Where are the Seven Hills, Anna?"

"I don't know, Mother, that's why I sent Ramon to the library to get this map, so I can find it."

Ramon kept silent staring at the map in deep thought. Anna, looked and searched on the map, trying to find the whereabouts of Seven Hills.

"Somehow I heard that name before."

"Show us where it is, Ramon?" questioned Anna.

"When I was twelve, my grandfather always told me that we are Indians, He told me that there was a land which cowboys were afraid of and they called it Seven Hills. My grandfather said that was the cowboys name, but the Indians had another name for it, black Hills."

"The Dakotas," said Raquel.

"That's it, then that's the place we have to go if we want to survive," Anna said.

"We go there now?"

"No, Mother, we wait until the signs are complete," said Anna.

"Do you honestly believe all this is going to happen?"

"Don't you, Ramon?" Anna said looking at him.

"No, Anna. I think your vision is only a dream that you are taking too serious"

"What about that vision I had about that lady, Nelly. That came ture Ramon."

"That was only a coincidence, Anna."

"I don't believe I'm hearing this from you," said Anna feeling frustrated. "Get out Ramon, I don't want to see you today," she said feeling rejected.

"I thought you said I was going to eat here?" questioned Ramon as he walked toward the door.

"Not anymore! Get lost!" shouted Anna closing the door behind him.

It's raining in California, but a little rain doesn't bother Oune. The man walked on the side of the road to the spot where an accident happened a few days ago.

Oune looked around, making his way to the tree. He moved around tall weeds which surrounded the tree an even walked beyond the tree.

"It's got to be here somewhere," he said to himself.

"Is this what you're looking for?" questioned Helcat, a female demon. She was sitting on a tree limb above Oune pointing to a spot on the ground.

"What belongs to Fotley is now mine," said he with a smile.

"I admire you, Oune. I like the way you got rid of Fotley, and that's why I'm here to serve you in anyway."

"The book says you are Helcat,' he said finding her name in the pages.

"I'm at your service, Oune. What can I do for you?"

Oune closes the book and looked at Helcat in which she smiled with her decayed teeth and snot ran down from her mouth.

"Can you tell me about the power of the third eye?"

"The invisible eye. He who has one should not fear in what he sees," said Helcat floating down from the tree to the ground.

"Does the third eye exist?" questioned Oune.

"Come with me, Oune," she said walking further into the woods. "The third eye has the power to see the invisible. What you see now, the third eye cannot see, and what you cannot see the third eye can see. The visible and the invisible."

"What can a person see with the third eye?" asked Oune as Helcat laughed and looked at him with bloodshot eyes.

"Demons, hell, and things that no mortal wants to see." She replied.

The both of them came to a tree stump with a small caldron pot upon it. There was no fire, yet the pot was boiling to the rim.

"What is this?"

"What you asked for, Oune, the third eye."

"I only wanted to know the power of the third eye, Helcat."

"You refused to receive the third eye? You would have been the only mortal in the world with a third eye. You could have seen above you, below you, x-ray vision, and would have known who the anti-christ was before anyone else."

"Let me think about it, Helcat?"

"There's nothing to think about, Oune, either you do it or you don't."

"If I do it, how will I be able to hide the third eye?" questioned Oune as Helcat smiled, stirring the pot with her finger.

"You yourself will be the only person to see the third eye nobody else can because the third eye is invisible."

Oune walked to a tree, kissed the *Book of Demonology*, and set the book on a tree limb. He then turned to look at Helcat with mixed feelings of hate and fear.

"Fine! You talked me into it, Helcat. Give me the third eye," he said.

"Remember this, to go back on your word would mean death, Oune," she said laughing like a witch. "You will be more evil than Fotley," continuing to laugh like a witch.

"Just do it, Helcat."

Helcat turned her back on Oune; she then pulled out one of her own eyes and tossed it into the pot. She stirred the pot with her fingers looking at Oune with one eye

"You look better with two eyes, Helcat."

"You have something of mine and I have something of yours"

"What do you have that's mine?"

"Your soul."

"I didn't tell you to take my soul?"

"It's an even trade, Oune, my eye for your soul. There are no returns, I get my eye back when you die," said Helcat giving out an evil laugh.

"So be it," said Oune showing anger.

"It is done," said Helcat giving Oune a fork.

"What do I do?"

"Stab the eye with the fork and eat it. Make sure your teeth sinks into the eye."

Oune stirred the pot with the fork and the eye looked at him, it also winked. Oune backed away from the pot leaving the fork in the pot.

"That eye is alive!" Oune yelled.

"Sure it is, just put it in your mouth and chew on it. It's tasteless," said Helcat.

Oune walked toward the pot and pulled out the fork with the eye attached to it. The eye was dripping black syrup as it was put into the mouth of Oune;

"Do not swallow it, Oune, bite into it," said Hellcat watching the man chew on the eye.

"You said it's tasteless! This is awful!" shouted Oune eating the eye. "It's leaving a bad taste in my mouth," said Oune spitting and gagging.

"Drink this? It will take away the taste in your mouth," said Hellcat giving him a chalice.

Oune drank from it and spit it out. "Blood!"

"My blood, Oune," said Helcat.

"Get it away, I don't like it," said Oune picking up his book, leaving the area, coughing all the way out.

Helcat laughed. "He belongs to me," she said fading away.

In the days of Aquarius, a strange occurrence had taken place. Some say it was a miracle, others say it was a phenomenon, but it was happening all over the world.

From out of the lakes and rivers, bubbles were rising from these waters raveling in the air. Millions among millions of bubbles were seen in the sky.

It attracted the people all over the world. When these bubbles came into contact with the flesh, it would pop curing them from diseases or sickness of all kinds.

Hospitals were being emptied, doctors were taking a day off, and patients were being cured. People in the thousands were thankful on this day.

Anna and Ramon entered her store watching the bubbles float by and bouncing off streets or walls. Many, many people were in the streets.

"I did have a cold, but now I'm feeling fine," said Ramon.

"My mother is in good health after being hit by a bubble," said Anna watching Nelly at work.

Nelly stood by a table surrounded by herbs. She kept silent and continued to crush and smash herbs into a fine powder. Afterwards, the powders will be mixed together.

"What are you doing?" asked Anna

"I'm making incense using your herbs in this store," replied Nelly.

"I didn't know I had the ingredients to make incense. I didn't even know that you knew how to make incense," said Anna watching her.

"I would like to burn some here, if you don't mind?"

"No, go ahead, Nelly," answered Anna.

Ramon walked up to the ladies after hearing the news on the radio. He looked at both ladies and looked down at the herbs.

"Scientists are saying that they can't figure out why bubbles came out of rivers and lakes or the cause of it."

"It's a sign," said Nelly.

"It's the work of the antichrist," Anna said.

"How can you say that when you don't even know?"

"Ahh, but I do know, Ramon," replied Anna.

"There's going to be more miracles coming," said Nelly wiping her hands with a paper towel.

"If what you say is true, Anna, Why is he doing it?"

"He's trying to convince the world that he is Jesus and that he has returned to the world in the flesh."

"I would like to see this Jesus or antichrist."

"You will, Ramon, and sooner that you think," said Nelly finishing her work. "Did you know that the antichrist is the devil himself," lighting the incense. "Let me ask you something, Ramon, and you, Anna? Do you know why we are here?"

"To create life," questioned Ramon.

"No, that's not it," said Anna hitting Ramon on the shoulder

"What then, Anna?" questioned Nelly.

"I don't know," answered Anna.

"Did you know that mankind is being tested by God?"

"Why, Nelly?" asked Anna.

"So that we can take the place of the fallen angels."

"That doesn't make any sense. God made us and it's up to him to watch over us. If we fail in the sight of him, then it's his fault for letting it happened," said Ramon.

"The angels of God is protecting us Ramon. That's why there's a war between heaven and hell with mankind in the middle," said Nelly.

"I don't want to hear this anymore,' Ramon said leaving the store.

"Sometimes, Nelly I just don't know why I love him so much," said Anna confused, learning the ways of making incense.

At the beginning of a new week, Bibles were being distributed around the world, all other bibles were taken away from homes, Libraries, churches, and anywhere else it could be found.

Agents left the apartment of Nelly taking her Bible away. Agents also left the house of Anna taking away two Bibles, but what they didn't know was that Raquel had a Bible hidden between the walls.

Fourteen days into Aquarius became a special day. It was to be Candle mass and a second miracle did come. The hungry and the poor were overwhelmed to see an abundance of food had grown overnight. Again, this happened all over the world. People gathered around to eat, drink, and be merry.

Somewhere in France, a young man, working hard in his laboratory, retired for the night a well known doctor of anatomy was being bothered by a voice.

A warm night, a restless night for the doctor. He twisted and turned in bed opening his eyes to see a specter standing by the bedroom door.

"Go away; I don't like to be bothered by such things."

"Do you know who I am?"

"A stubborn spirit who won't leave me alone," the doctor said.

All of a sudden, the powerful voice shook the room, throwing the doctor to the floor. He sat up on the floor wide awake.

"I am not a spirit!"

"I am an atheist! I don't believe in you or God! Or whatever you are!" shouted the doctor.

"Very well then, since you don't believe in me, Jon Lafet, I can be myself. You can call me Devil, Satan, Lucifer, or whatever you like. I have many names," it said appearing to Jon Lafet as a terrifying beast.

"I gotta be having a nightmare," he said looking at a dog, with the head of an owl, and legs of a goat.

"Get up, Jon, and follow me," said the devil. "I've got something to show you."

Jon Lafet got out of bed and followed the Devil to the lab room. The Doctor yawned looking at the wall clock and sat in a chair.

"It's after midnight,"

"Can man be a god?" asked the Devil.

"I don't know? You tell me," Jon replied rubbing his eyes.

"God made man of his own image, so if a man made a man, he himself would be god," said the Devil smoking a crooked pipe.

"It can't be done," said Jon Lafet. "No way."

"I find this very interesting. A man created by God has a soul, but a man made by another man has no soul," said the Devil puffing smoke from its nose and mouth.

"What are you trying to say?" asked Jon Lafet in confusion.

"In my hand, I hold a notebook showing ways to make a man. I will give it to you Mr. Jon Lafet only if you agree to one thing?"

"You want my soul. Is that it, Satan?"

"No, I will soon have that in great quantities."

"What then?" questioned the doctor.

"I want you to become a leader of my organization. Do everything that I tell you to do without question," replied Satan, setting the notebook and opened it. He looked at Satan with a smile infront of Jon.

Jon Lafet picked up the notebook and opened it. He was amazed in what he saw within the pages of the notebook. He looked at Satan with a smile.

"Cloning."

"The secret of making a man, what do you say Mr. Jon Lafet? Do you want to be a god?"

"No problem," he replied. "I can do this."

"You will be a very rich man, powerful, and perhaps a great leader," said Satan walking into darkness with his laughter echoing in the lab room.

So it came to be that Jon Lafet began to work on cloning a man without a soul. But what he didn't know was that he has the first stages for Mephistopheles.

XI

I AM HE, FOR BEHOLD the rising of the antichrist has come into the world. One who is gifted with the knowledge of the great one and speaks with wisdom. Nothing holy could touch him; no magic of those who dislike him could work on him. He is feared by Christians, for the power of him is greater than man had ever seen.

He who believes in his spoken word would be saved, for those who did not were to be condemned. He prepared the world for the coming of the beast.

This man who is the antichrist knows the secrets of the elements, his power comes from hell, and the demons stood beside him obeying his every command.

In the days of Capricorn in the year of the antichrist, Nelly has been conquered by loneliness. She sits alone surrounded by strangers, drinking coffee, remembering the curse of Mitsy.

She stares and hears a voice in her ear, but the voice is within her. "I Nelly, am a woman in distress, the curse of Mitsy is upon me. I can feel my heart and soul being torn apart, fear is overcoming my emotions I need help, and I need Anna to help me end this curse," she said sitting alone in the dark at her apartment while smoking a cigarette.

Outside on that same night, Anna arrived at Nelly's apartment after receiving a phone call. She walked upstairs to her apartment and knocked on the door.

"The door is open Anna! Come right in!" shouted Nelly.

"Why are you sitting in the dark, Nelly?" questioned Anna turning on the lights.

"Do you know what to do?"

"Only what you told me over the phone, Nelly."

"Do it now, Anna."

On the table, Anna saw a pile of white powder. She took parchment paper and put small amounts of powder on the paper. She then added a few drops of oil and a drop of blood from the left hand of Nelly.

After this was done, Anna wrote a chant on a red piece of paper. All this was folded from corner to corner and placed into a red flannel bag.

"Alright, I'm done. Now what?" Anna asked.

"Give me the bag," replied Nelly as Anna gives her the bag.

"What are you going to do with it?"

"I'm going to keep it for one day and one night, Anna. After that I will burn it over a hot coal with incense."

"Will the curse be broken then?"

"Yes, Anna."

"Well, at least your feeling alright," she said walking to the door.

"Thank you for helping me, Anna."

"Glad I could help, Nelly," she replied as she left the apartment.

At long last, the day of sorrow has come. It began in the hospitals where all patients, babies, doctors, and nurses were all marked.

It started at schools, colleges and universities, where students and teachers were given the mark. Many employees quit their jobs, while others took the mark at factories.

Throughout the days of Aquarius around the world, people gathered into the churches to receive the mark. It's being announced on radios, televisions, and newspapers to come and get marked.

Ramon hurried down the road in his car, stopping by the store. He finds Anna, who stood behind the counter looking at him as if he was frightened.

"Come with me so you can be marked."

"I don't want that number on me," said Anna walking away from Ramon.

"What's wrong with you?" asked Ramon looking at her crossly.

"Don't look at me like that. You know how I feel about that number," being suspicious. "Oh my gosh, don't tell me you have the mark?" questioned Anna.

"Yes, I do," he answered showing his hand to Anna with a number on it.

"Why did you do it, Ramon? After all this time talking about it and going to church together."

"I only went to church because you wanted me to, Anna."

"Do you know what you have done, Ramon?"

"Hell yes and I want you to have one, Anna."

"Well, I'm sorry, but I will not take it, so you can get out of my life."

"Is that what you want, Anna?" said Ramon in anger.

"You took that number instead of me, Ramon, by doing that you ended our relationship," said Anna, walking to the backroom with an attitude.

"Alright then! It's over! But you're going to be sorry, Anna!" yelled Ramon leaving the store with such anger.

In the backroom, Anna sat on a stool depressed and crying. Soon she heard her name being called. She wiped the tears from her face and turned around to see a vision in the mirror.

She saw a grave, a woman surrounded by light, and another woman running from the devil. Anna did not know what it meant or understand it, but only stared at it.

It's a cool sunny day in France. A man came out of a church hearing his name being called. He stopped by a woman who was standing in line.

"Greetings, Madam Mozat," he said standing next to her.

"I see that you already have your mark."

"Yes, and I suppose that is why you're here?"

"Of course," replied Mozat, looking at him in a lab coat. "What have you been doing with yourself?" she asked.

"Keeping busy," answered Jon.

"You care to tell me about it?"

"Not really," replied Jon yawning.

"Mr. Jon Lafet you don't look so good. You're tired; you're working long hours, why don't you let me help you in your work?"

Jon Lafet hesitated, scratching his head. "Well, I don't know for sure, madam Mozat."

"You can't do it alone, Jon, whatever you're working on. You need me," she said as if she was begging.

"That is true, I do need a partner."

"Let me be at your side, Jon."

Jon looked at her with ease. "You know where to find me," he said walking away.

"I'm going to get my mark first! Then I'm coming to see you!" shouted Mozat watching him.

An hour before closing, Anna was having trouble with her customers. She was confused and couldn't think straight. Nelly noticed this and walked up to the counter.

"I'll do it for you, Anna," said Nelly.

"Thanks," she said heading toward the backroom.

A few minutes later, Nelly entered the backroom and saw Anna wiped the tears off her face. At that point she knew her feelings had been hurt.

"Is everything okay, Anna?" she asked.

"I don't want to talk about it," she replied with her head held low.

"I think you need a friend right now, Anna. Let me be that friend, talk to me, Anna," said Nelly.

She looked at Nelly with her sad eyes. "A few hours ago I had a fight with my boyfriend"

"You mean Ramon?"

"Yes, and we ended our relationship."

"What started the fight, Anna?"

"He took the number Nelly and he wanted me to be marked. I said no and the fight started."

Nelly kept quiet, not saying a word. She slowly walked out of the room leaving Anna alone. At this time, the woman quickly got up and walked out of the room.

"I thought you were going to cheer me up?"

"I can't, Anna."

"Why not?"

"Because the worse is yet to come. All I ask is that you be strong in faith, Anna," Nelly said closing the store.

"You know something?"

"So do you, Anna," replied Nelly looking at her. "Do you want me to close the register for you?"

"Yes, do that for me," said Anna walking toward the backroom.

"See you tomorrow."

"Bye, Nelly," said Anna leaving the store.

Its early afternoon when madam Mozat entered the property of Jon Lafet. She sees him standing by the door smoking a pipe.

"Are you ready to work for me, Madam Mozat?"

"I'm always fascinated working with you, Jon,"

"Good, then I will show you my work," he said entering through the door. "Are you willing to spend a few months here with me?" Jon asked.

"Are you telling me that I should live here?" questioned Mozat.

"Can you?"

"Yes, I suppose I can," replied Mozat entering the laboratory.

"I want you to stay her and study my notes and blueprints. We begin work tomorrow."

"Alright, Jon," said Mozat sitting down. "Where will you be when I'm finished?"

"In my study room," answered Jon, leaving her in the laboratory.

Twenty one days into Capricorn a third miracle came about. People who were rich became drunk with power. They could do anything and everything without question with the power they have received.

The average people became rich with their bank accounts somewhere in the millions, no more work, and out of debts.

The poor people became average. Once they were homeless, now they have homes. They now could lead a life on their own, start a family, buy whatever they wanted to buy.

All this was available to them if they carried the number. There's no such thing as being poor. Only those who did not have the mark were poor.

Nelly and Anna were working at their store when suddenly they saw a fancy sport car stop in front of the store. Both stared at the fancy car as they saw Ramon coming out dressed in an expensive suit.

A woman also got out of the car. They both entered the store with Ramon looking at Anna. He smiled at Anna the way she looked.

"See what your missing, Anna?" this could have been you," said Ramon.

"Never, Ramon. Get out," replied Anna becoming angry.

"I would, but my lady friend wants to do some shopping," Ramon said.

"Yes, I do," she said looking around the store.

"Look around, baby, if you see something you like I'll buy it in cash. In fact, if you like the whole store I'll buy Anna out and put her out of business," said Ramon with a smile.

Nelly and Anna kept quiet looking at each other. Both ladies walked behind the counter as they watch Ramon walk around the store.

"I like the smell of this incense. I think I'll buy it," he said taking a bag.

"I don't like anything in this store, Ramon, there's nothing evil to buy."

"Well, then, I guess we have to go someplace else and leave these Christians alone"

The lady laughed and looked at them with a serious look on her face. Nelly looked back at her with a smile on her face.

"Are you really Christians?"

"Why does it surprise you?" questioned Nelly.

"If you are, I feel sorry for you both. Ten days from now, it will be open season on all those who don't have the mark."

"I'm looking forward to that," said Ramon with a smile.

"Let's go, honey, I'm ready to leave," said the lady friend heading toward the door

Ramon walked with her and turned to look at Anna. He had the look of a killer in his eyes. It gave Anna a frightful chill.

"I'll be back in ten days," he said leaving.

"What are we going to do, Nelly?" asked Anna.

"Ten days from now we better not be here, Anna."

"Where will we go?"

"As far away from this town as possible," replied Nelly hearing the back door open.

Raquel came out from the backroom looking worried. She looked at both ladies and sat down on a chair holding her bank book.

"Mother, what's the matter?" asked Anna.

"Heard something awful on television," answered Raquel.

"What did you hear, Mother?"

"The banks are going to be closed down; money is soon going to be worthless. Computers will take over the currency; they say the hours of the clock will be used for money. The mark, Anna, is what will be used to buy things," she said feeling disturbed

"When is this supposed to happen, Mother?"

"The money is good for thirty more days."

"We better get our money out of the bank before they close out accounts, Anna," said Nelly.

"You're right," she said putting on her coat. "I'll close the store for now and take my mother to the bank." Anna said walking together out of the store.

A thunderstorm is in progress in the state of California and the sound of thunder excited Oune. He sat in his office alone, but his third eye was at work. He saw a demon in the lobby and knew that he was not alone in the church.

The demon made his way down the stairs to where the gold was. Inside the room, the demon saw a ferocious beast sitting on top of the golden bars.

"I know that you are not what you are. Deep inside your heart and soul is a young maiden."

"How is it that you can see me, for I am invisible?"

"You are invisible to the human eye. I myself am a demon known as, Vine," he said walking in front of her.

"Go away, Vine. I await my master to change me back to what I am."

Vine laughed out loud "Do you really think he will change you back?"

The lovely girl, Christina, now a beast changed by black magic by the works of Oune, looked at Vine with suspicion.

"I did what he commanded me to do. He no longer needs me the way I am."

"You are so wrong, ugly beast. He doesn't intend to change you back. You are what you are."

"You're lying, Vine!"

"Am I? Well, two days from now it will be a full moon that's the night that you should be changing back, but Oune will not perform magic."

"If you are right, Vine, what should I do?"

"You're asking me what do to, beast? If I was a beast I would kill Oune. Then this gold is yours, the spell would be broken, and you would be what you once were. The *Book of Demonology* will also be yours."

"Is that what you want me to do?"

"That is what I would do, beast, but that's up to you, ugly beast. After two days have passed and you are the same as you are then I say kill Oune," replied Vine waking through the wall.

Oune stood in the dark lobby watching the demon come up from the basement to the lobby. Oune walked behind Vine being detected by the demon.

"Good evening Vine."

"Your third eye is at work Oune." He said looking at him with the *Book of Demonology* in his hands.

"What were you doing in my secret room, Vine?"

"Do you really want to know?"

"Yes, I do because I don't trust you."

"Oune, I'm not here to take away your *Book of Demonology*, but your pet is hungry," retorted Vine and then disappeared.

Three days passed when Oune saw a family hiding behind the walls of his church. He watched them through a window an opened the back door.

"Come this way," said Oune dressed like a deacon.

"Thank you father," said the man.

"Who are you hiding from?" asked Oune.

"Agents," replied the man.

"I have a secret place where agents won't find you," said Oune leading them to the basement. "This way."

"Thank you for helping us father," said the man following him down the stairs with his wife and teenage daughter.

Oune opens the hidden wall and turns around to the family with a smile on his face. The man looked into the darken room as the woman smiles at Oune.

"You'll be safe in here until the agents are gone."

The family walked into the room where it stood cold, dry, and smelled of death. At this time the man turned to Oune looking at him very strangely.

"Father, why do you carry the mark?"

"Everyone carries the mark, unless you are Christians, as for me, I'm the father of Satan," answered Oune closing the wall. He then opened the intercom to hear their voices.

"Dad! There's gold in here," said the teenager hearing the sounds of a beast.

"There's something else in here!" screamed the wife as she was being attacked.

Oune heard the screams of the family as he shuts off the intercom. "Eat well my pet," walking away.

On the stair way, Oune saw two demons in armor standing and a third demon standing on top of the stairs. Oune, showed no fear to them.

"So you're the man with the third eye," he said.

"Who are you?"

"Don't you recognize my voice?"

Oune stood silent for a moment, not making a sound in deep thought. Then he remembered the voice which the entire world has heard.

"The voice in the churches. You're the antichrist," said Oune excitedly, walking up the stairs. "I've been waiting for you a very long time."

"I am here, Oune so now you can worship me in the flesh." He said shaking hands.

"A demon in the flesh, how did you achieve this?"

"I created a body in which I could take. I caused his death and took over his body, which now has risen with all the powers of hell at my grasp."

"I don't understand. The prophecy says that the antichrist is to be born."

"Lets us go to your office, Oune, and I'll explain it to you,' he said walking together toward the office.

"What name do you go by?"

"In this world, Oune, I'm known as Mr. Lived," he answered as they entered the office. "Before my coming, there is a Christian family very devoted to Christian life. This family had a fourteen year old daughter and a son at eighteen years of age.

With the help of demons, the brother had sex with his sister. She became pregnant and gave birth on Six, Six, Sixty seven in the eighteenth hour, which is six in the evening.

The family was is disbelief, of what has happened and gave up the child. A few months later, the child was baptized by the devil, and I cam possessing the child.

At the age of fifteen, my demon friends became my teachers and taught me their knowledge. At the age to thirty three, I became a senator, but resigned in order of become an important religious person.

At the age of forty one, this body dies in an accident, but six hours later I rose from the dead in front of my friends so that they can witness a miracle. I became in full control of this body."

"Let me be at your side, Mr. Lived," said Oune, kissing is feet.

"You will be at my side, Oune, but first I am told by Helcat that you are displeased with your church?"

"I have no power of my church, the government has taken over, Mr. Lived, and I want power of my own church."

"You shall have it, Oune, and one hundred ten days from now I will be here. The world will see me as you see me now."

"I am thankful, Mr. Lived."

"Do not thank me, Oune, I hate to be thankful and I don't like to be pleased."

"My church is your church, Mr. Lived, come as often as you like," said Oune watching the man leave right through the glass door into nothingness. "I would love to have that much power," he said to himself.

Aquarius is coming to an end, and time is running out. Pisces is about to begin, one hour from now it will be open season on all those who don't have the mark.

The law will stop in an hour. Police were arming themselves, agents were arming themselves, and people who have the marked were armed.

At the store, Nelly, Anna, and her mother, Raquel, took all that they wanted from their store. Their trunk of the car was full.

"I think we got everything, Anna," said Nelly.

"Help me," cried out Raquel, carrying two large boxes, she quickly walked toward the woman and helped toward the woman and helped her out by putting the boxes into the car.

"We have forty five minutes, Anna."

"You go ahead, Nelly, I gotta lock up the store."

"I'll meet you at my place," said Nelly taking Raquel with her.

Inside the store, Anna locked the door and walked to the back door seeing her gun on top of the counter. She picked it up and puts it in her purse.

As she was about to leave a vision appeared in the mirror. Anna saw a burning cross and the face of Jesus Christ appeared on the mirror.

"My people are being destroyed for lack of knowledge," he said.

At this time, Anna left the store, went to her car and made her way to Nelly's apartment. For some unknown reason, she felt worried and disturbed.

Fifteen minutes away, a pick-up truck stopped by and Ramon got out with a gun. He saw a car in the driveway and walled toward it. Raquel got out of the car.

"She's not here, Ramon."

"Do you have the mark, Raquel?" he questioned looking at his watch.

"Why do you ask me, Ramon? You know I don't," she replied seeing her daughter's car stop by.

"Time is up."

"Ramon, No!" shouted Anna, getting out of the car.

A shot was fired and Raquel falls to the ground dead with a bullet in her head. Nelly came out of the door and a second shot is a near miss.

Anna screamed like a mad lady out of hell. With such rage in her heart, she forgot that she's a Christian, she forgot the laws of God, and anger darkened her soul.

Ramon turned around and saw her coming toward him with a gun in her hand. Before he could fire a shot, three shouts sounded out, Anna stood near him watching him die.

Neighbors came out of their houses with guns to see Anna standing on the drive way with a body lying in front of her

"I know you're a Christian, Anna," said one neighbor.

Upon hearing this, Anna saw Nelly at the top of the stairs. They could not help each other so Anna ran to her car being fired upon, and she left at a high rate of speed.

Being left alone, Nelly hurries down the stairs trying to reach her car. Once she was at the bottom of the stairs a voice sounded out behind her.

"Freeze or I will kill you!" shouted an agent as Anna stood still. "No mark on you."

A second agent handcuffed her. "Take her away," he said dragging Nelly to their car.

Now it had begun, the terror of the beast. Christian homes were burned down, many were put to death, and all this was happening all over the world.

XII

ANGELS KNOW ABOUT THE *Book of Demonology* and they know it's a book that no mortal should have. Demons from within the book will haunt the minds of the living stealing their souls

Somewhere beyond the minds of mortals, where man have yet to learn about the dimensional zones of time, where times of the past, present,, and future is controlled by Father Time.

It was here in these time zones that Father Time recorded of seeing the Book of Demonology. It was said that the book was over five thousand years old.

Its contents are like nothing man has never seen before with its pictures drawn in blood and writings done in many kinds of languages.

How did this book get into the organic world is another story, but legend has it that the writings is of the devil's own hand. His darkest secrets lie within the book. Each demon that had the book wrote their stories of what they did to humans when on earth. The battle of good and evil continues to exist.

It's a cloudy afternoon in the twenty second day of Pisces. Oune was standing in front of the church watching a car park near by.

Agent Bane walked out of the car and saw Oune standing by the church doors. Agent Bane walked toward him with papers in his hand.

"You got something for me, Bane?"

"I don't know how you did it Oune, but this church is no longer under government control. It would seem that you have control of your own church."

"When you come to know the antichrist personally things do happen, Bane."

"You saw the antichrist?" he questioned.

"Stick around, Bane, he's going to show himself to the world soon," replied Oune taking his papers and entered his church.

Approaching his office Oune saw Helcat, a female demon, sitting in his chair. He entered his office looking at her.

"It's about time you got in here."

"What's going on, Helcat?"

"I'm taking you on a trip, Oune."

"Now?"

"What's the matter, Oune, afraid to come with me?" she questioned getting up from the chair.

"No."

"Follow me, Oune," heading out of the office.

Oune picked up the Book of Demonology and hurries out of the office toward Helcat. Down the basement into the dark hall, where Oune saw a door on the wall.

"This door will always be here, Oune. You are not to enter unless told to," replied Helcat opening the door.

Inside Oune sees nothing except darkness, below him lies thick black mellifluous moving about giving off a strong sweet smell. It's being mix with a darkness that surrounds it.

"Take my hand, Oune, and don't let go," said Helcat entering the room together.

Oune felt the coldness of evil around him, being submerge into the mellifluous feeling himself being blend into it. Fear overwhelms him tightening his grip on Helcat.

"Where are we?" questioned Oune finding himself standing near the falls. He looked at the blackness of the water and saw body parts flowing over the falls.

"You are now in the world of the infernal regions, Oune."

"Are you saying I'm in hell?"

"This is my world, Oune," said Helcat walking into a cave.

Inside the cave stood burning lamp oils. Oune sits on the ground with human skeletons all around. He watched Helcat disappeared into the darkness and another female demon comes through the wall.

Oune saw this demon female once before in the *Book of Demonology*. He opened the book trying to find her name. The female demon saw him in what he was doing.

"I know I've seen her before."

"Do not bother for I am, Heresy," she said looking sexy sitting on a rock, wearing a see through gown.

Oune closed the book and began to blush, feeling very uncomfortable to see a sexy demon in front of him acting like no female woman on earth could.

"Why am I here?"

Hersey looked at him with her bluish green eyes touching the man's face with her ugly hand, yet it felt like sandpaper to Oune. She takes the book away from Oune and opened it.

"I'm going to show you a story about myself," turning the pages with her sharp tongue. "Here I am. I wrote this story myself," said Hersey.

Oune looked into the pages of the book and the story is told to him as if the book is talking. Hersey lying on the ground showing her beautiful naked body to Oune and he listened to her story.

THE MAGIC OF EMILY K

It was nine in the evening on a lonely freeway, a car with four passengers drive up to a tavern on the side of the freeway. Two males and two females having a good time enter the tavern laughing and giggling. Sitting by a table near the wall they looked around the bar.

A jukebox played music, but no one dance. There was a small crowd, each to themselves. It's very quiet for a Saturday night, not what the couples were expecting to see.

'What would you like?' asked a barmaid standing near them.

'I don't like it here, Carl,' said Wanda.

'Why not?'

'I don't know why, but something is not right.'

'It doesn't matter if you like it or not, your car won't start anyway,' said the barmaid as she sits down with the group.

'What do you mean?' questioned Carl looking at her.

'This night is a mystery to all,' replied the barmaid as she got up and smiles at them, walking away.

'What do you think, Alfred?' asked Carl as he got up.

'Go ahead and see if the car starts,' replied Alfred smoking his pipe.

'I'll be right back,' said Carl walking out the door.

At this time Alfred got up from the table being looked at by the two ladies as if they didn't want to be left alone.

'Where are you going?' asked Liz.

'We forgot to tell the barmaid to bring us some beer?' he replied walking away from the table.

Liz watched Alfred walked up to the counter to buy beer for the table. Wanda leaned over toward Liz who kept watching Alfred.

'Do you know what's strange here?'

'What?' questioned Liz.

'Everyone is wearing black,' replied Wanda.

Hearing what Wanda had said, Liz got up from the table and looked around the tavern. She then sits back down facing Liz.

'You're right, maybe this is why it's so quiet, somebody died.'

'I don't think so, look at the table napkin,' said Wanda.

Liz looked down at her napkin to see four different kinds of pentacles in which she thought was only designs, but now she has second thoughts.

'Do we have witches here?'

'It's the sign of evil,' replied Wanda seeing Carl enter the bar.

Carl stood standing by the door to see the ladies table empty and that Alfred was up at the counter buying beer. He walked up to Alfred.

'The barmaid is right, the car won't start.'

'Take the pitchers of beer to our table. I'll join you later,' he said turning to the barmaid. 'What did you mean by this night is a mystery?'

'The mystery starts here and never ends. It only gets more and more mysterious,' replied the barmaid all dressed in black. 'Car won't start?'

'No,' replied Alfred.

'There you have it, a mystery,' she said picking up the money.

'This happened before?' asked Alfred.

'Many times,' answered the barmaid giving Alfred his change.

'Whatever happened to those people who got stuck here?' Alfred asked.

'I told them like I'm telling you. Go to the mansion in the swamp, there's plenty of room to spend the night,' replied the barmaid.

'Where is this mansion?' questioned Alfred.

'Go behind the tavern and you'll see a trail. Follow the trail and it will lead you to the mansion,' answered the barmaid.

The barmaid walked away to help a customer. Alfred walked away from the counter toward his table where his friends were waiting.

'What did you find out?' asked Carol.

'This whole place is a mystery,' replied Alfred sitting down.

'Wanda wants to leave this place and so do I,' pleaded Liz.

'What's wrong with you two?' questioned Alfred pouring beer into his glass.

'This place is evil, it has devil markings everywhere,' replied Wanda being disturbed.

'Tell them we can't leave, Carl.'

'Is something wrong?'

'Car won't start, Liz.'

'Now what are we going to do?'

'Don't worry, we got a place to stay,' replied Alfred.

'Where?' asked Liz.

'At a mansion,' answered Alfred as he drank his beer.

'What mansion?' asked Liz.

'A mansion the barmaid told me about,' replied Alfred.

Liz, Wanda, and Carl looked at each other not knowing what to say. Alfred pours his second glass of beer as Wanda becomes curious.

'When I finish this beer I want to see this mansion,' said Wanda
'So do I,' said Liz.

Curiosity fades away and the four of them sat at their table talking
and laughing making noise at the tavern.

The jukebox kept playing music nonstop. The tavern itself becomes cold being felt by the couples. By two in the morning they had
finished their beer.

'Well I'm ready to go,' said Liz.

'Let's get out of here,' said Carl.

'We've been here three hours and no one came to this bar except
us' said Wanda as they get up from their table.

'Come to think of it, no one left either,' said Liz.

'Another mystery to solve,' said Carl leaving a tip on the table and
they all walked out of the tavern under a moonless night with a warm
wind blowing.

'Which way to the mansion?' Liz asked.

'Around the back,' replied Alfred waking behind the tavern.

Once they all got behind the tavern they see a trail. They also see
an old lady standing by the trail; she had a cane on one hand and a
lantern on another.

'Good evening,' said she with a smile. 'You will need this to stay
on the trail,' giving Carl the lantern. 'All you have to do is follow the
sandy trail to the mansion. Stay on the trail cause there's poisonous
snakes in the swamp,'

'A tip for you kindness old woman,' said Alfred giving her ten
dollars.

'Beware of her, cause she's here, she's there, she's everywhere, so
beware,' said the old woman as she walked toward the tavern.

'What do you suppose she meant by that?' asked Liz.

'I don't know and it's morning not evening,' replied Alfred.

'Let's get started and find this mansion,' said Carl following the
trail.

The morning sky and the sounds of creatures from the swap cause
the trail to look frightful. Both ladies held their hands with their boy-
friends walking down the sandy trail.

'This place gives me the creeps,' said Wanda.

'I do believe were coming out of the swamp,' said Carl coming to a clearing.

The trail becomes a pavement leading to a gate, behind the gate stood the mansion. Standing in front of the gate is an old man waiting for their arrival. They all walked up to the gate and heard the old man speak.

'I've been expecting you,' holding a torch and he opens the gate letting the couples inside.

'Who are you?' Carl asked.

'I'm the caretaker and everything in that mansion is to your liking. If not please let the butler know.'

'Are we being expected?' asked Carl.

'No sir, no one is present at the moment,' replied the caretaker closing the gate.

'Are you saying that we are the only ones in that mansion?' questioned Liz.

'No ma'am, but you are the only guest in that mansion.'

'We might as well make ourselves comfortable,' Wanda said as she walked toward the mansion.

Alfred puts his hand into his pocket and the caretaker knew what he is about to do. Pulling out a pocket full of change as he heard the caretaker.

'No tip please,' he said with a smile.

'Well if that's what you want, it's alright by me,' said Alfred turning his back on the caretaker.

'Beware,' said the caretaker in a soft voice.

'What?' questioned Alfred turning around.

'Beware, cause the first time she talks to you, the second time she warns you, the third time she will take your soul, don't let her catch you alone,' he said.

'What are you talking about?' asked Alfred.

'It's better that you stay away from here,' replied the caretaker coughing.

'Alfred! Were waiting for you!' shouted Liz.

'I'm coming,' he said hurrying down the pavement to join the group.

'What was that all about?' questioned Liz.

'Nothing important,' answered Alfred as they walked together toward the mansion.

All of them reached the thick door and didn't bother to knock because the door opened itself. A bald headed butler stepped put.

'My master welcomes you.'

'Where is your master?' asked Carl.

'My master is out at the moment,' answered the butler.

Wanda and Liz entered a large beautiful room. They stood in the middle of a waxed floor and looked at Carl and Alfred.

'This is quite a place,' said Liz.

'A rich man's home,' said Alfred.

Carl looked around the room, but he was especially interested in the priceless paintings that stood hanging on the wall.

'This guy does well for himself.'

'Are you hungry or should I show you to your rooms?' the butler asked taking hats and coats.

'I'm going to bed,' said Wanda looking at her watch.

'Were all tired,' said Carl.

'I will show you to your rooms,' said the butler as they all walked up the stairs.

On the second floor each person is introduce to their rooms. Each and every room is in luxury which made the ladies feel classy and the men felt like gentlemen.

'I'm going to sleep like a king,' said Carl.

'Goodnight everybody,' said Wanda entering her bedroom.

There is silence on the second floor in a twenty eight room mansion. Every room had early American furniture and antiques from all over the world. Every room is decorated to its perfection.

It's ten in the morning when a knock on the door awakens the guest to a breakfast being served in bed. Wanda calls the room next to her.

'Liz, on the line.'

'How does it feel to be treated like a queen?'

It was then that Carl opened the door to Wanda's room to see here sitting up in bed talking on the phone, drinking coffee, and eating breakfast.

'Aren't you dress yet?' he said smoking a cigar.

'What's the hurry?' she asked hanging up the phone.

'What do you think?'

'You look great,' replied Wanda seeing Carl all dressed up in style.

'I feel like a millionaire.'

'Where did you get the wardrobe?'

"Look in the closet, Wanda, there's many to choose from,' replied Carl.

'I'm ready when you are,' said Alfred as he walked up to Carl.

'You can join us at the game room, Wanda, and tell Liz,' said Carl closing the door.

Within a few hours Wanda and Liz got all dressed up in their new fashions. Soon they join the men at the game room. They all began to explore the other rooms of the mansion. They came to a recreation room where they see a little girl watching television.

'Were not alone,' said Liz.

Upon hearing the voice of a woman the seven year old turns around and sees four people standing in the room. She looked at them in a friendly way.

'Hi,' said the little girl with a smile.

'Hello,' said Liz.

'You must be the new people my father told me about.'

'What is your name little girl?' asked Liz.

'Do you want to go to the bar room?' she asked not answering Liz.

'That sounds good to me,' replied Alfred.

'Follow me,' said the seven year old leading the way.

The four of them noticed the little girl is limping. They all looked at each other as the little girl made her way out of the recreation room and down the hall.

'Did you hurt yourself?' questioned Wanda.

'It doesn't hurt much, I fell off the tree yesterday,' as she walked into the bar room.

'This is my kind of room,' said Alfred heading toward where the liquor is at.

Alfred began to mix drinks for the four of them as Carl looked down at the little girl who happened to be standing next to him.

'You live here?'

The little girl got up on the couch so that she could look at Carl eye to eye. She had very spooky eyes that it gave Carl a hypnotic trance.

'You must be the man name, Carl; there is much greed in you.'

'Are you a mind reader?'

Not answering his questioned the little got off the couch and walked toward the man who is pouring drinks into four glasses. They looked at each other.

'Your name is, Alfred, and you strive for power.'

'Did you tell her that Liz?'

'I said nothing to her,' replied Liz sitting on a couch.

The next person the little girl wanted to see was Wanda. Both kept silent, but Wanda observed the child by staring at her and the girl stared right back.

'Well go ahead and say it,' said Wanda.

'You hate to be old; beauty is the most important thing in your life.'

'How about selling me your youth,' said Wanda laughing.

'Didn't you know that beauty is only a skin deep,' as she walked away from her and approached Liz.

'I guess it's my turn now,' said Liz batting her eyes at the little girl.

'You, Liz only think of yourself and nobody else.'

'Any harm in that?'

At this time Carl walked toward the seven year old girl holding a drink in his hand. He stands behind her and the little girl turned around to look at him.

'Now that you know all about us, how about tell us about you?'

The little girl smiled at him and walked to a sofa and sat down. Everyone wanted to know something about her and the little girl knew this.

'My mane is Emily K. I live here in this house, and I do magic tricks.'

'If you do magic, then show us one?' questioned Carl.

'Alright,' answered Emily taking an empty glass and walked up to Carl. 'Hold this,' she said as Carl hold the empty glass and Emily put a black cloth over the glass. 'One, two, three,' said Emily taking the cloth off and the glass had water.

'Show me another?'

'I will turn this water into wine, just for you, Carl,' replied Emily placing the cloth over the glass.

Suddenly the sound of the car honking its horn is heard by every-body. Emily K. quickly takes the black cloth off the glass water.

'That's my ride, I have to go to school,' she said as Emily exits the room in a hurry

'Hey!' shouted Carl as Alfred laughed. 'I knew she couldn't do it,' taking a drink of water. His face becomes astonished looking at the group.

'What's the matter?' questioned Alfred.

'It's not wine its whiskey,' replied Carl passing the glass around.

'How did she know it's your favorite drink, Carl?

'It would seem that, Emily K knows more than we think,' said Alfred.

'Let's get away from here, Alfred,' said Liz.

With out and hesitation Alfred walked out of the game room and out of the mansion being followed by the rest of the gang. He stood standing by the door way looking at the gate.

'You ladies wait her while me and, Carl, bring the car,' he said walking toward the gate.

'Open the gate!' shouted Alfred arriving to it.

'Good idea,' said the caretaker.

'What's a good idea?' asked Carl.

'Staying together, you should never let, Emily K. catch you alone.'

'You're not making any sense,' said Carl trotting, catching up with Alfred.

Both men arrived at the tavern by the way of the trail. They see their car just as they had left it as Carl walked toward it.

'I hope the darn thing starts,' he said.

'I'll get some drinks,' said Alfred as he walked into the bar. To his surprise he sees the same amount of people sitting on the same table, wearing the same clothing, as last night, nothing had changed.

'What can I do for you?' asked the barmaid, which was also the same lady as of last night.

Outside the tavern Carl got the car started closing the hood of the car. It was then the man walked up to the car and stared at Carl.

'Do you want to say something?' he asked as he walked away.

'Do you want to say something?' asked Carl.

'Don't let Emily catch you alone or the same thing will happen to you as it happened to me,' he replied as he walked away.

Carl got into his car and rolled down the car window. 'For your information I'm leaving this evil place!'

The slow walking, the strange looking man heard what Carl had said. He entered the tavern and me Alfred who was leaving.

'Excuse me sir, but is that you friend?' he said pointing out the window.

Alfred looked out the window to see Carl drive the car He quickly stepped outside waving his hand at Carl trying to make him stop.

'Hey! Wait for me!' he shouted.

'You stay here! I'm going to get the ladies!' shouted Carl driving away.

'He'll be back,' said Alfred to the man who is now standing by the door.

'No he won't,' touching Alfred on the shoulder with his icy cold hands. 'He's going to meet Emily K. alone.'

'What's the big secret about Emily K.? To me she's a nice little girl,' said Alfred.

'Did she show you her magical tricks?' asked the man looking like the walking dead.

'Yes, she did.'

'She knows the tricks of the devil,' said the man.

Alfred looked at the barmaid who was also standing by the door behind the man. She looked at him as if she was the devil herself.

'Can you tell me who Emily K. is?'

'Not who? What has become of Emily K.?' questioned the barmaid. 'You and your friends are doomed.'

'You people are strange,' said Alfred as he walked behind the tavern taking the trail to the mansion. All this time he's thinking about the possibility of who is Emily K.

Carl drove down the hi-way and turned onto a dirt road leading through a swamp onto pavement that leads to the mansion. He sees the gate up ahead with Emily K. behind the gate.

Emily K. sees the car coming toward her. She raises her hands up in the air and the gate opens itself. She stood standing on the pavement with her head turning around counter clockwise. Soon there appeared an eerie dark tunnel in front of Emily K.

Carl stopped the car, but the force in the tunnel pulled the car into the tunnel. Carl tried to get out of the car, but the doors would not open. The tunnel closes and the car is gone with Carl inside. Emily k. made her was to the mansion.

A few minutes later Alfred arrived at the gate. He sees the ladies waiting outside the mansion as he reached them breathing hard.

'I was so certain, Carl, would be her already.'

'Why didn't you come with him?' Wanda asked.

'Because he told me to wait at the tavern and that he would be back with you ladies. I did not want to wait,' answered Alfred.

'Look,' said Liz seeing Emily K. coming down the pavement road.

'She's not a little girl, she's something out of a nightmare,' said Alfred.

Emily approaches the trio, wearing a colorful dress. She looked at each one with a friendly look and a smile talking to all three.

'I thought you were gone already?'

'We're leaving right now,' replied Wanda.

'Emily, will you do some more magic for us?' asked Liz.

'Liz, no.'

'Yes, Wanda.'

'Do you have some silver coins?' asked Emily.

Liz looked into her purse and found six coins. She gives it to Emily like giving money to her own daughter. She smiles at Emily K.

'Let's see if you can make them disappear.'

'I'll do better than that,' said Emily, holding the coins in the palm of her hand. She made a fist in front of Liz and smiled at her. 'You can open my hand now.'

Liz opened her hand to find six gold coins. Is it real?' Wanda asked.

'Of course it's real,' replied Emily going inside the mansion.

'Where in the hell is, Carl?' questioned Alfred.

'Something must have gone wrong,' said Wanda.

'I'm going to walk on the road and see if I can find him. You ladies wanna come?'

'Sure, why not, maybe we'll meet him on the way, Alfred,' replied Wanda.

Liz put her six gold coins in her purse and all three walked together when all of a sudden Liz tripped on the pavement falling on the hard surface.

'Damn it!'

'You alright, Liz?' asked Alfred, picking her up.

'My foot hurts.'

'Let me carry you back to the chair,' said Alfred as he walked back with Liz to the chair.

'You two go ahead I'll wait here.'

'Are you sure about that, Liz?'

'Yeah, I'll be alright, Alfred,' she said as she relaxed in the chair.

'Don't you go anywhere, Liz, we'll be right back.'

'The way my foot is, I'm not going anywhere Wanda.'

'Let's go,' said Alfred as they leave being watched by Liz.

The caretaker finished trimming a bush and walked toward Liz. He saw her two friends walking away as he looked at her.

'What?' questioned Liz.

'You should have gone with them.'

'I hurt my foot?' said Liz rubbing her foot.

'Your friend, Carl, will not be here,' said the caretaker looking at her without a smile.

'You know where he is?'

'He met Emily K. alone, just as you will meet her alone.' He replied walking toward the next bush.

'Hey you!" she shouted. 'What wrong with Emily k.?'

The caretaker stopped by the bush and turned around to look at Liz. The lady felt the cold chill from his stare.

'Emily can open doors to other dimensions and your soul will be sucked into it with no way out.'

'Well you're here with me, I'm not alone,' said Liz.

The caretaker stared at her with a smirk on his face. 'I'm already damned,' he said walking away.

'Wait!' shouted Liz standing up from her chair.

All at once Emily came out of the mansion with a ball. She bounced the ball in front of Liz and saw her limped back to her chair.

'Are you hurt?' asked Emily holding the ball.

'Yes I am.'

'I can fix it so that you can catch up with your friends,' said Emily.

'More magic?'

'My father calls it healing,' said Emily touching her foot.

Emily rubs her painful foot with her hands and within a few minutes Liz got up from her chair and began to walk normal.

'Your okay, Emily,' feeling no pain. 'I will forget what I'm thinking about you.'

'Now you can catch up with your friends?'

'That's exactly what I'm thinking about,' replied Liz running across the lawn.

Emily K. stood very still watching Liz vanish under the ground, she screamed, but no one was able to hear it or help her.

'I guess she didn't make it,' said Emily bouncing her ball.

Alfred and Wanda had walked away from the mansion and are now walking on a dirt road. The sun seemed to have lost its brightness and everything around stood very quiet.

'He couldn't have left us here,' said Wanda.

'No. I don't think so, Carl wouldn't do that to us,' as they saw a car on the side of the road.

'There's our car,' said Wanda as the both of them ran toward the car.

'We've found the car, but no Carl,' said Alfred looking around.

'What could have happened to him?'

'I don't know, Wanda,' answered Alfred.

'Let's pick up, Liz, and come back here.'

'Yeah, we'll do that first,' said Alfred as they get into the car and drive forward.

On their way back to Liz, they see the gate which was left opened and they drive through heading toward the mansion. When they approached the Mansion they find Liz is no longer sitting on the chair.

'Where can she be?' questioned Alfred.

'She must be inside,' replied Wanda.

'I'll wait here and you go get her.'

'Alright,' answered Wanda getting out of the car and hurries into the mansion.

Within a few minutes, Emily K. came from around the mansion. She stopped in front of the car and made her way to the driver's side.

'Hello, Emily,' said Alfred with a smile. 'Do you know where my friends are?'

'Yes, I do. Do you want to be with them?'

'Just tell me where they are,' said Alfred stepping out of the car.

'Will you take my hand and I'll take you to them,' said Emily K.

'Sure,' said Alfred taking hold of her hand and the both of them disappeared into a hole in the pavement.

'Carl! Liz! Anybody?' shouted Wanda walking around the rooms of the mansion.

'I'm here, Wanda,' Emily said standing behind her.

'Do you know where they are?' turning around.

Emily stared at Wanda with her frightful eyes and gave out a smirk. Wanda did not like what Emily was doing to her.

'Let me see now, Carl is in the third level, Liz is in the second level, and Alfred is on level four.'

'What the hell are you talking about?' retorted Wanda.

'I'm talking about the infernal world,' answered Emily.

Wanda began to panic and pushed Emily aside. She ran out of the mansion to the car only to find it empty. She saw Emily come out of the mansion.

'Where is, Alfred?' she called out loud

'I already told you,' replied Emily standing by the door.

Wanda walked away from the car and toward Emily with such anger in her eyes. Emily remained calm showing no emotion whatsoever.

'You are evil, Emily K. What are you?'

'I'm the butler, the caretaker, the barmaid, and anybody whom I choose to be.'

'I want my friends back, Emily?'

'Okay, if that's what you want,' she replied walking back into the mansion with Wanda behind her.

They enter a room that had a large mirror on the wall. Emily looked at herself in the mirror and then she stood next to it.

'I don't see my friends?'

'They are in there, Wanda.'

'Is this another magic trick, Emily?'

'No, Wanda, it's no trick, all you have to do is put your hand into it and pull out your friends,' replied Emily.

Wanda walked up to the mirror seeing herself in the mirror. She looked at Emily and then put her right hand through the mirror.

'I feel something.'

'If you feel a tug, then you pull,' said Emily.

'I feel a hand,' said Wanda as a tug is felt. 'I got you,' she said pulling hard, but the tug was stronger than her that she herself went through the mirror.

'Too bad,' said Emily K. walking out of the room.

THE END

Oune closed the book, rub his eyes, and stared at Hersey. A black candle burns in front of him as Hersey stood next to him.

"Are you Emily K.?" he asked.

"I was Emily K." answered Hersey playing with his hair.

'Whatever happened to those people you killed?"

Hersey licks the face of Oune with her long ugly tongue. She got off the table and made her way to a dark wall. Turning around she smiled at Oune.

"Oune, you sexy beast, they are here," she said showing her finger to Oune.

Hersey lit her finger and brought her finger to the wall. Oune saw several vails on the wall with the souls of people within them.

"My personal collection."

"Time is up, Oune," said Helcat leaving the cave.

"Call me, Oune, you animal, you know how to reach me?' said Hersey in her naked way.

'Where to now, Helcat?" Oune asked following her.

"There's another who wants to meet you," she replied as they headed toward the City of Dis.

"I wonder how you live here, Helcat."

"You don't want to know," she said loudly.

XIII

Mexico, a country of beautification, now it's nothing, but wickedness and evil. Deep in the farmlands, a man took a woman by her hair out of the house.

"You can't do this, Pehamo!" cried out another man coming out of the house without a shirt.

"You and your family do not have the mark, Lopez!" as the man killed him with a shotgun.

Lopez was on the ground in a pool of blood. The woman screamed and cried pleading to a man who has a shotgun on her head.

"Please don't kill my child!"

Pehamo kept silent momentarily and looked down on a woman on her knees crying. He couldn't kill a woman in cold blood, but he had other ideas.

"You are right I will not kill you or your child," he said.

"Let me go to my child. I am begging you," said the woman.

"Go then," said Pehamo, watching the woman run into her house.

The man takes a five gallon gas can from his truck and walked to the house and set it on the floor. He walked out of the house and shot the gas can with his shotgun setting the house aflame.

Pehamo stood by his truck and watched the house burn. From a distance he saw a black man walking toward him the black man stopped by the house to see it burn down. He then walked to the man who caused it.

"You want something here?" questioned Pehamo.

"I want you," he replied.

Pehamo reloads his shotgun and looked at the black man from head to toe. With a serious look on his face he notices something about the black man.

"You don't have the mark?"

"I do not need the mark, Pehamo."

"What makes you so special for not wearing the mark?" Pehamo asked pointing the shotgun at the black man

"Go ahead and shoot, Pehamo. I can't be killed," said the demon. A shot was fired and the black man remained standing unharmed. "I am Zagan a demon from the darkest world."

Being silent Pehamo walked under the shade and sat down on a pile of logs. The demon followed close behind him and the both of them watched the house burn down.

"Is that what you really look like, a black?"

"No, Pehamo. What do you want me to look like?"

"I don't care about that Zagan, but what else can a demon do beside not be killed?"

"We demons can excite tempests and lightning. We can transport organic matter from one place to another. We can transform into man or animal. We can induce diseases as well as cure them. We can reveal hidden treasures; make man invisible, and possess man. We can render man impotent and women sterile. We can even make beast talk.'

"If you're so powerful, why do you need me?"

"I want you to become like me, Pehamo," he replied looking at him with evil eyes.

"You want me to become evil like you?"

"I want you to go to California and seek out the Book of Demonology and bring it back to Mexico."

"Do you know who has the book, Zagan?"

"A man called Oune, find him and end his life."

"California is a long way from here, Zagan?"

"That's why you should start you trip now, Pehamo," said Zagan fading away.

At the place of the infernal regions, Helcat and Oune reached the city of Dis. Every kind of sin was being committed there, which made Oune impressed in what he saw.

They entered through a stone wall and found themselves in a bar like surrounding. The entire place was filthy, smelly, and unpleasant sights.

"What happened here?" asked Oune as he heard a voice.

"Mortal! Over here!" it said in its most hideous form.

"Go to him," said Helcat.

Oune walked toward the demon as if he knew him. What he looked like he did not care. What he smelled like did not bother him.

"Sit and have a drink with me."

The demon watched Oune looked downward and immediately knew what Oune was thinking. Oune did not see any chairs or anything to sit on.

"I think I'll stand."

"I said sit down!"

"There's nothing to sit on," replied Oune.

"See how stupid you are. You have the *Book of Demonology* use it."

Not looking at the demon Oune opened the book and found what he wanted. He recited a chant then sat on air, closing his book. He stared at his drink that stood before him.

"Drink up!" shouted the demon.

"What is it?"

"Dirty water," replied the demon.

Oune picked up the mug and took a sip of the water. He turned his head and spit out the nasty tasting drink. It left a bad taste in his mouth.

"Taste like toilet water."

"That what it is."

"I can get sick drinking this," stated Oune. At once the demon slams the block of stone with his fist.

"Are you denying my drink?" asking angrily.

"No!" answered Oune loudly drinking the water.

"Let me see that book, so I can see if my story is still there that I wrote," said the demon looking through the pages.

"What do you call yourself?"

"Here I am," said the demon, turning the book around to Oune. "Listen to the story it tells," he said drinking his toilet water.

THE SACRIFICE

In the of the year of the millennium, it is said the devil will come not as a man, not as a beast, but a thing of beauty. How can this be done? What the devil needed is living organic matter to possess.

Here is a lady obsessed with the black arts going by the name of Monica Hallmarkus. She was dressed in black from head to toe; she was wearing a red cape sitting in a dark room gazing into a crystal ball. A demon stood next to her playing with her mind in a room that is so cold, yet the presence of evil exits.

'My day has come, at long last, after months of suffering and days of complication. Tonight I shall let the devil take my body and soul, letting it walk the earth.

I remember my friend Betsy who told me that I was the chosen one. I didn't know what she was talking about and I didn't believe in her religion.

I remember that night when Betsy picked me up and took me to the midnight witches. When I saw what went on there, it amazed me. From that point, I became obsessed; I wanted the devil to possess me.

On the eve of Candlemas, the midnight witches performed their spells. Betsy welcomed six teenagers brought to the coven by the way of spells.

Betsy dressed them in black, purple, green or red. Each teenager was given a charm which would bring them to the coven against their will.

On the eve of Walpurgis, the six teenage girls were present, but they did not know why. The midnight witches performed conjurations to each girl.

Betsy watched six girls spill their blood into six cups and each girl sold their souls to the devil by signing their name in blood. Finally, each girl had a demon as a guardian and protector.

It may sound strange, but during the day of Lammas, the mother of each teenager killed themselves. On the night of Lammas each teenager killed their fathers without mercy proven themselves to the devil.

I myself did not participate in the ritual, but the long wait had ended. Hollows eve is just around the corner,' said Monica

She heard a squeak and knew that the door is being opened. The light brought brightness into the dark room which made Monica angry.

'Shut the damn door!'

Betsy quickly closed the door and walked toward her looking at her face to face. She could not believe in what she saw in her.

'Did you look at yourself at how evil you look?'

'That's because I'm devoted to the devil,' replied Monica.

'I came here to tell you that they are waiting for you downstairs,' said Betsy.

'Let's go,' Monica said walking out of the dark room.

Both girls walked down the stairs to where six teenage girls were waiting. They did not know each other, not even their names, and it remained that way.

'Where are the midnight witches?' asked Monica.

'They are at the coven,' replied Betsy.

'You are Monica,' said a blond girl talking like a robot. 'We all know the codes of the sixes.'

'Let me hear them?' asked Monica.

'The first six means that 666,000 souls are needed to be killed within a two year period. It's for the devil, which is needed to be release from the pit.'

A red headed teen spoke out. 'The second six is referred to us. We are the keys to bring the devil into this world.'

Finally a Hispanic teen walked up to Monica and looked at her eye to eye. Monica felt a hypnotic power within her eyes as she spoke out.

'The third six tells the time, date, week and month which all this to be done,' she said turning away from Monica.

'The third six tells the time, date, week, and month which all take my body and walk the earth in the flesh,' said Monica joining with the six teenagers.

'Come, time is short,' said Betsy.

'The time is now, I'm the chosen one who will let the devil take my body and walk the earth in the flesh,' said Monica joining with the six teenagers.

They walked outdoors, into the backyard, onto a path that lead into the woods Deep into the woods, near a swamp, stood the midnight witches, thirteen in number all dressed in deep red robes.

'We are here to show homage to our master,' said the high priestess.

'I am here to surrender my body,' said Monica.

'We are the key to bring forth the devil,' said the six teenagers together.

'So it shall be done.' said the high priestess. Everyone walked together keeping silent on a ninety minute journey to the forgotten cemetery of Collenstick. Legend has it that this cemetery has been here for more than two centuries. A burial ground for witches and warlocks.

The Collenstick cemetery was always covered with smog. It was said that the smog comes from the graves, a gateway to hell. On a hot day Collenstick would be cold, on a cold day, Collenstick would be warm. It was here on this cemetery that the group entered.

'We are here,' said the high priestess looking at a broken down crypt. 'You will wait here, Monica Hallmarkus, and Meditate. We will prepare everything inside for you.'

In the hours of the night, Monica and the six teens sat on the ground in a circle meditating. Soon Betsy came out of the crypt and walked toward Monica.

'The room is ready, according to the Book of the Dead.'

Monica stood up from the ground and walked up toward Betsy, and whispered into her ear. The six teenagers got up and entered the crypt.

'No matter what happens to me, I want you to be at my side,' she said.

'You won't be yourself,' said Betsy.

'Say to the devil it's my wish to let you be at my side,' said Monica.

Betsy stared at Monica and them she smiles at her as she saw the midnight witches come out of the crypt. She then looked at Monica a second time.

'Alright, I will be at your side,' she said.

'We will wait here for our master,' said the high priestess.

Everyone hears the sound of thunder as Monica looked at the dark sky. The cemetery began to be covered with a misty fog coming from the ground.

'My time has come,' she said walking inside the crypt, followed by Betsy.

Once inside, Monica saw the six girls in a circle. Monica knew what she had to do as she walked into the circle. The girls went down on their knees, reciting a chant over and over again. They held hands while Monica sat on the ground meditating.

Each teenager took a knife and cut their left hand. The girls now began to walk around Monica counterclockwise. Monica stood up and her clothing was being torn off. Blood, from the teenagers, was being shed upon her.

Outside, the midnight witches watched an electrical storm without rain or wind. Gravestones were exploding in the cemetery. Trees that stood up burst into flames. Inside the crypt, the girls were holding black candles, the room was full of incense, and a cold air was felt. The flesh of the teenagers melted like was and one by one they disappeared without a trace.

Monica Hallmarkus felt the pain of possession as she lay flat on the ground, naked to the elements. She screamed, and the circle exploded in to flames.

Outside the midnight witches were kneeling when all of a sudden everything stood quiet. A green and black smoke rose from out the crypt.

Betsy came out coughing, falling to the ground, trying to catch her breath. The high priestess picked her up from the ground.

'Where is our master?' she asked.

'We've been lied to there is no devil and yet they took the souls of the teenagers and took away Monica,' replied Betsy.

'What could have happened? What did we do wrong?' said the high priestess looking very confused.

THE END

"By the way Oune, my name is Seere, and what I did on earth was splendid work of the black arts."

"You took the souls of those six teenagers and gave those midnight witches nothing in return, Seere."

"That's to show them what fools these mortals are and that includes you, Oune."

"Whatever became of Monica Hallmarkus?" questioned Oune closing the book.

"Do you want to know?"

"Yes, I do," answered Oune.

Seere pounded on the stone table and a woman came running toward him and kneels to Seere. She was naked in front on Oune.

"We need more drinks, Monica!"

"I should have known," said Oune.

"Time to go, Oune!" shouted Helcat walking up to the table.

"Have a drink with me, Helcat?"

"If it pleases you, Seere, why not," she replied taking the mug of dirty water and drank it with one swallow.

"Goddamn! That demon woman can drink!" Seere called out loudly.

"That was good, Seere," said Helcat as she smashed the mug on the floor. "Let's go, Oune."

"You're good at that," Oune said following Helcat out of the bar.

XIV

L OOKUP, AND BEHOLD THE heavens, which holds the secrets of the universe. It may never be known.

Look beyond, and behold life after death, a mystery that can't be solved. We may never know.

Look into the unknown, and behold the future, a time which is yet to come. We may never see it.

Be wise, be active, be alert, look among humanity and believe what is to be forgotten for behold the destiny of man is at hand.

Pisces had ended and Aries has begun. A police with two agents walked to a jail cell where Nelly is at. They looked at her with disgust.

"She's in your custody now," said the police officer.

'I'm not to be executed?" questioned Nelly.

"You're being transferred to California," one agent said.

The police officer opened the cell door and grabbed Nelly with force. She is then handcuffed and pushed out of the cell.

"Why am I taken to California?"

"There's someone who wants to see you," replied the agent.

"Let's go," said the second agent walking together out of the cell room.

Hundreds of miles away driving through the country roads, Anna had to keep away from the freeways. She knew police had put road blocks checking people to see if they carry the mark.

Long hours of driving came to an end when Anna enters a Christian town. She knows this by the way the town is destroyed, a sight of terror and horror, bodies lying everywhere some were castrated; stores were looted or burned down.

Anna drives slowly in her car trying not to run over obstacles lying in the street. She sees a mother and a daughter hanging on a telephone pole. Not a single living soul is ever found in that town as Anna kept driving away.

Somewhere in California, Bane drove on a gravel road to see a long time friend. He knew this man very well, they grew up together, and went to school together, but today it would be different.

Bane drove into the driveway reaching a fine looking house. He stepped out of the car being greeted by an eight year old girl.

"Hi, Bane!"

"Hello, Sally," patting her on the head.

"Bane! You have the mark; does that mean you can't be my godfather?"

"Who said I can't. Mark or no mark I'm still your godfather," replied bane reaching the house.

A tall heavy set man came out of the house to see her daughter holding hand with his friend. He waited on the porch for them.

"Go inside, Sally, your mom wants you."

"Hello, Timmy."

"I know why you're here, Bane. My family and I are not going to wear the mark."

"I'm surprised nobody found you yet. I was expecting to find you dead, so now I'm here to do one of two things. I can kill you and your family right now or you can become my property," said Bane.

"Are you saying we become slaves under your care?"

"At least you and your family won't be killed, Timmy. I'm giving you a chance to live."

"If I say yes, what happens then?"

"Well then you sign this paper," showing Timmy a document. You'll receive name tags saying that you are my property and no one can hurt you except me."

"What do we do as slaves, Bane?"

"You will become caretakers of my house just as you are doing now, but of course you also will be my chauffeur. Your wife will be my maid and your daughter will continue to go to school."

"So you want my family to take care of your house?"

"Yes. In time, your house becomes my house, this land, bank accounts, everything belongs to me. You have no choice, unless you take the mark, other than that you have nothing."

Timmy takes the document away from Bane and walked into the house with Bane close behind him. Victoria saw the two men as she sat on a rocking chair holding Sally with a concern look on her face.

"What are you going to do with us, Bane?" she asked

"That depends on your husband," he replied.

"What does he mean by that, honey?"

Timmy turned to Victoria looking at her holding the document. "What he's saying, dear, is that by signing this document we become slaves under his name."

"He's not going to kill us?"

"If we sign this document, no he won't kill us but we lose everything that we own Victoria, and we work for him. Do you agree with that, Victoria?"

"No! But for the sake of our daughter, Timmy, sign it."

"You must sign it to Victoria," said Bane watching her sign. "Thank you," said Bane as he walked toward the door He turned around to see them unhappy.

"Look at the bright side of it, at least you stay alive," he said with a smile.

Two days went by and a man entered a café. Who he was nobody knew, a stranger in town. He walked toward the cook and stands as if he is going to fight.

"Where can I find the Church of Lights?" asked the unshaven man.

"It's thirty miles from here Mr. In that direction," answered the cook pointing.

The unclean man did not thank the cook, but he had a mean look on his face. Dressed in farmers clothing he made his way out of the café.

That afternoon in the state of California, Oune entered the Hall of Pain. He approached a desk having a female agent.

"What can I do for you?"

"I'm looking for a girl between ten and thirteen years of age," said Oune.

"Yes we have some at that age."

"Must be a Christian girl," said Oune.

"We have some."

"That's fine. I would like to have one."

"For what purpose?" the agent asked.

"I need to do a sacrifice for my church and I know that the House of Pain has some people here that don't have the mark."

"I know who you are now? You're the guy from the Church of Lights?"

"Yes I am," replied Oune.

"Sign here," said the agent holding the tablet with paper forms.

"Are you going to attend my mass?" questioned Oune as he signs his name on the forms.

"When is your sacrifice?"

"This Friday at midnight," replied Oune.

"I'll be there just to see a Christian girl die," said the agent lady."Any specific girl you're looking for?"

"I like the fat ones if you have some."

"Do you want to take her now or wait until tomorrow?"

"Bring her tomorrow," replied Oune walking away.

After a long journey from Mexico to California, Pehamo finally reaches his destination. He stood standing looking at the Church of Lights. The church itself had demon statues outdoors, an upside down cross, and stain windows.

"Greeting my obnoxious friend."

Pehamo looked at him not willing to make friends. He still had that mean look on his face and Oune felt his feelings.

"Are you, Oune?"

"That's me and you are?"

"Pehamo," as he looked at the church.

"What is it that you want, Pehamo?"

"You have a nice church, Oune. When is the next mass?"

"Your not here to attend my mass. You came here from Mexico to do what? Why are you here, Pehamo?"

"You are good, Oune," he replied staring at him. "Is it true that you have the *Book of Demonology*?"

"Is that what you're after. Yes, I have such a book, but the book is sacred to me, nobody can see it," answered Oune being tough in his response.

"I think I'll come to your midnight mass tomorrow," said Pehamo giving off a bad breath as he walked away.

Oune made his way back to the church thinking to himself. "I wonder who told him about the book."

Somewhere in the states there is a driver driving on a country road, in the night, without lights, it's an eerie feeling. The driver doesn't know what to expect ahead on a lonely gravel road. This is what Annie is feeling at the moment. All would be fine for her until the worst has happened. A flat tire occurred.

Annie came to a complete stop on the side of the gravel road. She knows what had happened, but her fear of stepping out into the night sky is what's keeping her inside the car. She wiped her face with her hands and her fear is overcome by faith.

Annie gets out of the car and notice that her flashlight doesn't work. She hears voices in the dark and sees two figures walking down the gravel road toward her.

One had a rifle and the other had a flashlight. By the sound of their voices they were two men. Annie stood still, calm, and frighten.

"May God help me now," she said making the sign of the cross.

"You're a Christian?" asked a male voice.

"Yes I am," replied Annie.

"Don't be afraid. Were Christians too," said the young man holding the flashing on her.

"How can that be when you're wearing the mark?" asked Annie.

"My daughter is good with makeup, she puts these false markings on us," answered the man with a rifle.

"Follow us lady," said the younger man with the flashlight.

Annie takes her things out of the car and follows the two men. They do not follow the gravel road, but take into the fields under the night sky. They arrived at a burn down house.

"This use to be where I live until those devil lovers burned it down," said the older man with the rifle walking through the ruins. They walk down the stairs to the basement where the young man opened a floor board.

"We now live underground," he said going down the stairs.

Annie is next to go down the stairs followed by the old man. At the bottom they were standing on cement floor which gave Annie an idea that she was in an underground shelter.

"Nice set up you have here."

"I want you to meet my family," said the old man putting away his gun. "This is my wife, Dora, my son, Jerry, my daughter, Katie, and I, Denny." Annie shook their hands greeting them. It was then that she saw a priest in a wheelchair. She was not introduce to him, but wanted to meet him.

"Who might you be?" she asked.

"I'm Father Tony," he answered coughing. "Excuse me. You are, Annie, the woman with the visions."

"You can read minds?"

"No, your guardian angel told me," replied Tony.

"You know all about angels?"

"That and much more, Annie," answered the priest.

"Katie, go get your make up kit, she needs a fake mark," said Denny.

"Alright, Dad," she said walking to the next room.

Dora walked up to Annie and put her hands on her shoulder sitting her down on the sofa. Dora takes her coat off Annie and smiles at her.

"It's not safe to walk in the dark; you must spend the night here and have supper with us."

"Thank you. I think I will do that," said Annie knowing how tired she was.

"Come, Jerry, we have work to do," said Denny.

"We'll be back in time for supper, Mom," Jerry said leaving the room.

At this time Katie returns to the room with her make-up kit. She did her way toward Annie and sat down next to her.

"Where do you want it?"

"On my hand," replied Annie looking at her.

Katie set up a mirror so that Annie could see what she was doing to her hand. She began her work quietly as Annie watched by staring at the mirror.

Before long the image of Katie disappeared from the mirror and what Annie saw no one else could, but a vision appeared to her.

It's a furnace of red hot flames; four people were burning, and a demon pulling the heart out of a man who could not walk.

The vision quickly faded away causing Annie to jump from her seat. It also disturbed Katie from her work and Annie sat back down.

"I'm sorry if I frightened you," said Tony.

"He always scares people," said Katie continuing her work on Annie.

"I know you had a vision, Annie"

"How do you know I had one, Father Tony?"

"I just know that you did and I want you to tell me about it."

"It's all finished," said Katie.

Annie looked at the mark. "That's very good; I can't tell if it's fake or real."

"I'm going to help my mother," said Katie with a smile walking away with her makeup kit.

"About you vision, Annie?" questioned Tony.

"I saw you die and this whole family will die also," said Annie with a concerned look on his face.

Father Tony bowed his head and rubbed his eyes. He takes out a rosary from his pocket and hangs on to it in his hand looking at Annie.

"It's just as I expected," said Tony.

"What does it mean?"

"It means that this whole family has death all over them, they are waiting for the arrival of Katie's son. I'm here to do battle with her son."

"I don't understand?"

"Katie's son is the antichrist," he replied.

"How did that happen?" asked Annie as she was startled to hear it from Father Tony.

"Its a long story," answered Tony.

"Annie!" Jerry called out coming down the ladder. "Your car is ready"

"You fixed my car?"

"It's only a flat tire, that didn't take long," replied Jerry as he was joined by his father.

"I don't know what to say," said Annie feeling dumbfounded.

"Supper is ready," Katie said as everyone made their way to the table.

"I believe that our guest should say grace," said Father Tony.

"Alright," said Annie looking at the group, she bows her head. "God is great, God is good, let us thank him for our food, peace in heaven, peace on earth, and bless everybody in this house. Amen."

Delicious food on dishes began to be passed around as each and everyone filled their plates with food. They all began to eat.

"Where are you going, Annie?" asked Katie.

"The Dakotas," replied Annie drinking her water.

"Are you spending the night with us?" questioned Jerry.

"Yes, I am. I'll leave tomorrow," answered Annie continuing to eat.

Ten days into Taurus a feast was about to begin. It was not a feast to the Christian people, but to Oune it meant a day he had been waiting for.

The church of Lights was being decorated by witches in its most evil ways. Oune stood at the altar looking at his church and saw Pehamo inside his church.

"Do you like what you see?" he asked.

"A special occasion of some kind?" questioned Pehamo.

"You don't know what today is?" asked Oune.

"No! Damn it! So tell me?" retorted Pehamo.

"Today is Walpurgis, a feast for the demons. Tonight I will performed a human sacrifice."

"Will you be using the *Book of Demonology*?" Pehamo asked.

Oune gave a smirk smile and turned to Pehamo looking at him rather oddly. The man also gave Oune a cold stare of anger.

"You still want my book?"

"I want to look at it"

"Liar," said Oune. "You want to take it away from me, but I will keep that book with me at all times."

"What time does this feast start?"

"I don't think I'll tell you," replied Oune.

That's okay. I'll see this feast tonight," said Pehamo walking away.

A few minutes after Pehamo had left the church a woman in uniform walked into the church holding a clipboard. She stood and found the man she is looking for.

"Oune!" she yelled.

"Over here!" he called out as the lady approached him. "What can I do for you?"

"I have one thirteen year old Christian girl ordered by you. What do you want to do with her?"

"Follow me," Oune said as he made his way to the back of the altar.

During the afternoon hours, Bane walked down the hall of cells accompanied by two agents. They stopped by a cell room and he saw a lady kneeling, praying silently.

"He cannot help you," said Bane to her.

"I know that, so I'm praying that he will wait for me when you execute me," replied Nelly.

"Is that right," Bane said turning to the agents. "I want the execution of this lady to be stopped. She is to die of old age."

"It will be taken care of," said the agent.

Bane looked at the lady with a smile. The lady looked at him with anger in her eyes. She got up from kneeling and sat down.

"Do you think he will wait for you now?"

"I have nothing to say to you," replied Nelly.

"I think you would like to be tortured on national television," said Bane as Nelly looked at him, but didn't say a word. "Make a note of that, Agent Rodger."

"I sure will."

"That sounds real good to me, Nelly. We'll torture you, but not kill you, so that everyone can see you suffer some real pain," Bane said laughing and walked away.

By the coming of evening a strange occurrence took place. Every television, radio, and all forms of communication were taken over by voice. The entire world was hearing this voice, as well as to see him.

"Behold! Let the world know who I am, at first the world knows my voice, but now the voice has a face. I am the Christ! I am the one who performed the miracles! I am the one and only to be honored! I am Mr. Lived."

The voice of this man echoed through buildings, houses, underwater, every dark corner, everywhere in the entire world. Nelly stood still in her cell listening to the echoes of his voice. Annie parked on the side of the road, to hear his voice on the radio.

"Tonight is a special night. Tonight is to be Walpurgis Night! In California, at the Church of Lights, the world will witness a human sacrifice done by the high priest, Oune.

If you are in California I urge you to go to the Church of Lights and see this spectacle done in my name. Do not worry because the whole world will see Walpurgis feast at the Church of Lights," he said as his image faded away. Oune stepped out of his office after he heard what Lived had said.

"Did you know about this?" asked Bane standing in the lobby.

"I am going to do a sacrifice; but I didn't know the world was going to watch."

"You're going to have a security problem, Oune."

"That's why you're here, Bane. Help me out."

Not saying a word Bane left the church in a hurry. At this time Oune saw a demon coming out of a dark corner into the lobby.

"What are you doing here Seere?" he asked curiously.

"I'm going to attend the feast. Everyone is going to see me as I really am. The way you see me, Oune, is the way the whole world will see me."

"Who said you can do this, Seere?"

"The Christ himself, Mr. Lived. He also said that you better do it right. You don't want to disappoint Mr. Lived."

"Don't worry, tonight the antichrist is going to be astonished," said Oune walking back to his office. Seere passed through the walls of the church.

The sun has set and what everybody has been waiting for has come at last, Walpurgis Night. People gathered inside the Church of Lights which is to be the largest gathering Oune has ever seen.

Inside the church, the walls were decorated with signs of evil. Flags were present with the markings of Satan; there stood bon fires burning upon large clay pots. No lights, but black candles gave light to the church.

On the altar stood two table, one table had some instruments of death while the other had containers above and below the table. A Christian teenager was tied to a platform facing the audience. She was dressed in a red robe and was terrified.

Television cameras were set everywhere in the church so that the world could witness the feast of Walpurgis Night. The church itself had the smell of burnt flesh, a fountain stood at the entrance of the church which contain unholy water so that people could anoint themselves. Oune had two apprentices to assist him. They were well known for their evil works.

On this evil night, Nelly remained in her cell lying on the cold floor trying to sleep, but she was wet after being sprayed and only one meal a day. She felt sick and hungry, which kept her awake. A voice came to her.

"Have no fear, Nelly, I will comfort you."

"Who's there?" questioned Nelly sitting up to see Manna bread on the floor. She knew then that an angel had come and her hunger overcome by angel food.

The Black mass had begun and coming inside the door was Pehamo. Once inside he heard his name being called out in a dark hallway. Instead of going into the church he walked to where he heard his name.

"It's you again, Zagan."

"Come this way," said the demon leading him down the stairs.

"Is this a shortcut to the altar?" he asked.

"It is, but something else is here you need to see," Zagan replied approaching a wall. "Put your ear on this wall and knock."

Doing what he is told to do he knocked on the wall and heard a voice of a woman on the other side screaming like a wounded animal.

"Let me out!"

"Who is she Zagan?"

"An angry beast who wants to kill its master."

"Do you want out?" questioned Pehamo.

"Please open this wall. Look for a button somewhere on the wall," said the voice.

The man kept quiet as he felt the wall with his hand trying to find the button in a dark hallway. At long last he located the button and the wall opened.

Right before his eyes Pehamo saw a pile of one ounce gold bars. His eyes began to show the greediness within himself.

"Do not enter this room or I will kill you."

"I hear you, but I can't see you," said Pehamo.

"I'm invisible, I'm guarding this gold, and I want my life back. Oune tricked me, that good for nothing son-of-a-bitch," said the beast.

"What do you want me to do?"

"Bring Oune here in this room and I will kill him. The curse will be broken, I will have my life back, and this gold will be yours," replied the beast,

"All I have to do is bring, Oune in this room?" questioned Pehamo.

"That's the idea," answered the beast.

"Say no more," said Pehamo as he walked down the hallway anxiously in having the gold for himself.

The Black mass continued during the hours of Walpurgis Night. There stood a large crowd in the church, an unpleasant odor existed within the church, and no light only candles burned.

"Hail to the Watchtower of the West, Spirits of the Underworld, Guardian of the Western Gate, hear me!" Oune called out loudly.

He picked up a hot pot of incense, yet his hands did not burn. Oune walked to a large pentagram clock and he stared at it.

"Father Time," he said anointing the clock with incense.

The man then walked to a pile of dirt, Oune stood upon it and he meditated. He then brought forth an urn filled with ashes of a tree.

"Mother Earth," he said anointing the dirt with ashes.

Oune made his way to a fountain of water and he kneels to the fountain putting his hands into the water. From out of the water he brought out a jar of oil.

"Sister Water," he said anointing the water with oil.

Oune now walked to a flaming pot in which he put his hand into the fire. His hands ignited, but did not burn and he held up a cup of dust made from bones of an animal

"Brother Fire," he said anointing the flames with dust.

Finally Oune made his way to a tile floor. He lifted the title off the floor and a gust of wind blew about. Oune placed his hands over the wind and opened a bottle of strong, unpleasant perfumed

"Brother Wind," he said anointing the wind gust.

Oune now walked toward the teenager looking at her eye to eye. He turned to face the audience holding a bowl in his hand.

"Brother Sun," he said anointing the face of the teenager with paste mixed with lard.

The high priest, which is Oune, walked to the altar and picked up a hot pot and made his way back to the teenager again facing the audience.

"Sister Moon," said he anointing the teenager with the mark of Satan on her breast with ashes of blood.

Pehamo stood by the altar door making sure not to be seen. He saw Oune holding the *Book of Demonology* in his hand. He kept quiet watching and waiting for the right moment.

Seere came walking through the wall and kept walking down the aisle. Everyone could see him in its true form as he really is. It's ugliness frighten people, it's foul stench made other faint, and his evilness made people to act in such disorderly manner. With the power of the third eye, Oune could see other demons within his church.

The two apprentices brought the teenager to the altar table and strapped her down. Oune took a sacred dagger and stepped in front of the teenager.

"This sacrifice is dedicated to Walpurgis Feast. To the Prince of darkness, I give to thee her heart," said Oune, cutting into her body

One of the apprentice held a large glass container filled with flammable liquid. Oune pulled out the heart of the teenager and showed it to the audience.

Everyone clapped their hands as they saw the heart beating and the teenager remained alive screaming, not of pain, but of fear. Her heart was placed into the glass container with blue flame burning above it.

"To the antichrist, known and Mr. Lived, I give to thee her head," said Oune, picking up a razor sharp hatchet.

Once again an apprentice held a basket made of weeping willo bark. With one chop, the teenagers head fell into the basket.

"Hail to our Lord and Savior!" shouted the audience as they see a large glass container with the teenager's head inside. It was placed next to the heart.

"To the Queen of Evil ways, I give to thee her body. The blood from her body shall be spilled and this shall belong to the Church of Lights," said Oune.

An apprentice tied a thick black rope around the girl's legs. Both apprentices pulled on the rope and the headless body was lifted off the altar table. Oune placed a plastic tub underneath the headless body collecting the blood.

"The feast of Walpurgis has ended! Let the celebration of Walpurgis begin!" shouted Oune. The audience cheered and began to take off their clothing.

It was then that Pehamo hurries down the altar seeing Oune take the Book of Demonology. Pehamo bumped Oune to the floor and he took the book.

"Pehamo! I want my book you asshole!" retorted Oune getting up from the floor and chased Pehamo down the hallway.

Pehamo went down the stairway into the darkness toward the secret room. He looked behind to see Oune coming down the stairs.

"Here he comes," he said to the beast.

Oune immediately stopped running and stared into the darkness. He slowly walked into the dark being very cautious. His third eye is at work, but saw nothing.

"I know where you are! There's no place to hide!" he shouted to see the secret room opened.

"Goddamn it! You know about my gold."

"Yeah! And I like your gold!" Pehamo called out in the dark and pushed Oune into the room.

At that very moment the high priest was attacked by the beast. Both falls to the floor as Oune tried to fight the beast off him.

"I am you master!" he cried out, but the beast tore into his flesh

"What a mess," said Pehamo as he saw a naked woman come out of the darkness.

"I am, Helcat, and I come for my eye," she said picking up her eye from the floor. "See you in hell, Oune," said Helcat disappearing with laughter.

The beast appeared to the eyes of Pehamo and he watched it change back to a naked female. At once the woman saw herself naked and she saw Pehamo looking at her. She felt embarrassed and ran out of the room.

"You're free!" shouted Pehamo as he walked into the room toward the gold.

"The soul of the dead man belongs to Zagan," he said taking an ounce of gold and he closes the wall." This gold and the book are now mine," said Pehamo walking away.

XV

AND IT CAME TO pass, what is done will soon come to be in the ways of Mr. Lived, a man with a sick mind, the antichrist himself. In America there is corruption, blackmail, betrayal, and murder among the politicians.

It became a time of crises where Senators turned their backs on each other. Trust no longer exists, laws were broken, and the states were beginning to hate each other. America suffered and the outbreak of war is near.

Riots were happening in every state in the days of Cancer. America was out of control, but for Susan Walcot, a Florida Senator, was asleep in her private cottage.

Once a devoted Christian now her dreams are mixed with sinful thoughts. A restless night for Susan, turning around in her bed, a battle between angels and falling angels in who will control her mortal thoughts.

A new day has come. Susan got up and looked at her husband fast asleep. She takes a shower and got dressed; she came out of the shower room and finds her husband still asleep.

Susan walked to the kitchen and saw a pot of hot coffee already made. She takes a cup and pours herself some coffee sitting down on a chair.

The door opened and Mr. Lived entered with the morning paper. Susan looked at him rather surprised, she knew who he was, but wasn't welcomed.

"Did you like my coffee?"

"I didn't invite you Mr. Lived."

"I make my own invitation, Susan," sitting down.

"My husband will be awake soon."

"No he won't. He'll be asleep until I'm gone, Susan."

The woman drunk her coffee and looked at him. Lived stared at her like a hypnotist. Susan finished her coffee and could no longer stand the way she was being stared at.

"Alright then, what is it that you want?"

"I want you to become President of the United States," replied Mr. Lived as he smiled.

Susan could not believe in what she was hearing. She coughed and began to laugh as if it was a joke. Lived did not think it was funny.

"Not a chance in hell, forget about it," she said with laughter.

"If you had the opportunity would you consider it?"

"Sure I would. I think America could use a woman President," answered Susan.

"That's all I wanted to hear," said Mr. Lived as he walked out the door.

"Wait! There things you need to know!" shouted Susan, but Mr. Lived had already gone.

A sunny day in California, Bane is at his house having lunch with a friend who is also a Senator. Timmy and Victoria were servants.

"I should have thought of that, Bane, turning Christians into personal slaves."

"At first I couldn't care less, a good Christian is a dead Christian, but then I thought about it. I said to myself, why should I kill them, when they can work for me?"

"You have a good thing going here, Bane"

"I think so," he said as they walked out of the house.

"What I wanted to tell you is that there's a position opened for you, if you're interested."

"A seat in the Senate?"

"Maybe."

"Yes, I'm interested," Bane excitedly replied.

"I'll mention your name and let you know," said the Senator getting into his car.

In Washington DC, at the white house, Mr. Lived made his way to the office of the president, unseen by the agents or the secretary.

Mr. Lived walked through the door and sat in a chair listening to the president talk with the Vice President. The president turned around and saw Mr. Lived.

"How did you get in here?"

"I always find a way, Mr. President,' answered Mr. Lived.

"I better be going, Mr. President, and do what I have to do," said the Vice president.

"No!" shouted Mr. Lived. "Sit down, Vice president, this concerns you as well."

"What do you have to say, Lived?"

"You're going to make changes, Mr. President."

"What kind of changes?" he said as Mr. Lived stood up and paced the floor.

Listen to what I have to say. In the Judiciary system the Supreme Court will have one judge and only one judge. Whatever he says will be done, He'll be able to pronounce sentence and it will be carried out immediately." Mr. Lived stared at the two men. "In the Legislative System there will be one senator per state, three Governors per state, and many more mayors. There will be representatives, no congress, and the President will always have the final say. There are no elections, no voting, which means these offices will be appointed."

"That's the most ridiculous thing I've ever heard of," said the President laughing.

"Under the power of the Constitution we can't do what you say. That's not possible," said the Vice President.

"What constitution? It no longer exists!" shouted Mr. Lived angrily.

"It doesn't matter. What you said will never happen. I won't let it happen," said the President.

Mr. Lived stopped pacing the floor with his back on the President. Suddenly, his head turned around facing the President. He had the most freightful and most evil look on his face.

"I believe at this very minute you are about to have a heart attack, Mr. President."

"Once again the head of Mr. Lived turned around to its normal position. He then turned around to see the president dying on the floor. The man looked at Lived as he coughed out blood and died rather suddenly.

"You killed him," said the Vice president with an emotional disturbance.

"Did I? Can you prove it? Besides, that makes you President and you will follow my orders."

"If I follow your orders it doesn't make me President, only a Dictator."

"Damn right, and soon you will resign from office so do as I say or the same fate awaits you," said Lived.

The Vice President stood up from his chair and stared at Lived, but he is stared back by Lived which made his body to tremble.

"Alright. I'll do as you say."

"I will be there Mr. Vice President to hear what you have to say," said Lived as he leaves the room.

Evening hours had arrived in the state of North Dakota. Anna is in line with other cars in slow moving traffic, she then saw two agents by the bridge crossing.

"I got to relax, be calm Anna, don't panic," she said to herself approaching the bridge.

This is a code check," said the female agent.

Anna puts out her hand showing her fake mark to the agent. "Is it good enough?"

"Pass through," said the agent.

Anna felt peaceful once more driving onto the bridge heading toward her destination. She stopped at a cheap motel to spend the night, her first restful night at a motel.

Bane continued to work as an agent, but he also waited patiently for three days until he received a phone call. It's the call he has been waiting for.

"Bane speaking."

"Just the man I want to talk to."

"Senator Milcox."

"There's a Legislation meeting at one o' clock today. Be here at my office about noon."

"That's fine with me Senator. I'll see you at noon," said Bane hanging up the phone.

After what happened three days ago a doctor came to the white house to see the vice president, now president. They both had a private meeting.

"Well doctor. I want to know how the president died."

"That's what I want to know, Mr. Vice President, what happened to him?" said the doctor looking at him puzzled.

"What do you mean?"

"It's hard to explain it, but his heart burst."

"What you mean burst?"

"Mr. Vice President, the President didn't die of a heart attack. His heart looks like someone squeezed it. I don't understand it at all," said the doctor.

The vice president walked away from the doctor and turned to one of his officials. They looked at each other as he held a cup of coffee.

"Is it true that our Constitution is missing?"

"No sir, that's not true, it's there except it has burned to ashes," he replied.

Soon a knock came to the door. "Who is it?" the Vice president called out.

"Mr. Vice President, we have an emergency!"

"You may enter."

"Mr. Vice President, the ambassadors are walking out of the United Nations. We are no longer United," said the general.

"Damn, that Mr. Lived," said the vice president walking out of his office with the general.

A few hours later it became one in the afternoon, Bane and Senator Milcox were at the meeting with the other Senators and congressmen. News was spreading to each other as to what happened to the president and what has happened at the United Nations.

"Ladies and Gentlemen, the Vice President of the United States," said the spokesman.

Everyone stood silent watching the Vice President approach the podium. He took a drink of water from a cup and looked at the audience.

"What you all have heard is true, but I advise you to keep it to yourselves. There's going to be many changes coming about."

"That's correct, Mr. Vice president!" shouted Mr. Lived walking toward him.

"I am not the president of the United States. I am only a vice president and I'm going to resign my office."

"Well said Mr. Vice president," said Mr. Lived stepping up to the podium and the vice president stepped down. "Since the constitution no longer exists I say you resign from office Mr. Vice president as of right now."

"I accept my resignation from office of vice president of the United States." He said and he left the room.

"Alright ladies and gentlemen, what we need here is a powerful leader not a weakling. Senator Susan Walcott come up here!" Mr. Lived called out.

At once everybody began to talk to one another as Susan Walcott made her way to the stage. She was being stared at as she approached the stage.

"You sent for me?"

"I choose you, Susan Walcott, to become President of the United State," replied Lived.

"I accept the office of President of the United States."

"Are there any questions?" asked Mr. Lived.

"You can't do this!" shouted a senator as others stood up and began to argue.

Mr. Lived looked at them at how they were arguing toward him. He took his middle finger and pointed at each one. Immediately they all fell dead and the room remained silent.

"Are there any more questions?" asked Lived looking around the room and all stood at complete silence.

"I guess I am President," said Susan Walcott with a smile. Lived turned and looked at her.

"Tell them the changes that are to take place, Mrs. President?" he asked walking away.

"I don't believe this," said Milcox leaving the room.

"A lady president, of all people it had to be black," said Bane following Milcox.

Outside the meeting room Milcox saw the ex-president is about to leave the building. He quickly ran up to him in an angry mood.

"Mr. ex- president!" Milcox called out. "Why did you resign?"

"Are you kidding, did you see what just happened in there? If you saw what I saw last night, you would resign too Mr. Lived, is the devil himself, within a few minutes all hell is going to break loose in that meeting."

"It already has," said Bane.

"What's going to happen in that meeting?" Milcox asked.

"I saw your name on the list, Senator. You don't have a job," replied the ex-president walking out of the building.

"What does it all mean, Senator Milcox?" questioned Bane

"It means the democracy of America has collapsed and Mr. Lived is to blame," answered Milcox as he listened to the shouting in the meeting.

"There's always a way to stop a mad man," said Bane watching Senator Milcox enter the meeting room and he leaves the building.

At the agent headquarters, where Bane worked, a woman walked down the hallway. She is excited as she comes to an office door and knocked.

"I'm here,' said a male voice.

The door opened and the woman entered his office. "Congratulations on becoming my boss, Agent Rodger."

"You have got to be kidding, Agent Suzy," he said in astonishment. "Bane didn't get the position?"

"Nope, and he's going to be very upset when he hears about it," answered Suzy.

"I can't believe I'm boss and not Bane," said Agent Rodger coming out of his office as others came to the agent to congratulate him.

At long last the sun has set and evening came like a shadow had been cast. Bane was at home talking on the phone getting angrier and angrier. He now knew what had happened at headquarters.

Agent Bane slammed the phone down, and tossed it on the floor in anger and continued to clean his rifle that he owned. All this time he thought about Mr. Lived, Senator Milcox, the resident, and now his position at agent headquarters.

While he cleaned his rifle Timmy John sat down with him having a cup of coffee. He pours alcohol from a bottle into a glass and gives it to Bane.

"Drink, Agent Bane, you don't look so good," said Timmy.

"Why am I drinking whiskey and you have coffee?"

"You don't like coffee," replied Timmy.

"Drink whiskey with me, Timmy"

"Alright," said Timmy pouring whiskey into his cup.

"You know something, Timmy? I thought the world would change by wearing the mark."

"It has change, Bane, it made you rich, it separated the Christians from the non-Christians," said Timmy drinking whiskey.

"It's not what I expected to be, Timmy. Today I lost my power as an agent and the worst thing about it was some man younger than me told me I should resign.

Today the president of the United States resigned from office and a black woman was appointed President. Today the United Nations has come to an end, it doesn't exist anymore," he said putting the rifle together.

"What do you plan to do?"

"I have to eliminate the evil that's in America," replied Bane.

"You are going to assassinate the antichrist?"

"By doing that, Timmy, America will be the way it was before."

"Bane," said Timmy standing up from his chair. "You can't kill the antichrist."

"Why not?" asked Bane as he took a shot of his whiskey.

"The antichrist is a demon possessed in a body of a mortal. You are only killing an organic body, and another thing, the antichrist is very powerful. He will know what you are doing before you even do it."

"What then, Timmy?" Bane asked starting to slur his words and he was in the process of getting drunk.

"The number that you have, Bane, is the mark of the beast. Which means the beast is still to come."

"The antichrist is the beast, Timmy."

"No, Bane, the beast is much worse than the antichrist. More evil than you can ever imagine."

Bane picked up the bullets and put it into his pocket, he put the rifle over his shoulder, and takes his bottle of whiskey

"I don't care about the beast," he said stumbling out the door

Timmy watched Bane get into his car as he closed the door. He then began to clean up the table when he saw his wife, Victoria, come out of the bedroom.

"I can't sleep your making too much noise."

"We're free, Honey," said Timmy.

"Did he tell you that?" questioned Victoria.

"No, but I don't think he's coming back. He's on his way to assassinate the antichrist."

"What will happen to us, Timmy?"

"We can't stay here, Victoria, the agents will kill us. We have to leave now."

"Where do we go?"

"Anywhere as long as we are away from here," replied Timmy as Victoria returned to her bedroom to get dressed.

The sun rose from the east bringing light to a new day. Bane was on top of a building walking in circles. He was demoralized.

"Here I am on top of a structure with a rifle in my hand I looked down and see the antichrist making a speech, it was he who dispersed America.

A time not so long ago a friend told me I had a chance to be somebody, and that he would be at my side. He told me to come with him so I could make myself own. But that did not happen so; instead we were taken by surprise of what took place. America had changed under the power of the antichrist.

America can no longer take the pain of Lived, which is why I am here. I say onto myself the antichrist must be stopped no matter what. I cannot let this happen.

Today is a dismal day for me. I'm looking through my scope and five hundred yards away, Lived, saw me and I saw him, but he only smiled at me. I have a bad feeling about this, but I must finish what I started, there's no going back.

I die like a man as I aimed my rifle at the antichrist. If I live, America will change, if I die, God forgive me because I tried, and so may it be."

Bane is a man lost in time; he cannot think or knows what he is doing. His mind gone and the demon within him has a hold of his soul. The voice he hears is the demon talking within. The enemy he dislikes is now inside.

"Around and around your soul goes, where it stops you do not know. Spinning around between heaven and hell, not wanting to see the unknown.

The evil knows your faith is weak and they are coming after you. The good is willing to strengthen your faith only if you ask them too.

Your time is running out. Your life is on a balance between life and death. To be saved would be fine, but if not your own shadow becomes your worst nightmare." There is no end to the Angelic wars, just what is yet to come.